You

game anyway, right?

Your pen pal—and perfect soul mate—an eloquent, self-made millionaire, who could give Cyrano de Bergerac a lesson or two in sensual writing, is also a pretend persona, isn't he?

But then the blackout happens…and you find yourself face-to-face, in the dark, with him. What will he do when he finds out who you really are?

WHERE WERE YOU WHEN THE LIGHTS WENT OUT?

ROMANCE

Dear Reader,

I can vaguely remember the great blackout of 1965, when most of New York went dark for the night. My family was at home when it hit, but some people were trapped in interesting places!

That's how it is for the three couples in this exciting trilogy that asks the question "Where Were You When the Lights Went Out?" started by Mary Anne Wilson's NINE MONTHS LATER... and Linda Randall Wisdom's DO YOU TAKE THIS MAN... It's the Fourth of July, in the midst of a torrid heat wave, when a blackout darkens much of the West Coast. You're not going to believe the places and situations these couples get trapped in!

My sister and I spent our blackout night listening to the Beatles on the radio. Trust me, though, these couples make much better use of their time!

Regards,

Debra Matteucci,
Senior Editor & Editorial Coordinator
Harlequin Books
300 East 42nd Street
New York, NY 10017

Jacqueline Diamond

DEAR LONELY IN L.A....

Harlequin Books

TORONTO • NEW YORK • LONDON
AMSTERDAM • PARIS • SYDNEY • HAMBURG
STOCKHOLM • ATHENS • TOKYO • MILAN
MADRID • WARSAW • BUDAPEST • AUCKLAND

ISBN 0-373-16645-1

DEAR LONELY IN L.A....

Copyright © 1996 by Jackie Hyman.

Chapter One

Dear RNW,

You may find this difficult to believe, but last week you saved my life.

As I stepped onto a private plane in Rome, I remembered the words in your letter. "Even though we have never met, your inspiration gives my heart wings. You are the first woman I have ever known whose friendship was not a trap."

At that moment, I realized two things. The first is that you are a very special man, not because of the financial accomplishments to which you've referred, but for the warmth and insight revealed in your writing.

The second was that I was, quite literally, stepping into a trap. My client, who had provided the plane to carry me to his remote estate, was not seeking to solve a murder but to commit one. And I was the intended target.

Sitting on the living room carpet in her condominium, Dana Grant paused in the middle of reading the letter. It was her favorite of all the ones she had composed in her year of corresponding with a mysterious man she knew only by his initials, RNW.

Six months ago, when she wrote this particular piece of fiction, she had enjoyed pretending she was a glamorous detective. Now she wondered if she hadn't gone too far.

RNW had decided he wanted to meet her. It was unthinkable. Even if he didn't turn out to be an escaped convict or something equally undesirable, he'd be furious at learning that she was a high-school English teacher whose imaginary alter ego was based on a character in a soap opera.

Reluctantly Dana forced herself to read the rest of the letter.

It struck me that there must be a reason why my client had asked such detailed questions about my appearance when we spoke on the phone. Was he setting me up to die and be mistaken for someone else?

As we started down the runway, I wrenched open the door, leaped from the plane and ran for my life. I was badly bruised, but the injuries are healing. Tragically, the plane exploded in midair, killing the pilot.

Further investigation has revealed that the client owes massive gambling debts. His wife, who somewhat resembles me, recently took out life insurance in the amount of one million dollars. I notified the Italian authorities, who have taken them both into custody.

Even a veteran detective like me was deceived, but your words opened my eyes.

Please write again soon.

With deep gratitude,
DG

The ad in the Pen Pals Wanted column of the singles magazine had intrigued Dana when she came across it the previous year. It had begun "Lonely in L.A.: Man of mystery seeks adventuresome lady to create a world of our own."

From the wording, she'd assumed this was a game. One of her high-school English students was corresponding with another science fiction buff, each pretending to be a heroic character as they developed a private fantasy world.

Dana had been fascinated by the concept. After reading the ad, she'd leaped at the chance to exercise the same kind of creativity in a different context.

The problem was that over the months, the correspondence had ceased to feel like a game. More and more, as she hurried to her postal box in hopes of receiving another letter from RNW, she found herself trying to picture the flesh-and-blood man behind the mystique.

Was he actually a wealthy entrepreneur, as he said? As far as she was concerned, it didn't matter whether he was a CEO or a grocery clerk.

Despite her fantasies about globe-trotting, she had simple tastes. The things RNW wrote about—like walks in the woods—appealed to her more than ski trips to Switzerland and jumping out of airplanes in Rome.

Running her hand distractedly through her shaggy hair, Dana stared at the letters scattered across the carpet. How charming, she thought irritably. Here she was on her thirtieth birthday, daydreaming like a teenager.

She had to break off the correspondence. Maybe she could fake her own death and write a tearful letter, signing it with the name of a fictional secretary. Or perhaps she should mark his letters Subject deceased—return to sender.

No, that seemed awfully coldhearted.

Maybe she ought to arrange a meeting just to satisfy her curiosity. Dana chewed her lip, briefly contemplating the possibility and then dismissing it.

She knew what would happen when she told him the truth, that her character was based on a glamorous detective portrayed by her sister. Either RNW would stalk away in a cold fury, or he would ask for an introduction to Dominique.

It happened all the time. But in this instance, Dana had brought it on herself, she reflected as she put away the letters.

She hadn't thought it was significant when she based her alter ego on Dominique's character on the soap opera *Intimate Pursuits*. Now, in hindsight, Dana could see she'd been repeating a lifetime pattern of living in her older sister's shadow.

Where Dana was shy and ordinary-looking, Dominique had a bold character and a stunning face and figure. Not to mention sophistication that glittered from every pore.

Dana still hadn't fully recovered from the boyfriend who, two years before, had finally admitted he was attracted to her only because of her resemblance to her sister. Even her parents could never quite disguise their partiality toward their elder daughter.

Well, today was Dana's thirtieth birthday, as well as the Fourth of July. No more phony personas. She was going to take hold of her life and start making things happen.

The trick, of course, was to figure out how.

Her summer was free, except for a volunteer job helping run a national student writing contest. Tomorrow she would check the paper for special events where she might meet a guy to make her forget all about RNW.

And tonight, maybe her sister would have some helpful advice. Dominique had promised to bring a birthday banquet, complete with wine and flowers.

It would be fun, chatting together like old times. Who needed a guy, anyway? Especially RNW, who was probably nothing like he seemed in his letters.

But if he really was poetic and thoughtful, well, Dana couldn't help wishing *he* would be the one bringing the birthday feast.

She wondered what he would have looked like, standing on her doorstep tonight. Tall, dark and handsome—why not? She might as well give him broad shoulders and a gleam in his eye. This was *her* fantasy, after all.

He would balance the dinner and flowers without the least sign of awkwardness. His grin would light up at the sight of her, and then he would take her in his arms...

... and spill food all over her T-shirt.

Dana stared at her shirt in the mirror. It did indeed bear a small grease mark, the remains of lunch. Making a face, she changed into her favorite red-white-and-blue short-sleeved cotton sweater.

Over it, Dana fastened an antique cameo necklace. Her grandmother had given both her and Dominique identical ones on their sixteenth birthdays.

Adding a pair of pearl earrings, she swapped her jeans for navy slacks. A pair of red sandals would complete the outfit, but Dana didn't own any.

Impulsively she decided to head for the mall and buy a pair. Why not? If she planned to start a new life, she deserved a sexy image to go with it. Surely a few shops would be open, even on a holiday.

Lacing on a pair of jogging shoes, Dana added a baseball cap and a pair of sunglasses. She'd fallen into the habit of wearing a disguise because, although she didn't see much similarity, people sometimes mistook her for Dominique.

It was her above-average height, the shape of her head and the general proportions of her body and features, the art teacher at Dana's school had surmised. The woman had also pointed out that actresses look quite different out of makeup. How could fans be sure that Dominique's bright green eyes weren't actually hazel and that her chestnut hair wasn't really light brown?

Opening the door, Dana encountered a blast of late-afternoon heat. Pasadena lay inland, far from ocean breezes, and the Los Angeles inversion layer had turned the basin into a sauna. But it suited the Fourth of July.

She should have bought tickets for fireworks at the Rose Bowl, but it had never occurred to her, Dana mused as she paced along a tree-shaded paseo outside her condo. She'd never attended the Rose Parade in person, either.

Sliding into her dented green car, she headed for Plaza Pasadena. Her thoughts flying ahead, she nearly passed the Bain Mailbox and Copy Store before she noticed it was open. Open? On the Fourth of July?

Dana swerved into the parking lot. Visiting the postal store had become a treasured routine, and she regretted having been too busy to drop by the previous day.

Dana's mailbox at the condo was too small to accommodate packages of manuscripts for the writing contests she helped coordinate, so she had rented a mailbox. It kept RNW from knowing where she lived, too, in case he ever decided to drop by and check her out.

The store owner, Morey Bain, wrapped and mailed packages of manuscripts when Dana needed to send them to judges. She'd gotten in the habit of leaving all her outgoing mail with him, knowing it would be sent promptly from the city's main post office.

Only one car sat in the lot today, a large, ancient Buick. Dana parked in its shade and went into the store.

The discreet chime of the door aroused the attention of a woman sitting at the counter with folders and ledgers spread around her. Dana recognized the thin face and gray-streaked hair of Morey Bain's estranged wife, Nita, who used to help in the store before the breakup.

"We're not open," Nita said.

Dana hesitated. "It wasn't locked."

"The door's open, but I'm not working." Catching Dana's glance at the ledgers, Nita added frankly, "I'm snooping."

"Oh, excuse me." Dana didn't want to get involved in other people's marital problems, but she didn't want to leave without her mail, either. "I didn't get over here yesterday, so would it be all right if I just took a look?"

Nita shrugged. "I suppose so."

Dana walked briskly to her box, inserted the key and opened it. There was nothing of interest inside, just a bill and a catalog.

As she was leaving, Nita glanced up again. "Whoa!" the older woman said.

"Is there a problem?"

"I've seen you before." Mrs. Bain squinted at her. "Haven't I?"

Dana nodded. "I'm in here a lot."

"You aren't... I mean, with that hat and everything... You kind of look like what's-her-name."

"She's my sister," Dana said.

Nita's eyes widened. "There's something you'd better see," she said.

The woman poked into a drawer and pulled out a thick file. Dana opened it with mild curiosity, which was quickly replaced by horror.

Beneath a sheaf of notes lay photocopies of her recent letters—both the ones she'd sent to RNW and his replies.

"I don't understand," she gasped. "What on earth—?"

"The only good thing about my sleaze of a husband is that he keeps thorough records." Nita pointed to the handwritten notes. "Apparently, he began to suspect you were really... What's your sister's name?"

"Dominique," Dana said numbly.

"He must have been steaming open your letters before putting them in the box." Nita grimaced. "You left your outgoing mail here, too, didn't you? That's how he got both sides of the correspondence."

"Why would he do it? Is he some kind of pervert?"

"Morey never wastes his time unless there's money involved." Nita shook her head grimly. "He's got dollar signs scribbled all over his notes."

Dollar signs? Morey Bain, the chubby man who'd greeted her every day with a smile, had been planning to rip her off?

"He was going to sell them?" Dana asked. "How awful. I mean, I'm not Dominique, but if one of the tabloids thought I was..."

The possibilities sent shock waves through her system. She could picture the headlines: "Dominique stars in private soap." Or: "Postal passion arouses Dominique."

Dana would have to admit publicly that she'd written the letters, to the amusement of a whole high school full of gossipy students and a few snide faculty members. And RNW would learn the truth about her in screaming headlines at the supermarket.

Oh, no. RNW. *His* letters had been copied, too. What if the tabloids exposed his most private thoughts as public entertainment?

"Thank goodness you found these in time," Dana said.

Reaching for the file, Nita plucked out a couple of Xerox copy receipts. "As I said, my husband keeps good records. He even charged himself for the copies he made. According to this, he made two of each letter."

"Two?" Dana said. "Where's the other set?"

"That's a good question," said Nita.

"I've got to talk to him." Panic threatened to wipe away Dana's composure. "Once I explain that I'm not Dominique, I'm sure he'll back off."

"Or, you could sue him," Nita volunteered. "But please wait until I get my divorce settlement, okay?"

"I'd rather prevent trouble than mop up afterward." Not to mention the fact that her reputation would be in tatters, her sister would be furious, and RNW would hate her through all eternity. "Where is he now?"

Nita wrote an address on a slip of paper. "You can try to talk to him if you want to." She indicated the ledgers. "He's also been trying to hide income from my lawyer. Isn't it disgusting?"

"Very." Dana clutched the file. "Thank you for giving me these."

"I just hate to see the creep get away with anything." Then, as Dana went through the door, Nita added, "Be careful who you marry. Guys can be such liars!"

So can women, thought Dana, wincing as she recalled the fictional exploits she'd bragged of in her letters. At the moment, she wished she really did possess the skills and daring of her make-believe character.

She was going to need all that and more to prevent a major embarrassment to a couple of innocent people.

"HEY, boss," said the world's most unconventional butler. "You gotta talk to this dude from the copy shop. He's sweating bullets about something."

"On the Fourth of July?" Nick Lyon watched his luggage disappear into the depths of his eighteen-thousand-square-foot hillside home, toted by the latest of the street people his butler liked to hire. After a thorough investigation to make sure they had no criminal records, of course.

"The guy's called three times in two days," said Hitch Rickert, who wore a black tuxedo jacket, a stiff white shirt and a red cummerbund over torn jeans and huarache sandals. The only visible signs of his biker days were a scraggly ponytail and a tattoo extending up his neck and extolling the virtues of someone named Phyllis.

"Tomorrow." Today, Nick had too much to think about.

He'd just returned from negotiating a multimillion-dollar deal with a Japanese company involving the licensing and packaging of multimedia programs on CD-ROM.

"There's another message." Hitch trailed Nick toward his personal quarters. "A reporter from *Heat!* wants to get Mr. Williams's comment about something or other."

"The tabloids are always after him. Trash that one."

"Okay, boss," said Hitch, and then went to tend to his butler duties.

The first thing Nick needed was a hot shower to wash off the flight from Tokyo. Then a late lunch, after which he would review the plans for his party.

Tonight was going to change Nick's life forever and not, he suspected, in an enjoyable way.

His guests—the cream of the Los Angeles entertainment and business communities, plus a few elite reporters—had been invited to the Top Hat restaurant in Hollywood at 10:00 p.m. to meet reclusive billionaire Renfro Williams.

No one had ever seen Renfro Williams. Pursued by the ambitious, the nosy and the greedy, he was reputed to have a privacy fetish even more pronounced than that of the late Howard Hughes. Ever since the invitations had gone out, curiosity had risen to a fever pitch.

The face Renfro presented to the world was that of his right-hand man and chief negotiator, Nick Lyon. Everybody knew Nick, and nobody pestered him. People treated him politely, but they didn't hang on him, or try to manipulate him, or, heaven forbid, try to marry him for his money.

Until tonight, only Nick's old surfing buddy, Hitch Rickert, had known the truth—that Renfro Williams didn't exist. Or, more accurately, that his real name was Renfro Nicholas Williams, alias Nick Lyon.

As hot water sluiced over his bare body, Nick recalled the day he was born. Not many men could remember their own birth.

After inheriting his father's small video-packaging business, he'd expanded explosively, taking advantage of leaps in technology and his own business acumen. His first major acquisition, at the age of twenty-five, had been a multimedia company in New Jersey.

He had arrived without fanfare several hours before the first scheduled board meeting. Unrecognized, he'd had a chance to overhear conversations as he toured the building.

Both male and female executives had been jockeying for position, trying to figure out how to impress and co-opt the incoming magnate. They had spoken of Renfro Williams as if he were half deity and half demon.

The experience had left a bad taste in Nick's mouth. He didn't want to be surrounded by phonies. The only way to be sure of learning the truth about the people who worked for him, he'd realized, was to play the role of his own assistant.

So Nick had explained to his new employees that he was the eyes and ears of a reclusive genius, who never left his inner sanctum. He had introduced himself as Nick Lyon, impulsively basing the last name on the fact that he was lying.

He'd kept that identity for ten years. Sometimes Nick couldn't believe he'd pulled it off.

But the game was wearing thin. Rumors that Renfro suffered from health or mental problems threatened to damage his business credibility. So he'd decided to go public. And tonight was to be the night.

Toweling off as he stood on the lush bath mat, Nick glanced out the louvered window. Striped tents gleamed in the sunlight, and workmen were setting up chairs and tables.

He couldn't turn back now.

Still posing as Nick, he would greet his guests at the Top Hat and invite them to Renfro's estate. It was a device to foil yellow journalists, who, if they realized the true location of the announcement, would spend all day trying to circumvent his newly augmented security system.

He supposed a public restaurant might not be a bad place to reveal his identity. But Nick liked to keep a tight rein on his affairs. He could orchestrate matters with more authority here at his sprawling property in Pacific Palisades, an area of secluded canyons between Beverly Hills and Malibu.

After the announcement, Nick would treat his guests to a fabulous feast and spectacular fireworks. He wanted a touch of grandeur tonight, in honor of his rebirth.

Life would never be the same again. But if he was going to meet the intriguing DG, Nick reminded himself, he couldn't keep masquerading as someone he wasn't.

The bathroom phone began ringing. Frowning, Nick ignored it. He was in no mood for interruptions. Hitch could answer or a machine would pick it up.

Stepping into the adjacent dressing room, Nick pulled on a pair of safari shorts and a short-sleeved button-down shirt woven of black cotton. It made him look like an adventurer, he decided, which suited his mood today.

Someone thumped on the door. Nick barely had time to call out, "Enter!" before Hitch popped inside.

"That copy-shop guy is on the phone again," said the butler. "Fellow named Tom Wyatt. He seems to be in a panic."

Nick couldn't imagine what could be important enough to make the store owner call him on a holiday. The postal box was used only to receive DG's letters, anyway. "Did he say what he wanted?"

"Doesn't make sense to me." Hitch shrugged. "Somebody showed up asking about some letters, that's all."

"A woman?"

"No, a guy who owns another copy shop," Hitch replied. "He said something about big money and tabloids. Mean anything to you?"

"I think I'd better take the call," said Nick.

If the wrong person had gotten hold of the letters, his coming-out party might not be the most distressing experience of the day, after all.

Chapter Two

Dear DG,

I was concerned to hear about your near escape from death in Rome. If you didn't break at least one bone jumping from a taxiing airplane, you were amazingly lucky.

It's disconcerting to think of you lying somewhere bleeding, and me unable to help. I can only hope that you will learn from experience and be more discerning about the cases you take in the future.

It's hard to think of you as fragile, as someone who could be lost to me. These past few months, I've come to depend on our "conversations" to free me from the narrow realm in which I both rule and am imprisoned.

In a way, not being able to see you in person is liberating. People believe they know us simply because they know our name, our appearance and our voice. But they're ignorant of our real, inner selves.

I feel as if I'm coming to know that deep part of you, but there are still things I wonder about. What aspects of your thoughts would surprise others, if they could read your mind? What parts of yourself do you hide from the people closest to you?

Awaiting your next letter, I remain,

Your friend,
RNW

"Yes?" Nick barked into the phone.

He was greeted by a cough. "Sorry." The poor guy sounded nervous. "Is this Mr. R. Williams?"

"It's Nick—I work for Mr. Williams." He'd impulsively listed the box in his real name, figuring R. Williams sounded anonymous enough. "I'm the guy who comes in every week."

"Well, there's a problem." Tom's voice had a dry catch to it, either from a summer cold or from severe anxiety. "Yesterday, I caught my new receptionist giving out information to a fellow named Morey Bain. He owns a postal place over in Pasadena."

Nick felt a tick of discomfort. He mailed DG's letters to a box in Pasadena. "What kind of information?"

"Mr. Williams's name and address," said Tom. "It seems this Morey person read some of the letters. That's completely unethical. Most people in this business are like me, hardworking and honest, but we're not part of the U.S. Postal Service. We're private businessmen."

"In other words, unregulated," Nick growled.

"I fired the receptionist," Tom hurried on. "Then I told Morey this information was not to leave my store."

Obviously, the result had been less than satisfactory, or Tom wouldn't be calling on a holiday. "But?"

"He offered to cut me in on the money." Tom uttered a disgusted snort. "It seems your boss is an important man, and this woman he's been writing to is some soap-opera star named Dominique Grant. I don't follow those things, but my wife says she plays a glamorous detective on TV."

DG was a phony? Nick half expected to snap awake and find that he'd been dreaming, or to hear Hitch announce that this call was a joke.

He had placed the pen pal ad partly out of curiosity. He had also nursed the small hope that he might meet a woman who would appreciate him for himself.

Most of the answers Nick received to his Lonely in L.A. ad had been dull or overly cute, but one had grabbed his attention. With an almost instant sense of recognition, he'd found himself feeling as if he'd always known this woman, or been meant to know her.

A few times during the past year, he'd suspected DG might be exaggerating her exploits, but he hadn't held it against her. He, too, was taking advantage of anonymity, in his case to reveal his long-hidden loneliness.

DG also had slowly begun revealing her vulnerable side. It had been fascinating, fitting together a picture of her through the jigsaw puzzle of hints she had given him.

Beneath the tales of derring-do, Nick had discovered a woman of internal contradictions, a person struggling toward a deeper sense of self. DG managed to be at once bold and fearful, apologetic and rambunctious, clever and naive. She had revealed more than she realized, he felt sure.

He had decided it was time to go beyond letters and meet this fascinating woman. He had prepared himself not to be judgmental if DG turned out to be different from the way she portrayed herself.

But this wasn't a mild deception; it was outright betrayal. The woman was neither a detective nor a dreamer, but an actress playing a role. DG, his funny, brave soul mate, was the kind of exploitive woman he had been trying to avoid in the first place.

What had their correspondence been to her, a game? Was she planning to use Nick's feelings as fodder for her scriptwriters?

And now this Bain character had discovered RNW's identity. Nick's temper flared at the prospect of having his private correspondence splashed across newspapers and TV screens. Why did this have to happen just when he was planning to take Renfro public, leaving Nick nowhere to hide?

He had to run damage control, and the sooner the better. "How do I get the letters back?"

"I wish I knew," Tom said with a sigh. "The best I can do is give you Morey's address. I got it off the check he wrote my receptionist."

Nick jotted down the information. The house was located in South Pasadena.

As he hung up, every instinct screamed at him to rush to Morey Bain's house and confront the jerk. But there were a few matters he had to take care of first.

Nick Lyon never went anywhere unprepared.

REALIZING she would have to postpone tonight's dinner, Dana had stopped to use a pay phone. Now, after a long explanation, she could tell from her sister's voice that Dominique didn't know whether to cry or get angry.

"I'm sorry," Dana said for the third time in ten minutes.

"I know you didn't intend for this to happen," replied her sister, "but I'm so sick of seeing my name in the tabloids! And...well, I was going to tell you tonight. I've been dating Harmon Mason."

"The director?" One of Mason's films had been nominated for a best-picture Oscar several years earlier. "Surely he wouldn't take much notice of a silly scandal in a tabloid," Dana said.

"He can be touchy," Dominique admitted. "Besides, our relationship isn't well established yet. Something embarrassing like this might destroy it before it has a chance."

"I'll do my best to get the letters back," Dana said. "I promise." If she had ruined Dominique's chance at love, she would never forgive herself.

Her sister let out a long breath. "I'll put the flowers in the fridge, and we can have our dinner next weekend, okay? No, scratch that, I've got a fund-raiser and a charity golf game. Maybe in two weeks, okay?"

"Sure. Whatever. I'll talk to you later."

"I know you'll do your best," Dominique said.

Glumly Dana hung up. There went her birthday celebration and her chat with Dominique about changing her life. But it would be worth it if she could keep her sister's name out of the tabloids.

And prevent her innermost thoughts from showing up on school bulletin boards, annotated with raunchy comments. The very thought made her want to crawl into a hole and hibernate.

As she drove toward South Pasadena, Dana tried to formulate a plan. The first thing that came to mind was to threaten to sue Morey Bain, but she doubted that would dissuade him. Not when he could get a big payoff right away.

Perhaps she should notify the tabloids that the letters hadn't been written by Dominique. But she couldn't be sure of reaching them all. Besides, if Morey *hadn't* sold the letters yet, she might create a scandal where none existed.

She would just have to play it by ear.

Morey Bain lived on a hilly street shaded by large trees. Dana stopped a few houses down from his address and surveyed the place.

From here, she could see several shingles askew on the roof of the two-story structure, a partly open window on the second floor, and streaks discoloring the beige paint. A small sign on the lawn warned that the residence was protected by a security agency.

Either the place was wired with an alarm, Dana thought, or Morey had stolen the sign.

Gathering her nerve, she skirted an overgrown rose-bush that intruded onto the walkway, marched to the porch and rang the bell. There was no response. A further series of knocks and rings produced the same result.

Below her along the block, Dana could see a family partaking in a holiday barbecue. Children ran around, shrieking and waving sparklers, while parents enjoyed the lounge chairs.

She decided to proceed like a detective and interview the neighbors. It was possible Morey had left a key with someone in case he locked himself out.

A neighbor might let Dana in to retrieve her own letters. It was a long shot, but the only one she could think of.

For the next hour or so, she traipsed all over the neighborhood, knocking on doors. Before she could get past the question ''Do you by any chance have a key to Morey Bain's house?'' she received responses ranging from ''That creep? Are you kidding?'' to ''If I had one, I'd steal back the garden equipment he swiped from me!''

Reluctantly, as afternoon turned to twilight and she tucked away her sunglasses, Dana accept the fact that no one had a key. Nor had Morey returned, with or without her letters.

One thing the neighbors had confirmed—Morey possessed a security system. They knew because a couple of times it had gone off by accident.

It was well after seven, Dana's feet hurt, and her birthday was ruined. Determined to try every possible recourse, she returned to one house where a party was under way.

"I wonder if I could borrow the phone?" she asked the resident. "I need to call the police."

The woman's eyebrows arched. "Is something wrong?"

"Yes and no," Dana admitted. "It's about Morey. He stole something from me."

The woman didn't probe further. "If you can get that idiot arrested, you can borrow my phone anytime."

Alone in the kitchen, Dana dialed a police business number. The dispatcher connected her to the desk sergeant, who listened to her story with something less than enthusiasm.

"Sounds like a matter for the postal inspectors," the man said. "The postal service investigates thefts from the mail."

"Do they work on holidays?" Dana asked.

"You could give them a call." He didn't sound encouraging.

No one answered at the post office. Of course not, Dana thought as she hung up. It was nearly eight o'clock on the Fourth of July.

"No luck?" asked the neighbor.

"Afraid not," Dana admitted. "I'm sorry I intruded."

The woman regarded her with a comradely air. "Why don't you stick around for a while? From our yard, you can see if his car pulls up."

"Thanks," Dana said. "Maybe I will."

She'd been smelling charcoal-broiled hamburgers since she arrived, but when she stepped outside, she saw that everything had been eaten. There wasn't so much as an olive left on the relish tray.

The guests wore expressions of stuffed satisfaction. The shouts of the children playing kick-the-can barely muffled the rumbling of Dana's stomach, but she had, after all, arrived uninvited.

Gazing over the valley below the neighborhood, she could see an occasional sparkle and hear the popping sound of firecrackers. Although the sky hadn't grown dark yet, people were getting an early start.

She wondered what RNW was doing tonight. Surely he couldn't really be what he claimed, a man isolated by his success, living on a large estate in Pacific Palisades. He must have invented all that, just as she'd invented her alter ego.

Did he live in an apartment? Maybe he, too, was inhaling the scent of other people's barbecues and listening to the bang of their firecrackers. From his letters, he sounded like a man who spent much of his time alone.

She wished they had had a chance to know each other without their relationship being tarnished by Morey Bain. She wished she dared to meet RNW just once.

Well, maybe she could. That might be the first step in taking the reins of her life firmly in hand.

If she could just recover those letters.

IT WAS after eight o'clock when Nick finished his tasks. Hitch didn't bat an eye when informed that he was being left in charge of the party arrangements.

"The caterer's setting up in the kitchen." The butler clicked his tongue. "I don't see why you bother. Everybody will be snarfing down hors d'oeuvres and swilling drinks at the restaurant at ten o'clock. Who's going to eat again here?''

"I am." Nick didn't plan to spend more than a few minutes at the Top Hat before inviting everyone to follow him home. "Besides, trust me—the richer people get, the more they like to dine at someone else's expense.''

He knew it might take a while to run down this Morey person, but it wouldn't hurt Renfro's guests to stew for a while. They'd been drawn to the party out of curiosity and a desire to see and be seen, and they would get satisfaction on all counts.

Besides, show-business folks kept late hours. Real nightlife didn't get started until around midnight in Los Angeles.

Rising from his desk chair, Nick decided not to change clothes. He would switch to a tuxedo when he brought his guests home, thus underscoring the difference between Nick Lyon and Renfro Williams.

As he headed for the row of garages, Nick decided to take one of the sports cars, a red convertible. It suited his mood.

His fists clenched the steering wheel in a death grip as he gunned the car and shot down the driveway. His instincts screamed at him to pound the tar out of this weasely Morey Bain. But he'd learned long ago that playing on people's greed was the easiest way to get what you wanted.

Tucked into Nick's wallet was a cashier's check—messengered over by Renfro Williams's banker, who'd drawn it up personally this evening—for one hundred thousand dollars, made out to Morey Bain.

How ironic, he thought, that on his last night as assistant to Renfro Williams, Nick would do once again what he'd done so often before, smooth his make-believe boss's path with a little diplomacy and a wad of money.

Twilight was thickening into darkness by the time he reached Morey Bain's address. From this hilly street, the nearby lowlands formed a fairyland of illuminated houses, brightly colored signs and floodlit yards.

As Nick walked to the house, a check of his watch showed it was a quarter to nine. Jabbing the doorbell, he listened to it ring hollowly. Nothing thumped or banged inside the house, so he rang again. Still nothing.

Nick shifted restlessly on the porch. He had to track down Morey Bain. Maybe the guy had left something inside the house, like a party invitation, that indicated where he had gone. There was even a tiny chance that the letters were inside somewhere, practically daring Nick to break in and take them.

That was all he needed, to get arrested tonight. The publicity would ensure that the story of Renfro Williams's mail-order romance with an actress made every front page and newscast in America.

But this was Nick Lyon's last night of life, so to speak. At the stroke of midnight, or sometime around then, he would be officially dissolved.

Nick Lyon must die tonight, but he could go out in a blaze of glory. Or infamy. Burglarizing a house would fit the bill.

The sign sporting the name of a security agency gave him pause, but only for a moment. He was willing to bet a low-rent character like Morey Bain had gone for a cheapo deal, wiring only the obvious places—front and rear doors and first-floor windows.

What were the odds that the second floor had been secured, as well? He could only hope that his instincts were right, he thought as he eyed a window, right above a huge spreading tree. It had been left open a good three inches.

Nick grimaced, wishing he'd worn something more suitable for climbing. Safari shorts and Italian leather slip-on shoes weren't going to stand him in good stead, but he had no choice.

The lower branches of the tree were too high for easy access. However, the house next door was dark, and someone had left a ladder propped against the side.

He jogged down the slope, grateful that the properties weren't fenced, and borrowed the ladder. After retrieving a flashlight from his car, he planted the ladder in place and climbed upward.

Transferring into the tree proved awkward. In the dark, it was hard to see the dozens of knobby branches that clutched at him from every direction. By the time he reached the window, Nick's shorts were torn and the top button on his shirt had been wrenched away.

He also managed to knock the ladder loose, sending it thumping to the ground.

After a quick prayer, he leaned from his perch toward the window and tried to push up the lower panel. It groaned and refused to budge.

Nick's determination to find a quick solution to his problem did not extend to smashing glass. He had been counting on sneaking inside and departing without a trace. But he couldn't go back; he faced a ten-foot drop.

The window might be secured by nails, or it might just be stuck. Bracing himself against the thick branch, he grasped the lower rim again and shoved upward.

The wood creaked, resisted, and suddenly yielded, sliding almost to the top rail. Nick teetered off balance, bringing himself into equilibrium by sheer force of will and muscles honed in his private gymnasium.

Resting against the trunk, he assessed the few feet between him and the window. Even worse than getting arrested would be falling two stories and breaking something vital.

The safest course, he decided, was to lie on his stomach and back in. Lowering himself onto the branch, he extended his feet over empty space and inched backward.

Eternity passed before his shoes touched the sill. Relieved, Nick wriggled farther, supporting himself with powerful arms.

The branch groaned. Suspended in midair, halfway between tree and house, there was nothing Nick could do but keep pushing.

He heard another groan, and then a low cracking sound. Desperately he shoved backward until his hips cleared the opening. He half slid and half fell onto the floor.

Then the alarm went off.

The jangling sent Nick's heart rocketing into his throat. Bain must have installed a motion sensor. For once, Nick Lyon had underestimated his opponent.

Suddenly the noise stopped.

Not just the noise, but everything. Through the window, he could see that the world had gone black. The valley, partially visible through the tree, had become a dark bowl pierced only by car headlights, red taillights, and distant bursts of fireworks.

A blackout. Nick couldn't believe his luck.

There was no telling how long it would last. No more than a minute or two before the power came on, probably, but he would make the most of this chance.

Nick stood, flexing his muscles cautiously. He was slightly bruised where his thighs had hit the sill, and his arms ached from supporting his weight, but that was all. Not a big price to pay for justice.

Pulling the flashlight from his pocket, Nick went in search of his letters.

Chapter Three

Dear RNW,

Sometimes, in the midst of my daily work routine, I get a sense of displacement. Your letters have become more real than the places and individuals I see, hear and touch. Maybe it's because I don't have to disguise my moods and because I feel safe with you.

I've been thinking about what you said in your last letter, that people believe they know us simply because they know how we look and sound, but that in fact we conceal our inner selves.

You asked me what things about me would surprise others. That's hard to answer, because it means I have to place my full trust in you. But here goes.

First, I have to fight a tendency to get too involved in other people's problems, especially adolescents who are going through a difficult time. I want to rush in and make everything right.

But that's beyond my power and sometimes would do more harm than good. So I maintain a kind of Solomon-like distance, listening carefully and offering advice where it's requested, all the while pretending my heart isn't aching in empathy.

Second, I'm a bigger coward than anyone would guess. I know I write about brave deeds; like everyone, I cope with whatever life throws in my direction and try to put a calm face on it. But inside I'm a quivering mess. I wish I had more genuine courage.

Finally, here's the hardest part to reveal. I've never met a man who brought out my sensual side, yet I know I must have one.

When that special man takes me in his arms, I'll discover sensations I've never known before, and we'll explore each other in a thousand ways, and be attuned to each other instinctively. Is that crazy? Do things like that ever really happen?

Best,
DG

Sipping a cola that failed to ease her hunger pangs, Dana realized she'd been daydreaming in the midst of a party. Her cheeks heated as she wondered if anyone had guessed from her expression that she'd been wondering what it would be like to make love.

Two children ran by with sparklers, startling Dana out of her reverie. When had the last daylight vanished? How long had she stood here daydreaming?

According to her watch, it was about nine o'clock, which meant that soon fireworks would be spurting from the valley below. She was beginning to doubt that Morey Bain would ever return.

It was no use waiting any longer. She might as well go home and raid the refrigerator.

The shriek of an alarm startled Dana. It sounded as if it were coming from Morey Bain's house.

"The darn thing's set itself off again," muttered her hostess, who was relaxing on a recliner. "I sure hope we don't have to listen to it all ni—"

The alarm stopped. So did the hum of an air-conditioning unit and a radio that had been blaring country music. Along with the silence came darkness, broken only by star showers from the sparklers.

"There's a bit of luck," cheered the hostess, now merely a shape in the night. "It must have been a surge of electricity that set off the alarm. Maybe that's what caused the outage."

"It'll be up in a few minutes," said someone else. "We haven't had a blackout around here in ages."

"I like it this way," added another woman. "Look down there!"

In the valley below, fireworks danced into the sky. Without the competing lights of homes and signs, they took on an intensity Dana had never noticed before.

Nevertheless, she didn't intend to stick around to enjoy the show. It was possible that Morey Bain had arrived home and set off his alarm by accident, and she intended to go confront him.

She thanked her hostess and left. The walk to Morey's house took longer than it would have under ordinary circumstances, as Dana's eyes strained to adjust to the dimness.

Someone had parked a convertible sports car in front of Morey's house. It wasn't Morey's; he owned a van marked with the name of his store. Or had he already sold the letters and spent his money on a new car?

After pressing the doorbell twice, she realized that of course it couldn't ring without electricity. She knocked, not really expecting an answer and not receiving one.

Dana's spirits sank. Another dead end.

Or was it? Without the alarm system, she might be able to slip inside and take a look around, just in case the other set of letters had been left there. That is, assuming she could find a way in.

It was a crazy idea. Soap-opera detectives might break into houses, but high-school English teachers didn't.

Wishing she had the daring of her alter ego, Dana retreated toward her car. In her absorption, she didn't notice the rosebush thrusting its unpruned branches into her path until she felt a sharp tug on her sweater.

Instinctively Dana jerked her arm free. As she did so, she could feel the sleeve rip. It was only a small hole, but this was her favorite sweater, and it would never be the same.

Unaccustomed fury blazed within her. Morey Bain had stolen her letters, ruined her birthday and now destroyed her property through his carelessness.

Dana didn't stop to reason as her anger turned to grim determination. At this moment, she felt she'd be justified in doing almost anything to that no-good louse.

It wasn't Dana Grant who snatched a flashlight from her car and marched back to the house. It was that fearless, irrepressible detective, DG, already figuring out how to break in.

Maybe Morey was one of those people who hid a key in case he locked himself out. And the blackout had fixed the problem of the alarm.

Outrage and adrenaline powered her onto the porch. She checked beneath the mat, then under a vase containing a withered plant. No luck. Shining her flashlight onto the limp leaves, Dana wondered why the thing was in such bad shape.

Maybe because somebody kept forgetting his key and pulling it out by the roots.

With a silent apology to the hapless plant, Dana grasped it and tugged upward. Sticking the flashlight under her arm, she groped around in the dirt with her free hand.

Presto magico. A house key.

Dana glared at it in the darkness. How like that obnoxious man to hide his key where it would mess up her fingernails!

The pop-pop of fireworks in the distance reminded her that time was passing and the outage wouldn't last forever. Fumbling with her tiny ray of light, she located the keyhole and let herself in.

NICK SEARCHED the upstairs first, starting with the bedroom into which he had arrived. It had been stripped to bare wallpaper and carpet. The window must have been left open to provide cross-ventilation with the master bedroom, since the chamber was obviously unoccupied.

Moving down the hall, he found a second vacant bedroom. Beginning to worry that Morey might have moved out, Nick proceeded to the end of the hall.

One glance into the master bedroom reassured him. A garish velour spread lay rumpled along the foot of the bed, revealing sheets that gave off a sweaty odor. A TV and VCR were perched on a rickety table.

His flashlight beam picked out several issues of *TV Guide* littering the floor, along with yesterday's newspaper. The trail had not grown cold.

Nick flipped through the drawers in the bedside stand, but found only a few personal items. There was nothing of interest in the dresser, the closet or the bathroom, either.

He retreated, hoping he'd left everything as he found it but doubting Morey Bain would notice the difference. The guy didn't strike him as a fastidious housekeeper.

He was halfway down the stairs when he heard the front door open.

He froze, debating what to do next. From here, the front hall resembled a pit of blackness. For all he could tell, Hannibal and his elephants might just have tiptoed inside.

Common sense dictated a hasty retreat, followed by a departure through the window. If he hadn't knocked the ladder over, that was exactly what Nick would have done. But he didn't relish the thought of dropping out of a tree.

Instead, he decided his best bet was to hide and hope that Morey, or whoever it was, would get absorbed in some activity downstairs. Then Nick could sneak down and go outside, turn around and knock, as if he'd just arrived.

There was something odd about the movements in the hall, though. The newcomer didn't stomp through the house cursing the lack of lights, the way he would have expected Morey Bain to do. The guy just stood there as if getting his bearings.

Then a flashlight came on. Well, that wasn't surprising in a blackout. But why did the newcomer still hesitate?

Nick found out for sure that it wasn't Morey Bain when a slim figure slipped across the hall in the moonlight, opened a door and jumped back with a gasp as a vacuum cleaner fell out.

Whoever it was didn't even know which door led to the broom closet. But who would be sneaking in here?

Nick supposed Morey might have cheated more than one person. Perhaps this was a vindictive ex-girlfriend.

He weighed the merits of departing and decided he didn't want to go yet. Not until he found out exactly what the newcomer was up to.

When the figure vanished into the interior of the house, Nick released a long breath and made his way quietly down the stairs, trailing the intruder.

DANA FELT LIKE AN IDIOT. The bold and daring DG would never mistake a broom closet for a room. She was grateful no one had been around to witness her embarrassment. Or her attack of nerves, either.

On TV, Dominique's character prowled through office buildings and castles alike with no sign of anxiety. In real life, Dana had to force herself not to turn and flee.

Trudging through the next door beyond the closet, she found herself in the dining room. She scanned the room with her flashlight, but saw nothing suspicious and decided not to linger. She couldn't afford to waste time, when the blackout might end at any moment.

The dining room led to the kitchen. The flashlight revealed dirt lines where appliances had been removed, apparently by the soon-to-be-ex Mrs. Bain. A sack from a hamburger drive-through sagged on the table, and crumbs spilled across the wooden surface.

Beyond the kitchen, a combination living room—den ran along the back of the house and wrapped around the far side. At the back, Dana noted what appeared to be a short hallway leading to a rear exit.

DG would certainly have made herself aware of any possible escape route and then gone about her business without a second thought. But this wasn't DG, it was Dana, and she felt a wave of guilt at intruding in someone else's house. Even Morey Bain's.

She doubted more than twenty minutes had passed since the lights went out, but it felt like hours. The later it got, the greater the likelihood that Morey would come home.

She was also beginning to wonder whether, once power resumed, the alarm system might not sense her presence and go off again. Left to her own inclinations, Dana would have gone home. But there were two other people involved here.

She forced herself to concentrate. A newspaper lay scattered on the coffee table. A welter of papers, files, bills and ads cluttered the couch, an end table and a rolltop desk.

Dana aimed her flashlight at the desk. That was when she heard a shuffling noise near the front hall.

Someone else was in the house.

Her skin prickled. She had never believed the expression about hackles rising on one's neck, but she would never doubt it again.

It couldn't be Morey. She had heard none of the normal noises, the clicking of a door and the footsteps that would accompany a homeowner's return. Whoever was in here must be trying to stay hidden.

Dana remembered the way the alarm had gone off moments before the blackout. Was it possible a real burglar had broken in before her?

She must have been crazy to think it was a good idea to sneak in here. Just because DG handled such matters routinely in the world of make-believe, that didn't mean Dana Grant could deal with them in real life.

Jump off an airplane on the runway, indeed! Dana's knees were trembling so badly she could barely move.

She assumed the burglar was a man, probably stronger than her. The only chance she had was the element of surprise. And maybe her flashlight to conk him over the head.

Taking a deep breath, Dana scampered for the back hall. At least, she meant to scamper, but it felt as if she were hobbling. Sticks of furniture thrust themselves into her path, and she moaned as her thigh whammed the edge of a table.

A couple of heavy thumps were all the warning she had as the man came after her. Two strong arms grabbed Dana's shoulders, spinning her around.

She tried to duck through his grasp, and stamped on his foot to buy a moment's distraction. It didn't work. Or rather, it worked too well. The combination of pain and the man's forward momentum sent them both plummeting off balance.

They collapsed in a kind of mad whirlwind, arms waving in a vain search for support. Dana felt the breath squeeze out of her, and the next thing she knew she was lying on the floor with a man's body pressed to hers.

NICK hadn't been surprised to note that the intruder was female. He assumed she had some personal connection with Morey, and his instincts warned him to leave her alone. He had only wanted to observe, to make sure she wasn't taking any letters.

Unfortunately, the silence induced by the blackout blotted out the normal hum of electronic devices, making it possible for her to detect his faint footsteps on the carpet. He had noticed the way her silhouette stiffened, and waited with bated breath in the vain hope that she would dismiss the noise.

When the woman fled, Nick had given chase purely on instinct. Now, lying atop her with his leg angled painfully, he wondered why he hadn't simply allowed her to escape. She could hardly report him to the police, when she'd been sneaking around herself.

"Are you all right?" he asked.

"What the heck do you think you're doing?" She shifted position, or tried to, and he realized he was pinning her down. "Get off me!"

Nick pushed himself back and sank onto the floor, grateful that the darkness hid his grimaces. He had done something to his knee that was likely to feel worse before it felt better. "I'm sorry. I may have overreacted." A beam of light hit his eyes, and he raised his hand to block it. "Get that out of my face!"

"Who are you?" The woman's voice trembled as she lowered the beam. "What are you doing here?"

"Morey Bain stole something from me." Nick lumbered to his feet, grateful to discover that the pain in his leg had only been a cramp. "He wasn't home, so I thought it might be simplest if I took it back."

The woman also stood up, ignoring Nick's proffered hand, or maybe she didn't see it. "Well, he took something from me, too."

"Are you his girlfriend?"

"Certainly not!" Her chin came up defiantly. "What a revolting idea!"

"Then where did you get the key?" he pressed.

"Under the plant," she said, as if it were the most obvious thing in the world.

"The plant?"

"The one on the porch."

Nick felt like a fool. He'd risked life and limb, not to mention his clothes, to climb through a second-story window when there was a key hidden on the front porch. "I guess I'm not as experienced at these things as you are."

"That's not surprising," she said. "I happen to be a detective."

"Licensed?" he asked.

"Of cour—" The woman coughed, as if thinking the better of her reply in midutterance, then said, "No, I'm an amateur. A good one."

"I see." But he didn't. Or he did, and didn't want to. This story was a bit too familiar. "Close your eyes."

"Why?"

"Because I'm more polite than you are," he said, and shone his flashlight into her face so that he could see what she looked like.

Her eyes snapped shut, but not before he got an impression of green flecked with brown. In the ray of light, Nick studied her high cheekbones, the wavy light-brown hair escaping from a baseball cap and the distinctive cameo at her throat.

Among his activities earlier that evening had been contacting the publicist for the company that produced Dominique Grant's soap opera. From her home office, the woman had faxed him a picture of the actress, and this one matched in almost every detail.

Oh, the eyes weren't as brilliant, and the hair peeking from beneath her cap lacked some of the luster, but that was obviously because she hadn't visited any beauty specialists today.

How amazing. Dominique Grant had come in person to reclaim her letters.

It intrigued Nick to realize that she was, evidently, as eager as he was to avoid publicity. It appeared she hadn't simply been using him as a means to collect material for scripts, but he couldn't imagine what her real motive might be.

He restrained the impulse to confront her with the truth. Better to let her go on pretending to be a detective for a while. He liked having inside knowledge that he could reveal when it suited his purpose. "And what is it Morey stole from you?" he asked.

"Some letters," she said. "I mean, he stole them from my client."

"Whose name you can't divulge?"

"Naturally."

"Well, this is a coincidence." Nick snapped off his flashlight. "I work for a man whose letters were also stolen by Morey Bain."

"What's his name?" Even in the darkness, her eyes looked huge.

Nick wasn't ready to let her know that she'd hooked the famous, or infamous, Renfro Williams. "He goes by RNW," he said. "I'm Nick. And you are?"

"Dana," she said. "You work for RNW? In what capacity?"

"I don't just work for him." Nick wondered if Dana was a nickname for Dominique, and decided it must be. "I'm also a friend."

"A mighty good friend, to take this kind of risk." For a woman who'd been tackled while burglarizing a house, she didn't seem fazed. Perhaps, as she'd stated in one of her letters, she was an expert at appearing calm while shaking inside. After all, she was an Emmy-winning actress. "So who is he really?"

"His buddies call him R," Nick retorted. "Sometimes W."

"You have a quick wit," she said. "For such a clumsy man."

Her riposte caught Nick off guard. He wasn't used to people getting the better of him, whether in business or in verbal fencing. His instincts commanded that he come up with a topper, but he couldn't.

He didn't have to win every battle, he reminded himself. Just the war. "It appears we have something in common."

"The letters," Dana said. "How did you find out about them?"

He explained about Morey Bain turning up at the other postal-box establishment. She seemed genuinely distressed to learn that RNW had been dragged into this seamy business.

It was hard to keep in mind that he was actually talking to DG. Despite the skeptical glances she threw his way, Nick detected a softness about the woman that appealed to his masculine sense of protectiveness. Besides, they were in this adventure together now, weren't they?

These few moments might be the only time he would ever spend with the woman he'd been dreaming about for months, and he had no desire to hurry. Besides, joining forces, at least temporarily, might give him a chance to find out what her intentions had been.

"Since we apparently want the same letters, we should work together," he said. "Which do you want to search, the coffee table or the desk?"

"Both," she said.

"I'll take the desk, then." He turned to his task, leaving her no choice.

THIS MAN couldn't possibly be RNW. He exuded confidence, whereas Dana's pen pal was a loner who guarded his emotions. Besides, a man as handsome as this one would never need to find a girlfriend through the mail. He must, as he said, be a friend or a co-worker.

She had tried not to notice, but even when she was lying on the floor, trying to figure out ways to brain Nick with her flashlight, she couldn't ignore the fact that the man had a hard, muscular physique that sent shivers up Dana's spine. He smelled like soap and leather, and his voice had the kind of baritone richness that would sound terrific reading Shakespeare to her class.

If RNW really was a multimillionaire business executive, Nick might be his head of security, but she couldn't bring herself to believe that scenario. More likely, Nick was a buddy helping his mild-mannered pal out of a jam. Kind of like Cyrano de Bergerac.

The image appealed to Dana, and not only because she loved literature. Cyrano had been poetic, like RNW. He had also been bold, like Nick.

This was dangerous thinking. She had no interest in Nick, except that they were stuck with each other while they tried to recover their purloined letters.

Despite the clutter on the coffee table, Dana saw nothing resembling the letters. There was also nothing worthwhile under the couch cushions, although she did find a large assortment of coins, buttons and popcorn kernels.

"Any luck?" she called.

The only response was a mechanical whir. For a heart-stopping moment, Dana thought the electricity had come on, but then she realized it must be a battery-operated device. "What is it?"

"I took the cassette out of his answering machine," he said. "There was a tape recorder in the drawer. Care to listen?"

"Sure." The room no longer seemed so dark as Dana crossed to the desk. She hadn't realized how readily one could grow accustomed to the dimness.

She also realized as she moved that the air was losing its air-conditioned crispness. Drawing near, she could feel the heat of Nick's body and again experienced that unfamiliar stirring along her spine.

An urge seized her to move within the curve of his body so that they were touching, with his large frame sheltering her smaller one. Moonlight madness, she told herself, and then forgot what she'd been thinking as Nick clicked on the recorder.

The first message was from Nita, ordering Morey to contact her lawyer in the morning. "I know what you've been up to," she said. "I've got your ledgers. Don't try to hide."

"Nice guy," muttered Nick.

"And by the way," Nita continued on the recording, "you'd better get in touch with *Dominique.*" She gave the word ironic emphasis. "She may have a surprise for you."

"Now, I wonder who Dominique could be." Nick sounded as if he were party to an inside joke, but that fit with his generally sarcastic manner.

"Beats me," said Dana.

The next message was from a man. "This is Andy Adams at *Heat!* My editor says everything looks fine and he'll issue the second check in the morning."

That was the end.

"Damn," Nick and Dana said at the same time. They exchanged disgusted glances.

The letters had already been sold. They were at this very moment in the hands of the nation's most scandalous tabloid.

Heat! had dogged Dominique in the past, inventing a battle between her and a fellow cast member over the Emmy. It was the worst tabloid nuisance of the bunch, as far as Dana was concerned.

"Can we stop them?" she asked.

"Possibly." The faint light cast shadows along Nick's face, emphasizing his strong jawline and sharply defined temples. "If the blackout is widespread, they won't be able to to put the paper out on time."

"Isn't it a weekly?" Dana asked. "Maybe they're not even going to press yet."

"Tonight's their deadline," he growled.

"How do you know?"

"I make it my business to know things like that." His tone softened. "Let's just say handling public relations is one of the things I do for RNW."

"I doubt they'll listen to us." Dana couldn't imagine that even her insistence that the letters were hers and not Dominique's would stop *Heat!* Its editors had a reputation for publishing first and retracting later.

"Unfortunately, I doubt I could find a judge to issue a restraining order on a holiday," Nick said.

A piece of paper rustled beneath Dana's foot, and she bent to retrieve it. As she did, she felt herself kick something aside, and played the flashlight under the desk, where it had slid. All she came up with, however, was a slip of paper.

It was a bank deposit, in the amount of fifty thousand dollars, dated July 3. "He didn't waste any time tucking away his first check from *Heat!*"

Nick reached for it. "I'll keep that. It might be helpful to know where the guy stashes his money."

Dana stuffed the slip into her pocket. "Not until I've made a copy for his wife. She's got a right to know, too."

A grin broke across Nick's face, shifting the harsh planes. "Your heart's in the right place, I'll give you that."

"My heart's in the same place it's always been," Dana snapped. "On the side of fair play."

To her annoyance, the man chuckled. "This sounds like a job for Superwoman."

He was making fun of her idealism, and Dana wouldn't stand for it. Never mind that tonight she really *was* playing at being a superhero, or superheroine, and that normally she would have cringed at the very thought of breaking into a house.

"If you want to impress me with your wit, you'll have to try harder," she retorted. "There's nothing ridiculous about a woman risking her life to help someone else!"

"Risking her life?" he repeated sardonically. "Aside from being attacked by a vacuum cleaner, I haven't noticed you in any particular danger."

"Aren't you forgetting something? Like the way I was tackled by a two-hundred-pound lug?" she snapped.

"Two hundred and ten," he said. "Stark naked."

Against her will, an image took shape in Dana's mind. Heck, she couldn't see the man clearly in the dark, even *with* his clothes on. So why was she forming such a sharp mental image of broad shoulders, a muscled chest, narrow hips and other well-built parts? Very well built.

Before Dana could come up with a response, she heard a sound in the ominous silence. It was a vehicle stopping on the street.

She recognized the triple creak of the brakes. She'd heard it before, when she'd arrived at the mailbox store a few minutes early and heard Morey Bain pull up in his van.

Chapter Four

Dear DG,

I can't stop thinking about what you wrote, that you've never been truly awakened by a man. I suppose that's an old-fashioned term, but there is a kind of awakening to the deeper meanings of life that can occur when a man and a woman become intimate in the truest sense of the word. Or so I believe. You see, it's never happened to me, either.

Last night I took a walk through the canyon behind my home. The moon was full and coyotes were howling, an unearthly sound. As a child, I was fascinated by science fiction, and last night it was easy to imagine that I had slipped into an alternate universe.

I pictured you waiting in the shadows, stepping forward and smiling at me. I don't actually know what you look like, but it doesn't matter. The moonlight would turn your hair to silver and your eyes to gleaming pools.

I am convinced I would recognize a certain confidence in the way you move and a thrust of the chin that declares your spirit. We would meet as equals, the force of both our personalities bringing us together with an explosion more brilliant than fireworks.

Anticipating your next letter, I remain,

Your servant,
RNW

In that frozen moment when she knew Morey Bain was about to catch them, Dana confronted two truths.

The first was that she refused to let herself be treated like the bad guy. Breaking into a house might be illegal, but she and Nick had a right to recover their property.

The second thing was that if *Heat!* ever published that intensely personal correspondence, something inside her might shrivel up and retreat from the world forever.

Nick's hand clamped on to her wrist. "Let's get out of here," he said, and pulled her toward the back door. She needed no encouragement.

As she hurried with him, Dana's mind skimmed over the clues they'd left. Would Morey notice the disturbed plant on the front porch? She had intended to lock the front door behind her, but had she?

Then she remembered the alarm. Maybe when it went off in those last few seconds before the blackout, it had also rung at a security agency.

"Do you think he's brought a guard?" she asked. "Will they shoot on sight?"

"I'm glad you told me you were an *amateur* detective," Nick said as they fumbled over a pile of umbrellas, sneakers and beach sandals moldering in the back hallway. "If you were a professional, you'd know how hard it is to get a gun permit in California." He gave the doorknob a sharp twist. It didn't budge.

"Even if he doesn't have a gun, he might know karate." Worrying about physical injury kept Dana from dwelling on the possibility of getting arrested.

"He might even know how to open this door. Wouldn't that be handy?" Nick stopped fighting the knob as they both heard the front door open.

Morey's high, rather nasal voice rattled through the house. "Come out, whoever you are! We've got you cornered!"

He had said *we*. There must be at least one guard, Dana realized.

The crash of wood splintering beneath Nick's heel revealed that he had found a way to open the door. As it sagged outward, he pulled Dana behind him down a set of rickety wooden steps.

She tried to organize her frantic thoughts. They couldn't run to the front and get in their cars. The guard would nab them straightaway.

Nick must have been thinking along the same lines, because he lunged to the left, across the lawn and down an unfenced slope into the neighbor's yard. In the moonlight, Dana could see that he was limping. Kicking down the door had obviously hurt, but he didn't complain.

She could hear shouts and scuffling noises behind them. Dana gave silent thanks for the darkness, shielding them from view.

Then the neighbor's dog started barking.

It wasn't a big dog, judging by the high-pitched yapping. It must have been sleeping, and now it strained to the end of its rope, vociferously protesting this invasion of its territory.

Nick and Dana skirted its range and plowed through a row of potted plants that they hadn't been able to see in the dark. Terra-cotta smashed on the patio, and Dana felt grit clinging to the soles of her shoes.

She apologized silently to the house's absent owners. Later, she would send them some money anonymously to pay for the damage.

Behind them, footsteps clumped across the ground at a rapid rate. That couldn't be the sluggish Morey, so it must be the guard.

Nick grabbed Dana's arm and pulled her at a faster pace. "And you're the one who jumped from an airplane," he growled. "We could use some of that speed now!"

"That wasn't me!" Dana gasped. "That was my client!"

"Whatever."

They veered around a camellia bush and dodged into the next yard. The dividing slope was steep enough to shield them from view, and Nick crouched, keeping low as he veered and ran toward the rear property.

Dana didn't see how he could keep up this pace, especially while limping on an injured leg. But if he could do it, she vowed that she could, too.

She only wished she had taken more aerobics classes. Maybe then each breath wouldn't be pumping so painfully in her chest.

They reached a low fence. Nick vaulted it, then helped Dana over. She wondered if real investigators did this much running.

Being a detective was a lot harder in real life than in her imagination, both physically and mentally. It was hard to think clearly when her attention was focused on trying not to injure herself in the dark.

She didn't see how Nick could keep mentally one step ahead of their pursuers, but obviously he'd worked out a plan. They were doubling back, while the guard had stopped and was calling to Morey that he couldn't see where they'd gone.

From Morey's response, Dana located him somewhere near the broken pots. With a burst of speed she wouldn't have believed possible, Nick yanked her forward and around the far side of Morey's own lawn, straight toward the street.

Morey spotted their shadowy figures. "Back here, you idiot!" he yelled to the guard, and gave chase.

As they cleared the house and headed for the sidewalk, Dana's instincts ordered her to leave Nick's comforting presence and take her own car, but it was several houses away.

She scrabbled into the convertible beside him and barely had time to grab her seat belt before he switched on the engine. They roared down the street so fast, her baseball cap flew off and vanished.

As they whipped around a corner, she experienced a twinge of doubt. She had jumped into a stranger's car, putting herself at his mercy. For all she knew, Nick might be planning to kidnap her and force her into one of those slavery situations that end with FBI raids and appearances on daytime talk shows.

From behind them came the screech of Morey's wheels. It was too late to turn back now.

"He might have gotten your license number," Dana said. "And we probably left the house full of fingerprints."

"Morey's in no position to call the police," Nick returned. "If he does, he'll be glad to drop the charges by the time my boss brings his legal muscle against him."

They shot down one darkened, half-empty street after another. Apparently, people were staying put, enjoying their parties and waiting for the electricity to come on.

The valley below lay in eerie peace, momentarily returned to a primitive state. The occasional burst of fireworks in the night sky gave the scene a surreal air.

A couple of times Dana heard tires screech behind them, but the sound faded. Morey, it seemed, hadn't been able to overcome their speed and surprise.

"Do you think he knows who it was?" she asked. "It wouldn't take a genius to figure out what we were looking for."

Nick didn't answer. He leaned forward, focusing on their curving path.

"Maybe he'll quit while he's ahead," Dana continued hopefully. "I mean, he already got his money from the paper, right?"

"Not all of it," said Nick. "Besides, he might figure that we took something. As you pointed out, his wife would love to know where he stashes his dough."

Dana's hand touched the deposit slip crumpled in her pocket. She would take pleasure in handing it over to Nita.

"I think we've lost him," she said.

"Unless he figures out where we're headed," Nick noted.

"Which is where?" Dana hadn't planned that far ahead.

"You're supposed to be the detective. You tell me." He shepherded the convertible through its paces, handling the wheel like a man accustomed to taking charge.

She found his attitude irritating. After a moment's reflection, however, she could see what he was getting at. "The offices of *Heat!*—right?"

"With this blackout knocking out their computers, maybe we can catch them before press time." With barely a moment's notice, they zoomed around a corner. The car handled the sudden change of direction like an expensive European racer.

Dana glanced down at the name on the dashboard. It *was* an expensive European racer.

"Whose car is this?" she asked.

"A friend's," said Nick.

"RNW?"

He didn't answer. She hoped that meant no, because she didn't want RNW to be rich enough to afford a car like this.

Why had she ever entered into that correspondence? Friends had warned that the guy might be a con artist or a deviant. Dana was more afraid he might turn out to be exactly what he'd said, a wealthy recluse.

She liked the part of him that hung out in canyons, listening to coyotes. Driving hundred-thousand-dollar cars struck her as excessive. And inhibiting. What if she scratched the paint?

"Would that make a difference?" Nick asked at last, as they neared the freeway. "If it belonged to RNW?"

"To my client?" Dana said. "I don't think so. I mean, it's *his* money, not hers."

"Plenty of women have tried to make it theirs, too," Nick murmured.

Dana felt her heart sink. "He's got a lot of women after him? I thought he was shy."

"Shy?" said Nick. "I never pictured him that way."

Dana fell silent, but something nagged at her. It had nothing to do with Morey or the car. It was something Nick had said earlier.

She remembered what it was as they careened onto the Pasadena Freeway and headed south, toward downtown Los Angeles. "How did you know DG jumped out of an airplane?"

"Excuse me?" said the figure beside her.

"You mentioned it when we were running," Dana reminded him. "Are you telling me RNW let you read the letters?" She didn't try to hide her dismay. She would never have let anyone read *his* letters to her.

Nick waited a beat before answering. "He told me about it. He was impressed. Personally, I think she made it up. What do you think?"

"I don't know," Dana said.

"She's *your* friend."

"Client," she told him.

"Amateurs don't have clients."

The guy's arrogance was maddening. Particularly since he so often managed to be right. "What are you getting at?"

"Isn't it obvious?" He favored her with a ghost of a smile. "You're DG, aren't you?"

She hadn't done a very good job of disguising her identity, Dana reflected. She had to admit that even one of her students would have seen through the story. "Okay, yes. So what?"

"It would cause you a lot of embarrassment if the tabloid printed those letters," he observed. "Or would it?"

"Of course it would!" she flared. "Isn't that obvious?"

"I don't know." He kept his eyes on the flow of traffic. "It might have been some kind of joke to you. Or an intellectual game. Maybe you enjoy seeing your name in print."

On the point of denying everything, Dana forced herself to be honest. "It did start out as a game. But the feelings were real. And the only way I want to see my name in print is because I've achieved something worthwhile."

"Wouldn't you consider landing a rich husband worthwhile?" he asked.

"What do you mean, 'landing'?" Dana snapped. "Like a fish?"

"Sorry if I offended your sensibilities." There was not a trace of regret in his voice.

"Besides, RNW isn't rich any more than I'm a detective," Dana said.

"How can you be so sure?" That smooth tone irritated her more than a dozen insults could have.

"Well, is he or isn't he?" she snapped. "You never even told me whether this is his car."

"Oh, it's his car, all right. One of several." Nick skimmed around a slow-moving station wagon. "He owns a great many things. Including me, according to some people."

"You don't strike me as the kind of man anybody could own," Dana observed.

"What makes you say that?"

"You're too ornery."

He chuckled, but didn't answer.

She wished she could read Nick's expression. She wished he would tell her more about RNW. She wished she didn't keep getting the impression that he knew or suspected more about her than he was letting on.

Most of all, she wondered how he intended to persuade the editors of the nation's least scrupulous tabloid to kill the tastiest story they had come across in weeks.

NICK COULDN'T figure the woman out. She didn't act like a TV star, nor did she give the impression that the letters had been some kind of stunt. If he hadn't known better, he would have believed she was just an ordinary woman whose private correspondence had been stolen.

Well, not entirely ordinary. Her coloring was too subtle and her bone structure too pronounced for her to be conventionally pretty, but he could see that she would sparkle on camera. She had the kind of looks that the right clothes and makeup can transform from plain-Jane to knock-'em-dead.

Except that Nick liked the way Dana seemed now, unpretentious and honest. She had an inner glow that spoke of intelligence and, oddly enough, innocence. Nothing about her came across as jaded or hard, which surprised him.

She had hopped right into the car, trusting him without question, which also seemed odd. If she was famous, wasn't she worried that he would exploit the relationship? Didn't it concern her that this RNW possessed the originals of her letters and, once he learned her identity, would hold a certain power over her?

None of that appeared to have occurred to Dominique, or Dana, as she preferred to be called. Neither had she worried about the effects of their flight, which could easily have resulted in a twisted ankle or some other injury that would play havoc with her taping schedule.

He wondered why she hadn't tried to use the cellular phone in his car. The actresses he knew were rarely out of touch with their entourage—each having an agent, a publicist, a manager, a beautician and a personal assistant, at the minimum.

Nick gave up trying to figure her out and turned his attention to the interchange of the Pasadena Freeway and the 101. Traffic slowed to a crawl, complicated by tourists with out-of-state plates moving in confusion from lane to lane.

With the freeway signs unlit, the situation was even worse than usual. Traffic was getting markedly slower, and then, just as he applied the brakes and came to a halt, Nick spotted flashing red lights indicating an accident ahead.

Nearby, a carful of teenagers opened their windows, blowing kazoos and waving flags. In another car, a couple shook up bottles of soda, sprayed each other and laughed uproariously, silhouetted against headlights.

The blackout, in conjunction with the holiday, had created a festive mood, but Nick was more concerned with trying to figure out how to reach the shoulder and ride it to an exit. Two things worked against him. First, there was no shoulder, and second, there was no exit close by.

By the car's clock, it was already after ten, which meant his guests were beginning to trickle into the Top Hat. The kitchen would be closed due to the blackout, he suspected, but the bar ought to keep everyone happy for a while.

At least being stranded didn't render him incommunicado. There was nothing Nick could do about his torn clothing before he got to the tabloid's offices, but he wanted to change as soon as he arrived at the restaurant.

Picking up the car phone, he speed dialed his home number. Hitch answered on the third ring with a fake British "Cheerio. Williams domicile."

Nick filled his butler in on the evening's events so far, carefully editing his account, since Dana couldn't help overhearing. He asked that someone bring a change of clothing to the restaurant about midnight, which he estimated was the soonest he would get there. At least the blackout would provide an excuse for his lateness.

"Will do," said Hitch. "I'll come myself."

"How's it going there?"

"Lots of grumbling," said his friend. "It's a good thing we have gas stoves, although the caterer has to work by candlelight."

"Let's hope the power stays off," Nick said. "We don't want those presses to roll."

"I wouldn't worry about that," his butler replied jovially. "I heard on the radio the whole grid has gone out, the entire West Coast."

"Interesting." And reassuring, Nick thought. Such a massive outage wouldn't be fixed in a hurry. Then, remembering that Dana was listening to every word, Nick added, "Please tell Mr. W I'll do everything possible to get his letters back."

"Excuse me?" said Hitch. "Is somebody listening?"

"Yes." Nick was glad he'd used the handset rather than the speaker phone.

"Not Dominique Grant? The lady in the fax?"

"I have to go." Traffic was beginning to creep forward again. "I'll fill you in later."

"See you at midnight," said Hitch.

LISTENING to Nick on the phone raised a lot of questions. As Dana watched the traffic jam breaking up, she wondered what was going on at that restaurant he'd referred to, and who he had been talking to.

Still, she'd been reassured on one point. Dana had been forced to consider the possibility that Nick Lyon might actually be RNW, but his reference to Mr. W had helped reassure her.

So had the casual way he'd chatted with someone who appeared to be another of RNW's employees. If Nick was the boss, there would be more formality.

Besides, the personality didn't track. There was nothing poetic about Nick, and there had been nothing of Nick's masculine imperiousness about RNW.

On the other hand, it was almost certain that RNW hadn't been kidding about his financial status. Reluctantly Dana abandoned her image of a Clark Kent type.

She tried to replace him mentally with a wealthy recluse. The image she got was of someone thin and reticent, with an otherworldly expression. Definitely not this tall, solid figure who calculated plans at the speed of lightning and regarded her with a mocking edge to his smile.

Remembering his reference to jumping from an airplane, Dana felt a niggling sense of discomfort. How much of her letters had RNW described to this man?

They edged through the interchange, past flashing highway patrol cruisers and two cars with smashed bumpers. It didn't appear that anyone had been injured, thank goodness.

Nick exited at the first ramp. There was no sign, or at least Dana couldn't see one in the dark.

"Where are we?" she asked.

"Figueroa Street," said Nick as he veered right.

That would put them smack in the middle of downtown Los Angeles, a maze of one-way streets below the steep hill that separated the commercial area from the government center.

"How do you know where the *Heat!* offices are?" She hadn't seen him consult so much as a phone book, let alone a map.

"I make it my business to know everything I might need to know," Nick replied. "It's my job to run interference for Mr. W. Unfortunately, that includes dealing with the less ethical representatives of the press, as well as the more responsible variety."

"What exactly is your job?" she said.

"Kind of a glorified gofer." He zipped through a yellow light and turned right again.

"What kind of business is RNW involved in?" she asked.

"The legitimate kind," he said.

"And I'm supposed to believe it just because you say it?" It hadn't occurred to Dana before that RNW's activities might be shady, which she supposed was naive of her. It would raise even more problems for Dominique if she was linked, however erroneously, to an underworld figure.

"You'll have to trust me."

"No, I don't," she said. "I just have to go along with you."

"It's interesting, the way you turn my own words against me," Nick said. "But then, I knew you were a good writer, from your letters."

"You said you didn't read them!"

"Only one or two."

"You can tell your boss for me that he's a louse!" Dana grumbled.

"He knows I enjoy fiction," Nick replied steadily. "Especially detective novels."

"Ouch." There was no response for that, and Dana knew it.

In the silence that followed, she stared out the window at the bizarre setting through which they passed. In utter darkness, downtown Los Angeles resembled a city after some mythical World War III, intact but empty. Only a few headlights reminded her that they were still among the living.

She switched on the car's radio and found that it was tuned to an all-news station. "A Southern California Edison spokesman says that as yet no official explanation has been found for the vast power outage," the announcer blared.

"But we have no shortage of explanations pouring in from around the Southland," he continued. "Take your pick. It's a design flaw in the grid, overuse of air conditioners or an endangered squirrel that ate through a cable."

"I'll take the endangered squirrel," muttered Nick.

"Continuing with our human interest stories," the announcer said, "we have an account here from Pismo Beach."

A female announcer-type voice took over. "Mrs. Mattie Harrison of this seaside community claims her husband just disconnected from the Internet for the first time in five years.

"He reportedly was shocked to discover that their children had become teenagers and that his workshop had been remodeled into a sauna."

Nick glided into the driveway of a parking garage and slipped a twenty-dollar bill to the guard. Dana wondered how much of that amount was to cover the parking fee, and how much was a bribe to get them in.

Seeing the headlights pick out the tabloid's logo on a glass door gave her a sense of relief. At least they finally had a chance to explain about the letters and, just possibly, bring this whole mess to an end.

NICK had visited *Heat!* once before, at the request of its managing editor, Bob Worley. The guy had claimed he wanted to establish good professional relations, then proceeded to try to bribe Nick to spill the inside story about his boss.

Although tempted to call the editor a few unpleasant names, Nick had kept in mind that the man might return the favor, in print. He'd been firm but polite in his refusal.

Now he was glad that he hadn't gone off half-cocked. He might be able to make a deal with Bob Worley to disclose some hidden facts about Renfro Williams in exchange for killing the letters.

He was even prepared, if necessary, to hold off on tonight's announcement of his real identity and give the paper an exclusive. But only if he had to.

It might work. It might also blow up in his face. He supposed it was worth the risk.

They stepped through double glass doors and stopped at a guard's desk. Dana took a deep breath, as if preparing for an argument.

Nick touched her arm lightly, hoping the gesture would convey that he wanted to take charge. The fact was, he doubted the guard cared much who they were or why they had come, as long as they had no criminal intent.

"Nick Lyon." He flashed a realistic, if bogus, driver's license, which the guard glanced at by flashlight. "To see Bob Worley."

Nick also had an array of credit cards in his assumed name, as well as a real license in case a policeman asked to see it. So far, none had.

"And I'm—" Dana began.

"With me," Nick said.

"Sign here." The guard pushed a clipboard at them and turned up his transistor radio.

Nick signed, then pulled Dana toward the stairs before she could add her name. No need to provide more information than necessary.

"I don't understand," she said as they reached the stairs. "Why do they have so little security? I went to the *Los Angeles Times* once to place an ad, and it was like entering Fort Knox."

Nick tried not to limp going up the stairs. His leg wasn't seriously injured, but the muscles still smarted from kicking down Morey's back door.

"The *L.A. Times* tries to keep out weirdos," he said. "You know, the ones babbling about UFO babies and government conspiracies. *Heat!* invites them in and pays them for their stories."

It was dark, in spite of their flashlights, too dark to read Dana's expression, but a click of the tongue revealed her dismay.

"You're so cynical," she said.

"Realistic," Nick corrected as they passed the second floor, which he knew was devoted to the advertising department.

"Maybe some of those people are telling the truth," Dana said.

"About UFO babies?"

"Well, government conspiracies, anyway. You know, corruption, that kind of thing. Maybe they're just whistle-blowers seeking justice," she said. "They deserve to have someone pay attention."

Nick hadn't heard anybody speak so fervently about justice in years. Her words sounded naive, old-fashioned...and oddly appealing.

He wondered if he was starting to get soft in the head. Nick Lyon and Renfro Williams had seen too much of the world's failings to get worked up about the unfairness of life.

But hearing Dana's words made him realize that he missed his old idealism. Nick had lost it somewhere along the road to success, and until this moment he hadn't even noticed.

On the third floor, they stepped into a room entirely different from the bright, noisy place he had visited before. Amid wavering shadows, figures sat around desks conversing by the flickering light of candles. Only one telephone rang, off in a corner.

"My kingdom for a manual typewriter," muttered one silhouette, stumbling past them with a flashlight.

"You'd think they would have some kind of backup power source," Dana said.

"They're not an essential service," Nick pointed out. "Not like hospitals, for instance. And running their own generators would be prohibitive. It's not as if this sort of thing happens often."

"I suppose not." She gazed around with wide-eyed interest, then quickly shook her hair over her face as if only now realizing that someone might identify her. Nick wondered again how such an experienced actress could be so guileless.

He recognized the glass-fronted office that belonged to Bob Worley, but in the dark it was impossible to tell if the man might be in. "Stay here." Nick steered Dana to one corner. "I'm going to make some inquiries."

"I'll come!"

"Are you sure that's what you want?" The woman was incredibly green, if she didn't think the reporters at a tabloid, of all places, would recognize her in an instant.

"What do you mean?" she asked.

"Just sit here!" he snapped. "And wait!"

As he stalked across the room, Nick couldn't figure out what had made him so irritable. He kept getting this impulse to protect Dana, and he didn't like feeling that way.

She didn't need protection. She had money, fame, and no doubt a manager and agent hovering in the background. Plus, hot and cold running men, if she chose.

He was beginning to resent her pretense at innocence, more so because she played the role so convincingly. What *was* she up to?

Bob's office turned out to be empty, but nearby Nick collared a man whom he recognized as an assistant editor.

After a moment's hesitation, the man recognized him, as well.

"Oh, you work for old Renfro!" boomed the fellow, who had thinning hair and a pair of glasses bound together with masking tape. He peered dubiously at Nick's clothes, but refrained from commenting on their disheveled state.

"I have to talk to Bob Worley." Nick tried to look casual, as if assistants to millionaires always walked around in torn shorts and gaping shirts.

"I'm afraid he's not available," said the assistant. "You're here about the letters, eh?"

Nick winced. Apparently the story was already common knowledge among the staff. "That's right. They're a fraud. But I can offer him something better."

"Why should you offer him something better if they're a fraud?" The fellow adjusted his glasses, which kept slipping low on his nose.

"I'm protecting a lady," said Nick.

The assistant grinned slyly. "I'll just bet."

Nick yearned for a weapon, not literally, but something he could hold over the man. Such as a restraining order. Or enough time to buy the newspaper and put it out of business. He drew a blank. "This is urgent. Where is he? In the backshop?"

That, Nick knew, was where computer technicians set the paper's type, reproduced photographs and shot entire pages to send to the presses.

"He was," acknowledged the assistant. "Trying to rig something with chewing gum and an Erector set."

"How do I get there?" asked Nick.

"Whoa!" The man shook his head. "He fell on the stairs about an hour ago. Broke his ankle, from the looks of it. One of the secretaries drove him to the emergency room.''

"Which one?" Nick demanded.

The assistant shrugged. "Could be L.A. County-USC. Or Martin Luther King, Jr. Or maybe they decided UCLA would be less crowded.''

It would take hours to check out those widely scattered hospitals. And trying to locate Worley by phone would be an exercise in futility, even under ordinary circumstances. In the confusion of a blackout, there was zero chance of a nurse taking time to find a patient being treated for a relatively minor matter.

"Is he coming back?" Nick asked.

"Absolutely," said the assistant. "He wouldn't miss a deadline, even if they had to bring him in a stretcher. The way this blackout's going, he'll have plenty of time.''

"Does Bob have a pager?''

"He hates the damn things.''

"What's his direct phone line number?" Nick jotted down the number. "When he shows up, tell him I'll call back. Tell him not to print the letters until he hears from me.''

"I'll tell him.'' The fellow grinned again. "For all the good it will do you.''

Nick glanced across the newsroom. By the wavering light of candles, he could see that Dana was deep in conversation with a young woman, probably a copy girl.

He shuddered to think what sort of information she might inadvertently convey. Dominique Grant's publicist ought to be handling this. That was what those people got paid to do.

Gritting his teeth, he marched across the room to rescue Dana from whatever mess she'd gotten into this time.

Chapter Five

Dear RNW,

A shiver went down my spine when I read your last letter. That image of us meeting in moonlight and shadow keeps flashing through my mind.

You seem aware, as I have always been, of a deeper reality that parallels our own. Some might call it the realm of the spirit. I believe that for people to truly fall in love, they must bond at this level.

I know instinctively that you will understand what I mean, but I wonder how many people would. Thank goodness these letters are private. No telephone conversations that can be tapped, no E-mail that can be stolen electronically. Sometimes the old-fashioned ways of communicating are the best....

Dana hadn't intended to talk to anyone until Nick got back, but her stony face had apparently alarmed a copy girl. The young woman kept asking if she was having a panic attack on account of the darkness.

"No," Dana said. "Really, I'm not."

"But you're upset?" the girl probed.

"Just subdued." Dana tried harder to hide behind her hair, but it didn't work.

Still trying to draw her out, the young woman launched into an account of how her mother suffered from agoraphobia and wouldn't venture out of the house for years until her doctor prescribed a new medication.

"I'm not having a panic attack," Dana said emphatically. "I'm just waiting for someone."

"Well, you looked scared," said the girl. "Hey, my name is Mia."

"I'm Dana." She didn't see how it could hurt to reveal that much.

"You look kind of familiar. Have we met somewhere? I mean, I could swear I've seen you!"

"I get around." Dana decided she'd better seize control of the conversation before Mia asked any more questions. The young woman obviously liked to talk. "Do you know where we can find the reporter who's writing a story about some letters?"

"Letters?" The girl's round face moved rhythmically as she chomped a wad of gum. "Oh, yeah! The love letters!"

Dana winced. "I suppose you could call them that."

"Gee, I'm not sure who's working on it now, but the guy who found the story was Andy Adams," Mia said. "He's new here, right out of J-school. That's journalism school. He gets assigned to answer the phones a lot, and somebody called in. You know, wanting to sell the letters."

Dana couldn't help asking, "Did anyone read them? I mean, besides Andy?"

"Oh, sure!" Chomp chomp. "We all did! I mean, we kind of handed them around for a few minutes. Management won't let us make personal copies now that paper's gotten so expensive. They were kind of sweet, you know? I wish somebody would write to me like that."

Dana tried to harden herself against a sense of violation. It sounded like nobody knew who had actually written the letters, at least not yet.

She could see Nick heading this way, and her heart sank. The way he was glowering, it looked as if he hadn't had any luck with the editor.

As he reached them, she asked Mia if she had any idea where Andy Adams was, and explained to Nick about the rookie reporter.

"He's out covering the blackout," said the copy girl. "Everybody is."

"What aspect of the blackout?" Surely the reporters had specific assignments, or at least Dana hoped so. That might help her find him.

"People. How they're reacting," said the girl.

"Great." Nick's voice dripped with sarcasm. "He's talking to people in a county that only includes...what? Eight or nine million people? That should make him easy to find."

Dana wasn't ready to give up. So far, Nick had scored all the points, and she couldn't help feeling they were in some kind of contest. How would a detective go about finding a reporter? she asked herself.

Inspiration struck. "Where's Andy's favorite bar?" she asked.

"The Footnote," Mia replied. "Two blocks north, on the left."

"Thanks." Dana caught Nick's arm. "Let's go."

"You don't think he's there, do you?" But from the wry twist of his mouth, he was considering the possibility.

"It's a place to start."

They had nearly reached the stairs when Mia said, "I know who you remind me of! You're Dominique Grant!"

"No!" Dana released a nervous breath. "I'm her sister. Everybody makes that mistake."

"You sure?" pressed the copy girl.

"I ought to be. It's my thirtieth birthday, and I've been Dominique's sister every step of the way."

As they hurried down the steps, Dana wondered what Nick made of Mia's remarks. He hadn't commented or acted surprised.

But then, a man like him wouldn't watch soap operas. He'd probably never heard of Dominique Grant.

NICK DIDN'T KNOW whether Dominique was turning thirty today, or whether she had a sister. But he had heard of movie stars sneaking out in public and, when told they looked exactly like themselves, replying, "Everybody tells me that."

Claiming to be her own sister was even better. He had to hand it to the woman, she was playing this role to perfection.

As they reached the parking garage, he paused to consider their next move. "I'm not sure it will do us much good to find this reporter— What's his name?"

"Andy Adams," Dana said.

"He isn't even working on the story, he's covering the blackout," Nick pointed out. "And, obviously, Bob Worley has the letters, or at least copies of them."

"I see your point," murmured Dana. "But maybe we can convince this guy that it's a hoax and could damage his career, since he's the one who led the paper astray. If we get him on our side, he might figure out a way to help us."

"Or we could offer him an even better scoop," Nick mused as they headed for the car.

"Like what?" Dana strode alongside him.

"You'll find out," he said.

"Gee, thanks." She gave him a hard look. "I'm so glad you trust me, after all we've been through."

"I don't trust anyone," said Nick.

It was surprising how well one could see in the dark when one grew accustomed to it, he reflected, watching her eyes grow round with dismay. He could even see a tiny wrinkling of the nose that indicated she didn't quite believe him.

"You expect *me* to trust you," she said.

"No, I don't. As you said, you're just going along with me because you have no choice."

"Did I say that?"

"More or less."

"Well, I meant it."

They might not trust each other, but they had grown to depend on each other this evening, Nick admitted silently as they probed their way through the unlit garage. However uneasily, they had become allies in their quest.

He still didn't know what the woman's motives were, but he was willing to concede that she seemed genuinely worried about the prospect of seeing her words in print. Was it possible Dominique Grant had answered RNW's ad because she was lonely? Did she, too, have a hard time meeting people who could appreciate her for herself?

But that didn't explain why she had posed as a detective. Unless, of course, she felt so uncertain of being accepted for herself that she had to hide in a fantasy, even with a stranger.

Dana's attitude during the past few hours had shown a mixture of confidence and hesitation, boldness and naïveté. It was as if she didn't quite know herself.

The part that intrigued Nick most was the natural and unaffected sensuality that seemed so much a part of her.

He remembered what DG had written, about never having found a man to bring out her sensual side.

He had felt a longing surging through her letters, stirring a long-repressed need of his own to share something meaningful and lasting. Nick couldn't figure the woman out, no matter how hard he tried.

In the absence of light, he realized as he held the car door for her, his other senses had strengthened. He found himself keenly aware of the scent of Dana's hair, like spring flowers, and the smoothness of her skin as she brushed past.

Sliding onto the seat, Dana passed so close to Nick that he could feel the radiance of her skin. Wisps of hair tickled his throat, and he had a sudden urge to sweep her into his arms.

This wasn't the time, and he felt certain this wasn't the woman. She must be intentionally teasing him. Dominique Grant couldn't be that unaware of her effect on men.

Well, it didn't matter. Once tonight was over, he would never see her again.

As he took his place behind the wheel, Nick returned his thoughts to their destination. He doubted a rookie reporter could help their case, but the bar was close enough for it to be worth a try. And by the time they got through talking to him, maybe Bob Worley would be back from the hospital.

As THEY DROVE the short distance to the Footnote, Dana hoped the blackout would last a while longer, keeping *Heat!* on hold until they got this matter resolved. The way things were going, she hoped the darn thing lasted until Christmas.

On the radio, the announcer said, "Psychologists are predicting the birthrate will rise exactly nine months from tonight. In any case, folks, it looks like we're in for a long one. The authorities have no word yet on a cause.

"Here's another in our series of human interest stories. Mr. J. J. Wexler of Oxnard calls to say that a man with a long beard and a white robe just marched through his neighborhood ringing a bell and announcing the end of the world.

"When Mr. Wexler went to investigate, he learned the man was advertising a local pizzeria that uses wood-burning ovens and has remained open during the black-out. That's good old American capitalism at its best, folks."

They parked in a lot near the address Mia had given. As they crossed the sidewalk, Dana saw a pub blazing with hurricane lamps. Almost as bright as electric lights, they gave the place a surreal clarity.

Dana had been picturing a low-class dive, with perhaps a pool table in one corner and a risque painting over the bar. The Footnote, however, resembled a sandwich shop, with a sleek chrome counter and a handful of glass tables.

People were crammed inside. The absence of television might be the cause, or perhaps it was simply a dislike of sitting alone in the dark.

It wasn't hard to spot Andy Adams. He had a young, scrubbed look, in spite of his scraggly attempt at a beard, and he was writing furiously in a notebook as a heavyset woman regaled him with some sort of story.

Nick made a low clucking sound. "I can't believe it. You were right. He's doing research in his favorite bar."

"I know a lot of writers," Dana explained. As an English teacher, she made it a point to attend poetry readings and book signings. "This probably *is* his idea of real life."

"Well, let's see if we can get his attention." Nick strolled over and waited impatiently until the woman finished speaking.

As she drifted away, the reporter looked up. "Yes?" Then he spotted Dana. "Oh, hello! Look who's here!"

She stifled a groan. She didn't resemble Dominique *that* much! "We need to talk about the letters," she said.

He gave her a grin that bordered on a leer, obviously relishing his power over someone more important than he was. "It won't do you any good."

"I know you're working on another story, but I also know you haven't gone to press yet." Dana spoke quickly, not wanting Nick to take over. She could handle this herself. "Morey Bain lied to you. The story is wrong."

Andy flicked a glance at Nick, then apparently dismissed him as some kind of hanger-on. Youthful bravado crackled as he said, "Why don't you and I go somewhere private and discuss it, babe?"

Before she knew what was happening, Nick had seized the upstart by his lapels and jerked him to his feet. The reporter, a good six inches shorter than Nick, had to stand on tiptoe to avoid choking.

"Let's try that again, shall we?" growled Nick as the other customers stared in fascination. "Apologize to Miss Grant."

"Sorry," gasped the young man.

Nick lowered him to the ground. "Number one lesson in life, kid. Treat everyone with respect until they prove they deserve otherwise. Like you just did."

Andy Adams coughed and straightened his coat. "Yeah, well, soap-opera stars who run around confronting reporters in bars are fair game."

Dana couldn't believe the guy's churlish attitude. He had a lot to learn, and not just about news gathering, but she didn't plan to be the one to teach him. "I'm not Dominique, I'm her sister."

"Dominique Grant doesn't have a sister," he said. "I read the publicity her studio put out."

Dana could have throttled him. Now he'd made it clear to Nick that she was supposed to be an actress. She could just imagine how RNW would feel if he learned that.

"Yes, she does, and it's me," Dana said. "Why should she mention her sister in her publicity?"

"Her sister, huh?" said Andy. "How old are you?"

"I don't see what that has to do with—"

"It's her thirtieth birthday," said Nick.

"There!" Andy beamed. "Dominique Grant must be about thirty, too. I can't remember her exact birthday, but I remember her age. Don't tell me you're twins, and they left *that* out of the publicity!"

Dominique's bio had shaved four years off her age. Dana couldn't bring herself to tell the truth to this snotty reporter. No doubt he'd find a way to work it into his story. "No, we're just sisters. We're close in age, that's all."

Andy shook his head. "Well, you're wasting your time. They took me off the story and gave it to somebody else."

"Why?" Dana asked.

"Because I'm new, why else?" His voice rose into a whine.

"Who's handling it now?" Nick pressed.

"Jim Jasper." At Dana's blank look, Andy added, "He's one of the paper's stars. Come on, don't tell me you never read *Heat!* Everybody reads it!"

"Where is he now?" Nick snapped before Dana could figure out a way to enlighten this young man about the real world, in which most people didn't give a hoot about TV stars' private lives.

"He's at the Top Hat," Andy said. "Trying to get comment."

"Comment from whom?" Dana asked.

"Don't you keep up with the news?" Amazement made Andy's freckles stand out in the hollow light. "Everybody knows—"

"We're on our way over there now," Nick said, and hauled Dana out the door.

She wanted to kick him. "What's the big hurry?"

"The kid's wasting our time," Nick growled, and dragged her along the sidewalk so fast Dana had to skip to keep up.

"What's the Top Hat?" she asked as they jumped into the sports car.

"A snazzy restaurant." The car roared to life. They cut through the city streets with dizzying abruptness.

"Where is it?"

"Hollywood."

All of a sudden, getting information from Nick had become like pulling teeth. "What's going on there tonight?"

"How should I know?" he muttered.

"You knew where *Heat!* has its offices," Dana pointed out. "I thought it was your business to know this kind of stuff. Doesn't your boss go to fancy restaurants?"

"He hates restaurants."

What kind of man hated fine dining? Dana wondered. The picture she was forming of RNW bothered her. If he was a recluse, maybe he had chosen that life-style because of paranoia. Or perhaps he had a bad temper. Letters might reveal a man's innermost thoughts, but they didn't show how he interacted with people.

"What's he like?" she asked. "This Mr. W, who hates restaurants and has enough bucks to hire a bruiser like you as his bodyguard?"

"Bruiser?" he said. "What makes you think I'm a bodyguard?"

To Dana, the answer had become obvious a few minutes ago. "The way you handled that cheeky reporter. You're obviously the muscle in this operation."

"And not the brains?" Nick seemed to be suppressing a smirk.

"You're the underling, so I guess not," she retorted, even though she knew she was being unfair. "He must be smart, this boss of yours. But he doesn't like being around people. Why not? Does he kick puppies? Does he have a fetish about not taking baths?"

"Check the side mirror and tell me if anyone is following us," Nick said.

She couldn't believe he would stoop to such an obvious diversion. "Don't be ridiculous. Of course no one is following us. Is your boss a jerk? Does he drool? If he doesn't like good food, what does he eat, pizza three times a day?"

"He's only a jerk to his enemies, he only drools when he's hungry, and he has a cook," Nick said. "Now do what I asked."

Dana glanced in the mirror. Half a block behind sped a van that bore a strong resemblance to the one Morey usually drove. Not likely to be a coincidence, she thought. "Uh-oh. I think it's Morey. How do you suppose he found us?"

"Through your chatterbox girlfriend at the newspaper, no doubt," Nick snapped, and whipped around a corner so fast Dana left her breath in the previous block.

She checked the mirror. The van was gaining on them. Nick must have noticed, too, because he applied the accelerator liberally.

As they zipped across an intersection, Dana glanced down a side street and noticed a crowd of vehicles letting off passengers in front of a hotel. She could have sworn that among the cars waited several horse-drawn carriages, including a round coach straight out of *Cinderella.*

Either her imagination was running away with her or the crisscross of headlights was creating optical illusions.

"What could Morey possibly hope to gain?" Dana asked. "He's already sold the letters."

"Some guys don't appreciate it when you break into their houses," Nick said as he took another corner too fast.

"We can't possibly lose them," Dana said. "They're practically on top of us."

"Yes, but can they do this?" he asked, and made a turn so impossibly sharp Dana could have sworn they had cut a ninety-degree angle. Before she realized where they were, the car whooshed down a ramp and into a parking garage beneath the hotel.

It was pitch-black, and much larger than the garage at *Heat!* Their headlights showed row after row of cars, with no indication of where the exits or the parking attendants might be. With only a moment's hesitation, Nick located a down ramp and began spiraling in the depths of the earth.

Dana tried to swallow, and it took three efforts before she succeeded. She had never felt trapped this way before, yet all she could do was hang on and let Nick make the decisions.

They zoomed down to another level. Headlights searched behind them as Morey's van followed their path.

"We can't keep giving away our location," said Nick. He switched off the lights as he nosed the car down a third ramp.

Dana covered her face, then realized how pointless the gesture was, since she couldn't see anyway. And neither could the driver. "Stop!" she cried. "You're going to hit somebody!"

The car eased to a halt. "I think we lost them," Nick said with satisfaction.

"I hope so," said Dana, then nearly jumped straight out of the car as a gunshot reverberated behind them.

Cursing with ear-blistering fervor, Nick flung open his door. "Get out! Hurry!"

She could see headlights moving along an adjacent lane, and heard Morey Bain snap, "Do you see them? Damn it, what kind of guard are you?"

Dana pelted alongside Nick between two cars, then crouched out of sight. "I thought you said it was almost impossible to get a gun permit," she muttered.

"It is," he said.

"Then how did they get one?"

"Who says they have one?"

A shiver ran through Dana. She couldn't believe Morey Bain would carry an illegal weapon, let alone murder them in cold blood. And for what? Breaking and entering but not taking anything?

But, as Nick had said, some men got mad when you broke into their houses. And Morey couldn't know exactly what they might have taken.

Headlamps swept past them. Just when she thought the car would continue on its way and leave them in peace, Morey shouted, "There! That's the convertible!"

Brakes creaked, and the engine died. A deep silence fell over the garage, amplifying Dana's heartbeat until it echoed through the space. Footsteps rang out, pacing toward them.

Now she understood how a cornered rabbit felt. Her instincts demanded flight, even though she knew it was safer to remain motionless.

Two dark figures with flashlights moved along the lane, peering through windshields and beneath cars. How long would it take before they spotted Dana and Nick crouching against the wall?

"I think there's a staircase to our left," Nick whispered.

"How sure are you?" she mouthed into his ear.

"Sure that we'll get killed if we don't try something," was the response.

Dana didn't like the choices. She also didn't like the black void opening to their left, which might, to her bleary eyes, have contained an abyss as likely as a staircase. But most of all, she didn't like the memory of that gunshot.

"Go!" whispered Nick, and the two of them scrambled between the wall and the cars, keeping low. A guttural curse from Nick reminded Dana that his leg must be hurting.

They might have escaped unnoticed, except that the door to the staircase turned out to be as solid as a rock. It took all Nick's strength to wrench it open, and the effort sent a hollow thud slamming through the garage.

"There!" cried Morey from some distance away. "After them, you idiot!"

Dana scooted through, with Nick right behind her. Letting the door clang shut, he said, "Go on! Straight up, and don't look back!"

"I won't leave you! If your leg's hurt, lean on me," Dana insisted.

"My leg's not that bad. I'm going to hold the door as long as I can," Nick responded. "Get up there." He indicated a faint red Exit light above them. "They've got some kind of low-level auxiliary power source. Take advantage of it while you can."

"But..." She didn't know why she felt this unwillingness to abandon him. It wasn't as if she would be of any use against armed men, Dana had to admit.

She simply didn't want to go on without Nick. They were a team, partners, if only for one evening. She relished his sharp rejoinders. She liked the way he smelled. In his presence, she felt more keenly alive than she had in a long time.

"I'm staying," she said.

"Like hell." Nick released the door. "We'll both have to go, then."

He grabbed her hand and tugged her upward. Dana went along with a quiver of relief. She could face the darkness and the confusion, but she couldn't face not knowing what had happened to Nick.

What was she thinking? she wondered in alarm. Nick wasn't her type of man. Too physical, too macho, too arrogant. She wanted a poet, like RNW, except that she was no longer sure the real RNW matched the character she'd come to know through his letters.

What she needed was time to sort out her thoughts, but there was no time.

Aided by faint red lights, the two of them plowed upward. The first door they tried was locked. One story above, the door was locked, too.

"Why?" Dana demanded breathlessly as she heard the bottom door groan open, admitting their pursuers.

"The stairs are for emergencies." Nick spoke between clenched teeth. "From the inside, they probably open on the lobby level only. Limiting access discourages crime."

"Not in this case," Dana gasped as they hurled themselves up another flight.

Finally they shoved a door open and spilled into a corridor. The only light came from a dim red bulb.

"I'd guess the lobby's this way," Nick said, his hand resting lightly on Dana's waist. She wondered why his touch felt so warm and why a soft buzz ran along her skin, radiating from the point at which the two of them connected.

As they rushed on, the chatter of voices ahead grew louder. Dana submitted a silent prayer of thanks. In the cover of a crowd, they could give Morey the slip. That still left the problems of retrieving their car and recovering the letters, but nothing was more important than staying alive.

Then they turned a corner and the passageway opened into vast reaches. Torches flared from evenly spaced holders and candles glittered in sconces along the walls, an arrangement so artful it seemed impossible it could have been thrown together quickly.

Far more astounding, however, were the people filling the rooms: men and women in the white wigs, long gowns and breeches of an era two centuries past. Fans fluttered, diamonds sparkled and lambent light fell across painted faces.

Dana stopped in confusion. They had emerged from the parking garage into another world.

Chapter Six

Dear DG,

You asked how someone with a poetic bent could be so successful in business. I fear you're succumbing to the stereotype of the businessman as a fast-talking shyster.

Success at the entrepreneurial level results from a combination of ability, preparation and timing. You have to know when to seize the moment.

When that moment comes, you must give it everything you have. Sometimes that means taking decisive action. At other times, the most valuable step may be to spend a leisurely day socializing.

Get to know your associates and your opponents. Encourage them to open up to you. Listen carefully for contradictions. Watch their body language.

Sometimes you just have to go with your instincts....

Nick couldn't have planned it better himself.

He had simply hoped that he and Dana could disappear among the hotel guests. Until this moment, he had forgotten about the annual Colonial Ball, sponsored by a group of history buffs, who threw a great deal of enthusiasm, if not always the utmost authenticity, into their costumes and dances.

Nick had read about them in the newspaper with amusement, even toying with the idea of joining as another way of going out in public while submerging his identity. But then he'd decided to bite the bullet and schedule his coming-out party for tonight.

Now, fate had thrust him in this direction after all. What better way to hide than by putting on a costume?

Catching the eye of an imposing man in a red coat with a badge that read Hospitality, Nick waved him over. A second badge, he noticed, read "Sir Allenby."

"We were hoping to join tonight," Nick said, speaking directly into the man's ear in order to be heard over the hubbub. "Our costumes aren't appropriate, I'm afraid." Not to mention ripped in unmentionable places, he mused.

"That can be taken care of," said Sir Allenby, who issued tickets in exchange for a sum of money. "We were scheduled to have a masked ball, but only the rental costumes have arrived. No one seems to be able to locate the truck with the masks. It's probably stuck in traffic. I hope you don't mind."

"Not at all," said Nick, although a face covering would have been even more to his liking than a costume.

"We'll get you situated, then," said the red-coated man, who waved to a white-wigged woman whose face was covered with powdery makeup, harsh rouge and tiny black paste-ons. "Lady Alicia! Would you assist this young lady in dressing?"

"Indeed, good sir, it would be my pleasure!" said the woman with a curtsy.

Dana shot a perplexed glance at Nick, but he gestured for her to go along. The sooner she got into a disguise, the safer she would be.

She apparently hadn't noticed the two figures skulking through the crowd on either side of them, peering at shadowed faces. Morey Bain and his lackey were closing in.

After making a few arrangements for later, arrangements involving a credit card, a bellboy and a key, Nick followed Sir Allenby to the cloakroom, where he too could be transformed.

THE LADIES' ROOM swam in the glow of a half-dozen candelabra. "I can't believe they set up the lights so quickly," Dana told Lady Alicia. "This hotel was certainly prepared for a blackout."

"Oh, la!" Lady Alicia whacked Dana's arm with a Japanese fan. "We had this event planned for months!"

"What a lucky coincidence." Dana regarded a rack of gowns dubiously. She couldn't believe Nick expected her to change into one of these.

"We do this every year!" The lady, who spoke mostly in exclamation points, appeared to be in her forties, although it was hard to tell under the heavy makeup. "It's the highlight of our season, let me tell you!"

Two other woman swished by, heading for the door. One, an African-American lady, wore a high-necked gown of striped fabric, a ribbon trimming the curly hair piled atop her head. Her companion, who sported a circlet of rosebuds in her red hair, wore a cropped maroon velvet jacket over a white lace gown.

"People certainly do dress up." Dana fingered her own simple cotton sweater, trying to ignore the rip in the sleeve. She felt completely out of place here, and she saw no point in remaining. "This is wonderful, but really, we just stumbled in."

"Oh, no!" Whack went Lady Alicia's fan again. "Your gentleman has purchased tickets and rented costumes. You must, simply must, get into the spirit!"

Perhaps it was the flickering light or the hunger pangs that sent a wave of dizziness shimmering through Dana's brain. She and Nick had urgent business, and yet he obviously considered this diversion worthwhile. Remembering the gunshots, she supposed it was.

Lady Alicia selected a gown and held it up for inspection. Unlike the flouncy, puffy dress that Alicia herself wore, it was simple in design. Cut of peach-colored silk, the dress featured a scooped neck and an Empire waist. Around the waistline and hem ran ribbons embroidered with a Greek key design.

"It's lovely," Dana admitted, then shook her head as her helper produced a massive white wig. "I couldn't wear that." She nearly added that it was ugly, then remembered that Alicia was wearing its twin.

"You have good instincts," the older woman conceded. "Wigs went out of fashion around the turn of the century." Dana gathered that the century in question was the eighteenth. "Try this instead."

The lady presented a small hat. From its back tapered a light veil that would cover the hair but not the face. It reminded Dana of something an actress might have worn in a Rudolph Valentino sheikh movie.

"You must at least try this on. Your gentleman has paid, after all!"

Well, any disguise would help throw off Morey and the guard, Dana supposed, and reached for the dress.

SINCE ASSUMING the identity of his own right-hand man, Nick had found that he enjoyed the idea of disguises and camouflage. There was something intriguing about assuming a manufactured persona. If nothing else, it forced a man to see the world through fresh eyes, and that was the best way to make discoveries.

On the other hand, he had never gone quite this far before. The buff-colored breeches clung to his thighs, revealing every bulge of muscle and ending just below the knee. The silk stockings and black pumps that went with it would have embarrassed Nick, if he hadn't been too absorbed in trying to hook the button-front fly.

The jacket wasn't bad, though, with its stiff high-backed collar and cutaway waist. It made Nick feel like one of Napoleon's generals.

He didn't see the costume assistant approaching with the powder until it was too late. With a flick of the puff, Nick's hair turned white.

"Hey!" He gasped for air and waved away the powder floating about his head. "Give a guy a break!"

"If we did that, no one would let us powder their hair," returned the fellow, marching off with a jaunty step.

Nick regarded himself in the mirror. This was definitely one of the oddest of the many rather strange situations in which Nick Lyon, indispensable aide to Renfro Williams, had landed in the past ten years.

He had drunk sake with geishas while discussing business in Japan. He had skied down Alpine slopes while negotiating rights acquisitions. He had scuba dived off the Florida coast to gain the trust of a music magnate. The nature of what he might be arranging for Renfro at this moment, however, was beyond definition. Love? Adventure? Insanity?

Nick couldn't shake the sense that the blackout had put the ordinary world on hold. Judging by a discussion he'd overheard a few minutes ago, the authorities were no closer to finding its cause and restoring power than they had been two hours ago, when it began.

Perhaps the entire modern world was at this very moment sliding down a steep slope into a primeval swamp. Tonight might be the last gasp of civilization, as all the ages, past and present, jumbled together.

It was as good an explanation as any for the mood that had seized him. At this moment, Renfro Nicholas Williams felt more lighthearted and carefree than he had in years.

The guests left dangling at the Top Hat, the caterer and fireworks crew waiting at his estate, even the tabloid about to bare his innermost thoughts to a cynical world, faded into the background. As he exited the cloakroom, he discovered that the music in the foreground was a minuet.

Nick wouldn't have recognized the approaching lady, if not for the determined steeliness in the way she strode toward him. Other than that, she formed a picture of ethereal loveliness in her floating peach gown and gauzy headdress.

As he had imagined the first time he saw Dana Grant, the right outfit transformed her into a beauty. In the soft light, her eyes grew larger, her skin more radiant and her hair more lustrous. She unmistakably resembled the photograph of the glamorous Dominique.

"Have you seen them?" Dana sneaked a furtive glance over her shoulder. "Are they here?"

"Morey the Pain and his goon?" Nick inquired. "I suspect they're hanging around somewhere."

Accepting his arm, Dana glided beside Nick toward the source of the music. "They might be watching the car. We could catch a cab."

"Not until we've danced," said Nick.

"Danced?" she repeated in disbelief. "We don't have time."

"Tonight, time stands still," he said.

"You can't mean it."

"I refuse to relinquish you until you grant me the honor of a dance," Nick said.

Dana's lips pressed together in annoyance, but by now she must have learned that he could be as stubborn as she. "Well, what do I do with this?" She held up her free arm, over which lay her street clothes and purse.

He located a bellhop and transferred the items, along with directions for recovering his own garments from the cloakroom. He gave the bellhop the number of the room he had already rented, along with a tip.

"What are you doing?" Dana protested as the young man hurried away. "Where's he taking my stuff?"

"All will be explained in due time," said Nick, who had no intention of explaining anything just yet.

The History Buff Society, as they called themselves, had done more than hire a ballroom—they had taken over the hotel. This meant, Nick discovered as they left the corridor, that the central atrium had been transformed into a Georgian delight.

The brilliance of torches reflected from small pools and flared into the vast space. Above them, two dozen stories of plant-draped balconies provided viewing galleries for onlookers.

Among the participants on the ground level, not everyone had chosen attire from the same era. This group, unlike some meticulous societies of reenactors, obviously tolerated diversity. As he and Dana entered the atrium, Nick observed Marie Antoinette gowns, Victorian top hats, Edwardian frock coats, and one confused-looking fellow in a toga.

With the aid of platforms covering some of the pools and nooks, a large dance floor had been created. At the far end, elevated on a balcony of their own, a small orchestra in colonial jackets and breeches performed upon violins assisted by oboes, a bassoon, a piano and a large kettledrum.

Nick couldn't keep his gaze from Dana's face as she absorbed the scene. Wonder, amusement and disbelief appeared, vanished and reappeared. At times she started to pull away, and then the music and the splendor worked their magic and she nestled comfortably against Nick.

It amazed him that a woman in today's world could live thirty years without becoming disillusioned and skeptical, but obviously Dana had kept her childlike sense of awe. That might go along with being an actress, but Nick doubted it.

He wanted to understand what made this woman tick. That, he decided, was his goal in remaining at the hotel and tolerating this ridiculous outfit. He wanted to tease away Dana's artifices and find out what was going on inside her head. He had spent the past year corresponding with a stranger. Tonight, they would knock down the barriers.

With the supreme confidence of a man who has conquered the business world, Nick had no doubt that he could remain in control of his own feelings. He would unmask this writer of misleading letters, this ersatz detective. He would lure and reassure her until she admitted the truth.

And then? As always, he would have done his job, protecting Renfro Williams from the predators of the world. Including, sad to say, this exquisite young woman.

But not quite yet. The orchestra had segued into a new piece, and Nick escorted Dana onto the dance floor. People were taking their places, and his leg no longer hurt except for a twinge.

AS AN ENGLISH TEACHER, Dana had always found costume dramas appealing. They brought history and literature to life, although she regarded much of the men's attire as foppish.

She had never, however, been this close to a man in Georgian clothing. She could see that, far from being ridiculous, the garments emphasized the wearer's masculinity shamelessly.

She doubted many men had ever cut quite the dashing figure that Nick Lyon managed. His square shoulders and slim hips were displayed to advantage by the high-collared jacket, with its cutaway waist. The tight-fitting pants emphasized his muscular build, and his confident stride dispelled any hint of coyness about the tights and patent pumps.

Even the powdered hair gave him a distinguished air. With his height and self-assurance, he eclipsed everyone around him.

The man reeked of virility. Dana wondered how the ladies of earlier eras had managed to remain so chaste, then remembered that a lot of them hadn't. She could understand why girls had married early, and why widows had been notorious for their affairs.

Not that she would contemplate such a thing, Dana thought. Her interest in Nick Lyon was purely that of a fellow conspirator.

She wished she could figure out what he had in mind by insisting that they stick around the hotel in these disguises. Were Morey and the guard keeping such close watch that it would be dangerous to flee? Had Morey hired more goons who might, even now, be closing in?

Nick's refusal to confide in her was maddening. Dana didn't like the idea of a man trying to protect her by keeping her ignorant. She considered demanding that Nick come clean, but there was something about him that both commanded respect and warned that he expected his judgment to prevail.

That went along with her suspicion that he might be a bodyguard or security expert. If so, the obvious conclusion was that RNW needed protection—but from whom?

Despite Nick's assurances, she wasn't convinced his boss had no shady connections. It would certainly explain the man's fetish for secrecy.

It would also explain why Nick hadn't called the police, even though they'd been shot at.

If so, Dana might have stumbled into matters that were over her head. Still, she refused to leave everything in Nick's hands. Those were *her* letters that were about to be exposed to the world, and it was *her* sister whose life might be turned upside down.

Not to mention the giggling and snickering that would follow Dana through the halls of her high school once the truth was revealed.

Lost in thought, she allowed Nick to draw her onto the dance floor before she realized what was happening. Now Dana found herself standing in a line with other women, facing a line of men. Obviously, Nick intended for them to participate in this antiquated dance, although she couldn't imagine why.

She didn't have a clue what the steps might be. Distressed, Dana glanced at Nick's face, but couldn't read his expression in the dim light.

So what if they made fools of themselves? she told herself. In these getups, nobody would recognize them, anyway. By the time the dance was finished, the coast might be clear.

As the music began, it occurred to Dana that since this event had been staged to avoid electric lighting, they would have no way of knowing when the power went on in the rest of the city. At this very moment, *Heat!* might be starting its presses and sealing their doom.

There wasn't much she could do about it now.

The line rippled, and she realized that a woman had slipped in beside her. With relief, Dana recognized Lady Alicia.

"What kind of dance is this?" she asked as they curtsied to the gentlemen's bows.

"A country dance," responded the bewigged woman, sweeping her skirts about her and sinking so low she was barely able to scramble upright again. "We've taken a few liberties, but no one's quite sure exactly how the dances were done in the old days, anyway. There weren't any films, you know."

With some coaching from Alicia, Dana managed to keep up with the other women as they half turned and joined hands with their partners. From that point, Nick led her serenely through the dance, passing along the formation to its head and then separating to come back around again, as if he'd done this many times before. Only by close observation could Dana tell he was faking some of the steps.

Other participants, too, sometimes mistimed their turns and changes of partner, and after a few minutes Dana relaxed. She was reminded of a square dancing session she'd participated in at the high school, though tonight's maneuvers were executed with more grace and less adolescent cavorting.

The orchestra shifted into a faster tempo, and the melody changed. The dancers divided into smaller formations, with intricate steps that Dana could barely keep up with.

She felt Nick's hands on her waist, guiding her with good-humored assurance. The swirl of movement around them, far from putting them on public display, provided privacy. Lost in the mass of dancers, they were alone with each other.

The formal dance might have appeared sedate from a distance, but in the thick of it, Dana couldn't avoid having contact with Nick's boldly displayed body. At every turn, his thighs brushed hers and his hands steered and controlled her.

The formations had been designed to give the man dominance, forcing the woman to rely on him. It wasn't an arrangement Dana would usually have appreciated, but in these costumes, somehow it seemed like a treat.

Mostly she was aware of Nick's grip burning through the thin fabric of her gown. The femininity of the long skirt and the low neckline conspired to remind Dana that she was very much a woman, in the presence of the most desirable man she'd met in a long time. Maybe ever.

The warmth stirring within her came partly from the exertion, but more from her tingling awareness of Nick. Was he responding to her the same way? Impossible to tell from the faintly mocking smile that played about his lips.

When forced to trade partners, Dana could feel Nick's gaze on her until they were united again. No other man moved with such assurance. She seemed able to track his movements with an inner radar, keen for the moment when his hands would claim her once more.

She felt suspended, unsure what was happening. This silver yearning felt like nothing Dana had experienced before.

When the music ended, she struggled to regain her sense of purpose. "We have to be going," she said.

Nick leveled her a stern look. "Not before you grant me a waltz."

"I don't know if people waltzed back then." She remembered seeing a documentary about Strauss-mania sweeping Vienna, but wasn't that later in the nineteenth century?

"The waltz came into fashion in England about 1815," offered Lady Alicia from nearby, then bobbed away in search of a new partner.

"I guess that answers your question," Nick murmured. His breath whispered across her cheek, and Dana could smell his spicy fragrance.

He wasn't the Nick Lyon she had met earlier this evening. Transformed along with the setting, he had ceased to be an ordinary modern male and become an adventurer, a plunderer and a brigand.

The amazing thing to Dana was that Nick appeared to relish the role. She would have expected him to be impatient with this delay and at this whole masquerade. Instead, he seemed to have nothing more urgent in mind than claiming his waltz.

When the music resumed, Dana discovered that the colonial style of waltzing bore only a passing resemblance to the one-two-three shuffle of the modern school prom. Couples formed a large circle and began with a promenade in three-quarter time, circling the dance floor.

When the gentlemen spun the ladies halfway around, Dana felt as if she were part of the workings of a great clock. Seen from the balconies overhead, the dancers must form a pattern in constant motion.

Then the participants squared off with their partners. Nick's hand rested on Dana's hip. He offered the other hand palm up, and she placed her right hand on it, palm down. Following the example of the other ladies, Dana lifted her skirt with her free hand.

Nick whirled her around the circle with such suddenness that she could barely catch her breath. She was vaguely aware of other couples swirling in a grand design, like a living kaleidoscope, but nothing seemed real except this man and his influence over her.

Dana didn't know this aspect of herself, the coquette who glanced flirtatiously up at Nick as they waltzed. It might have been the dress that drew out this more wanton side of her, or the tacit permission provided by their costumes to pretend she was someone other than her ordinary self.

Had this woman always lurked inside her, sensually aware of her own grace as she twirled, attuned to the whisper of air across her partly exposed bosom and to the subtle twitch of a muscle in Nick's cheek? Dana had read about a woman feeling undressed by a man's eyes, but it had always sounded like an exaggeration before.

Yet she was safe here, in a public place, free to give rein to her newly discovered feelings. There was no harm in smiling at Nick alluringly just as she spun away, and no danger in leaning toward him ever so slightly when they rejoined, even at the risk of revealing more of her breasts.

It bothered Dana a little that she was dallying, however innocently, with Nick Lyon, when it was his employer who had captured her heart. Or at least her imagination. She supposed it was RNW's own fault for sending a stand-in to recover his letters instead of doing it himself.

She couldn't blame him for relying on Nick, however. The man paused from time to time to survey their surroundings, never losing track of possible danger. As bodyguards went, he must be a good one.

The waltz ended, and she swept into a curtsy that no longer felt awkward. Dana wished she could cool herself with one of those fans that other women were employing with such skill. She felt engulfed by heat, and it hadn't come solely from exertion.

She had forgotten the need for caution until she saw alarm flicker across Nick's face. Following his gaze, Dana spotted Morey Bain's chubby form wading toward them through a knot of onlookers.

"Look!" She indicated Morey's direction with her head, not wanting to point and make it clear to their pursuer that he'd been spotted.

Nick's hand clamped on Dana's wrist. "Let's head for the other side of the atrium."

"But we need to reach your car!"

"I know somewhere better to hide," he murmured, trying to penetrate a sea of bodies washing toward them as newcomers took to the dance floor.

In the crush, Nick had to release her wrist or risk injuring her. Immediately Dana found herself propelled away from him.

"Where are we going?" she called over the oblivious newcomers, hoping that Morey couldn't hear her words amid the noise.

"Meet me on the fourth floor, near the service elevator," Nick responded as they were pulled in different directions.

To Dana's surprise, he didn't try to stay parallel to her as she continued toward the rear of the atrium. A moment later, she saw Nick's stratagem. He was pointing Sir Allenby toward Morey, indicating the man's lack of a costume.

With surprising speed, the red-coated gatekeeper reached Morey and began a harangue. Beyond them, Nick vanished.

Dana searched in vain for a sight of him. She had no choice but to follow his directions, even though her instincts demanded that she leave the hotel and get as far away from Morey Bain as possible.

When she was with Nick, Dana hadn't paid much attention to the layout of the atrium. Now she found herself lost in a sea of surging shadows. She couldn't spot an elevator, but then remembered that even if she found one, it wouldn't work.

Her breath squeezing in her chest, she pushed and prodded her way through the mass of bodies. Another dance had begun, and people thrust toward the formation, blocking Dana's escape. The cluster of heavy garments obscured her line of vision, and the scents of perfume, powder and musty fabric overwhelmed her senses.

Dana forced herself to think calmly. Although the staircase from the parking garage had ended at the ground floor, there must be another set of stairs leading upward. The entrance most likely lay off the corridor where she and Nick had entered.

As she squirmed through the assembly, occasionally bumping a passerby, Dana became aware that men were regarding her in an unfamiliar way. Their gazes alit first on her heaving bosom, then traveled with interest to her face, which, at the moment, felt feverishly aglow. Several times she heard the beginnings of an invitation to dance, but she gave each suitor a quick twist of a smile, along with her regrets.

Somehow their interest didn't surprise her, although in her normal selection of baggy clothing, Dana rarely rated a second glance. Tonight the entire world must be able to see the sensations that Nick had aroused. In a way, she supposed, Morey Bain had arrived barely in time to rescue her.

But precisely what he had rescued her from, and whether she wished to be rescued, remained to be determined.

Reaching the corridor, Dana tried a succession of doors, all locked. None bore a label, and she wondered how hotel workers could keep them straight. At least, she told herself with grim humor, she hadn't beaned herself with any falling vacuum cleaners.

She turned a corner into a quiet hallway and heaved a sigh of relief. At least now she could proceed without having to elbow aside the mass of partygoers.

A few sconces provided faint light, and at the end Dana discovered a glowing red sign reading Stairs. Thank goodness for the hotel's emergency supply of electricity.

She moved forward, only noticing the branching corridor as she passed it. There was a man coming toward her, Dana noted, and instead of a costume he wore a dark-blue security uniform.

Maybe he worked for the hotel, she thought frantically, quickening her pace.

"Wait!) Miss!" The man loped toward her.

Hoping he wouldn't recognize her, or was the wrong man entirely, Dana paused. Running away would only force him to give chase. "Yes?"

"I'm trying to find a couple who've left their car in the the garage." At closer range, the fellow was almost as tall as Nick, although thin to the point of gangliness. "They're blocking me."

"I don't work for the hotel." Dana backed away.

"I know, but you might have seen—" He broke off and stared at her. "My God, it is you! Dominique Grant!" He didn't sound like an eager fan, but rather a hunter seizing on his quarry. At that moment, candlelight flickered, giving his face a demonic cast.

Dana fled toward the stairs.

Chapter Seven

Dear RNW,

Thanks for offering to send me flowers for Valentine's Day, but they'd never fit in my p.o. box. Especially since my favorites, calla lilies and birds of paradise, are huge. That's why I like them—because they're so dramatic.

Since you ask, my tastes in food would make a nutritionist blanche. If I could, I'd eat shrimp in garlic-butter sauce, fettuccine Alfredo and asparagus every day, with chocolate mousse ice cream for desert. And a glass of white zinfandel to wash it all down!

My arteries might wind up clogged, but I'd die with a smile on my face....

Dana heard the man's feet thud on the carpet and knew it would take only a few steps before he caught her. She couldn't move quickly in this confining dress, and her dainty slippers skidded as she ran.

Just as she reached the stairs, the door opened. Dana barely stopped in time to avoid being smacked in the face.

"Oh, my dear!" boomed Lady Alicia, stepping out with a portly gentleman in tow. "We watched you waltz from the second story. How wonderfully you dance! Dana, may I introduce Sir Gerald?"

As the man swept into a bow, the guard's hand clamped onto Dana's upper arm. "Unhand me!" she cried, instinctively slipping into the language of an earlier time, and praying that he wouldn't produce a gun.

"For shame!" Lady Alicia whacked her fan against the guard's hand, startling him into releasing his grip.

Instantly Dana darted past him and up the stairs. Behind her, she could hear the guard protesting as Lady Alicia and Sir Gerald blocked his path, both scolding loudly.

She knew she ought to take some form of evasive action, but couldn't think of anything except to head for the fourth floor, as Nick had instructed. She felt her way up the steps in utter darkness, keeping one hand on the banister and hoping she hadn't miscounted the doors along the way.

Three flights up, Dana opened one and found herself on a walkway marked by rooms on one side and the atrium on the other. Sprightly music wafted from below, along with the rustle of dancers.

She gulped, unable to avoid imagining what might happen if the guard caught her and tried to throw her over the railing. It was a melodramatic idea, but didn't seem too farfetched, considering the events of the evening.

The light came solely from flickering torches in the atrium, so faint and changeable that Dana had to peer closely to determine that one of the room numbers was indeed in the four hundreds. She was on the right floor, but where was the service elevator?

Dana's heart was pounding, and she fought to catch her breath—and to get her bearings, more internally than externally.

Tonight, she didn't feel like herself. The past few hours had stripped away the woman she knew, the high-school teacher who lived in a condominium and shopped at the mall, leading a quiet life in familiar patterns.

Tonight she had broken into a man's house, fled with a stranger and barely escaped being shot. Now, strangest of all, she found herself behaving like some headstrong creature from another era, lost between the past and the present.

Nick was the only safety she knew. She had to find him.

A few people in costumes hung over the railing, watching the activities below, too absorbed to pay any attention to Dana. She doubted they would know where the service elevator was, anyway.

Nick might have picked the fourth floor at random. All they needed was some prearranged point at which to meet, Dana reflected. And perhaps he figured the hotel's scarce power supply would target that vital elevator, which could whisk them down to the garage and his car.

On the other hand, Morey and the guard would probably be checking the car frequently, unless they'd had it towed. Or planted a bomb in it.

You will not panic, Dana ordered herself as she fumbled down a side corridor in search of the service elevator. *You will find Nick. Or your clothes. Or something.*

There were no sconces in this part of the hotel, and the halls provided only a minimal source of light from small bulbs set into the baseboards. It wasn't even strong enough for Dana to read the room numbers.

She stopped, afraid to venture farther. Maybe she should go back. At least downstairs there were people who could help her. Lady Alicia, for instance.

The problem, Dana discovered, lay in retracing her steps. Each junction of corridors appeared identical to every other, and twice she had to guess blindly, unable to remember which way she had come. Within moments, she was hopelessly lost. Worse, she came to a dead end and knew without a doubt that she couldn't have come from this way.

Behind her, a door scraped open. Dana whirled to face a silhouette looming against interior candlelight that, by contrast to the darkness, hurt her eyes.

"Excuse me, I'm looking—" she began, and then the man pulled her into the room and locked the door.

TONIGHT Nick felt like a sorcerer. Every time he waved his wand, events tumbled in the right direction.

The very existence of this ball, falling into their laps, had been a stroke of magic. Then Dana had somehow been persuaded to go along with changing into a costume, and dancing with him, and now here she was at his front door, saving him a trip to the service elevator, several corridors away.

She seemed vulnerable, standing in the hall, her eyes wide with shock and her lips quivering. A man couldn't help noticing such details, even when he knew he should try to distance himself.

As he steered her inside, Nick realized from the way she drew back that Dana hadn't recognized him. "It's me," he said.

She let out a long breath. "Thank goodness. But what are you doing here?"

"Hiding," he said, which was partly true.

"Who does this belong to?" She paused beside him, peering at the setting in the candlelight. The living room encompassed a circular couch, a bar and a dining table. Beyond French doors lay a private balcony overlooking the central court, four stories below.

It was impressive, Nick reflected with a touch of pride. "My boss," he said.

"RNW? Is he here?"

"He keeps a suite for visitors," Nick said.

"At all the hotels? Or just this one?" She ran her hand over the rich fabric of the couch. "That's a bit coincidental, don't you think?"

Nick ducked his head, embarrassed at being caught in a lie. "All right. I made arrangements when we got here. I thought we might need somewhere to retreat."

"I thought you were in a hurry to recover those letters," she said challengingly.

How could he explain? He certainly hadn't rented the room in order to seduce her. Nick didn't take advantage of women. More often, he had to fend them off to keep them from taking advantage of him.

He simply wanted a chance to be alone with Dana, to get to know her better, but that didn't sound very believable. "I think we should let our friends cool their heels. Maybe they'll get bored and go away."

"Maybe we should call the police," she said.

He shook his head. "We're burglars, remember? Besides, even if they agree to investigate, it will be hours before they get their paperwork done. Believe me, we'll be on our way quicker without them."

Dana bit her lip as she considered. It was an unstudied and oddly endearing trait. Nick wondered why the studio makeup artists hadn't warned her against it.

"I don't see how we can wait another minute," she said stubbornly. "The electricity could come on, and the paper will go to press. Besides, that reporter might have left the Top Hat by now."

"No, he hasn't."

"How do you know?" she asked.

"Because he's waiting for someone who hasn't arrived yet." If he wanted Dana to trust him, Nick was going to have to tip his hand a bit.

She shot him a puzzled glance. "Who?"

"Me."

"I don't get it."

Nick experienced a sudden longing to kiss away the look of confusion from her face, and wondered at this unfamiliar instinct. He wasn't used to playing the role of protector for anyone but his alter ego. "I'm supposed to be there when RNW reveals his true identity tonight," he said. "He's decided to stop hiding."

"Hiding?" she asked. "You mean he hides from other people, too? I mean, I know he's reclusive, but I didn't know he carried it that far."

"Well, he does," said Nick. "At least he has, until tonight, but he's decided to go public."

"Why?" Her forehead furrowed. "It doesn't have anything to do with me, does it?"

"It's because of rumors," he said. "About his mental health." Seeing her frown deepen, Nick added, "He's fine, by the way. Just a trifle eccentric. But reputation means a lot in business."

"So that's what Andy Adams meant about the Top Hat, that everyone knows what's going on. Except me." She made a face at Nick. "And you didn't bother to tell me."

"I'm telling you now," he said. "My boss is hosting his own coming-out party. He's invited half of Hollywood."

"He should have invited me," Dana said, only half joking.

"Consider yourself invited."

"You can speak for him?"

"I do it all the time," he said.

Gliding away from him, she walked to the open French doors and peered down into the courtyard. Below, the orchestra was playing a minuet. "Nick, I don't know what to believe about RNW. He must be someone important, then?"

"Yes." He wondered how much that mattered to her. Dana didn't behave like a status seeker, but she didn't behave like an actress, either. She might be playing some complex game, or simply be very good at submerging her real personality.

She turned to face him. "Who is he? How about a free preview?"

"I'm not allowed to say." The remark sounded pompous and stiff to Nick's own ears, so he added, "It would be a breach of trust. He wants to make the announcement himself."

"Why did he write to me?" Her eyes searched his.

"Loneliness," he suggested, unable to resist moving toward her. "Boredom, perhaps."

She crossed her arms, as if protecting herself. "I suppose I should have expected that. I mean, that the letters were a way of amusing himself."

"What were they for you?" Nick stopped where he was, in the middle of the room. "What did you hope to gain?"

"At first, I thought it was a fantasy game." The partial veil made a halo behind her soft brown curls. "The kind where you each assume an identity and create a make-believe world between you. After a while, I realized he might not be joking."

Her words reassured Nick. Dana hadn't meant to exploit him. But she also hadn't been searching for love. "Did that annoy you?"

"What? The fact that he wasn't joking?" The idea seemed to startle her. "No, I wasn't annoyed. I was touched."

"You pitied him?" Nick probed.

"Oh, no." Dana came forward and sank onto the couch. On the coffee table sat a candelabra of polished silver, its many branches creating a tree of light. "He writes so beautifully, I thought he might be a poet. What's he like?"

"He's a mystery to almost everyone." Nick remained standing, maintaining a physical distance that mirrored his emotional reticence. He couldn't have said what held him back. Perhaps the years of hiding his identity had made him wary. Besides, Dana still hadn't confessed to being an actress. He wanted her to come clean first, so that he knew he could believe the rest of what she said.

"What does he look like?" she asked. "How old is he?"

"In his thirties," said Nick. "About my height. Would you like a drink?" The suite came with a fully stocked bar.

"No, thanks." Dana's hand fluttered. "I don't drink much, except a bit of wine on special occasions."

"Don't worry," he assured her. "It's coming."

"What is?"

The distant music changed to a waltz. "The wine. And here's your birthday dance," Nick said. "May I have the honor? Our last waltz wasn't exactly what I'd planned. Let's try something a bit less organized."

She laughed—it was a spontaneous bubbling of delight—and rose to accept his offer. "You can be persuasive when you're in a good mood."

He quirked an eyebrow. "And when I'm not?"

"You're stubborn and maddening." Dana slipped into his arms as if it were the most natural thing in the world. And, to him, it was.

"Then I promise to make myself agreeable." Nick stopped talking as he drank in her teasing scent and felt the tickle of her hair against his cheek.

DANA KNEW it was dangerous to dance with Nick alone in a hotel suite, but she couldn't resist. It was her birthday, after all.

Oh, it wasn't dangerous in the same way as confronting Morey Bain. But this man posed a threat to her peace of mind, all the same.

For one thing, he was still wearing that rakish costume cut to emphasize his virility. It was hard to imagine that, two centuries ago, men had gone about in skintight pants and jackets practically pasted to their chests. She had always assumed society was more demure back then.

There was nothing demure about the way Dana felt. Despite the long skirt, her dress was constructed of tissue-light fabric that clung to her waist and dipped low at the bosom.

With his hand on her hip, Nick must be able to feel her body as boldly as if she wore nothing but lingerie. Despite his rigorously upright stance, the way his breath caught in his throat and the hardening of his thigh muscles told their own story.

She wondered why he kept dissembling on the subject of his boss. Was Nick acting from a sense of loyalty? Did he intend, like a good servant, to bring the fair maiden home to his lord without yielding to his impulse to ravish her?

Dana suppressed a chuckle at the image she had summoned. She was no Guinevere, and she doubted Nick would compare himself to Lancelot.

The whole scenario was hugely self-indulgent, she thought, resting her cheek against his strong shoulder and letting the heat of his body percolate through her thin dress. Down-to-earth Dana Grant would never permit herself to be so vulnerable, especially not with a man who was as much a mystery as his boss. But tonight she was someone else, someone she didn't know very well.

From the masterful way he expected her to follow his lead at every turn tonight, Nick clearly was a man accustomed to power. She doubted he was merely RNW's lackey. As a security chief, he probably came from a background in law enforcement, or perhaps something shadier.

He was definitely the wrong sort of man for a high-school English teacher to entrust with her safety. But just for these few minutes, Dana didn't care. It was her birthday treat to herself, to nestle in his arms, to press her lips lightly against his jaw and inhale his faint scent.

Nick's mouth brushed along hers, and then he was kissing her, slowly and deeply, his hands sliding up her back and fluffing her hair beneath the demiveil. There was nothing boyish or awkward in his movements. He angled her easily against one arm, tilting her face upward so that he could explore her mouth more thoroughly.

With a moan, Dana felt his lips trace a fiery path down her throat. She knew that if she didn't make him stop, they would quickly reach that unspoken point from which a couple did not retreat. She willed herself to speak, and found no words. Her hands fluttered, intending to push him away, and instead stroked his upper arms.

He pulled her hard against him, and she felt his arousal, which his costume did nothing to conceal. She understood now the Victorian belief that for a man and a woman to be alone together was tantamount to making love. She could almost believe the costumes had been designed for the express purpose of seduction.

A brisk knock at the door startled her. Nick uttered a click of annoyance, but shifted her gently from his arms.

"Who's that?" she asked as he strode to the entrance.

"A surprise," he said.

The surprise, from what she could see in the dimness, came in the form of a bellhop and a cart. The service elevator must indeed be working, she noted, and she wished it and everyone else could disappear into another dimension while she and Nick finished what they had started.

A few deep breaths, however, brought Dana to her senses. They also brought her the aromas of garlic and cheese and a blending of other delights that reminded her she hadn't eaten dinner.

The heat ebbed from her skin as she came forward to investigate. Nick had, in the meantime, dispatched the bellhop with a bill folded into his palm.

"Happy birthday," he said when the man had gone and he'd removed the covers from the plates.

Dana's nose told her even more than her eyes. Here was her birthday feast, in every detail—shrimp in garlic-butter sauce, fettuccine Alfredo, asparagus and chocolate mousse ice cream. She could only imagine what it must have cost Nick to summon such a meal on short notice in the midst of a blackout.

A vase on the cart offered a huge selection of bird of paradise flowers, calla lilies and orchids. "Orchids," she said. "What a lovely touch."

"I thought I'd add something extra." Nick gestured her to a seat on the couch, and Dana was only too pleased to comply.

He poured her a glass of white wine from a bottle cooling in a silver bucket. The glasses had an expensive, hand-cut feel.

Everything was perfect—a little too perfect. Dana felt a vague discomfort at this sudden appearance of exactly what she wanted, but at the moment she was too hungry to worry about it.

She came up for air after several mouthfuls of shrimp. "How did you know?"

"Know what?" Nick was digging into the fettuccine as if he, too, hadn't eaten in hours, which she supposed he hadn't.

Dana set down her fork. She hated for cold reality to intrude, but she couldn't ignore it.

"Do you expect me to believe RNW also described my favorite meal and flowers?" she said. "Along with telling you about my jumping out of an airplane? Or did the description of my favorite meal just happen to be among the few selections he let you read?"

Nick winced. "Do you really want an answer to that?"

"I do."

"He let me read your letters. All of them."

"Why?" Tears of anger pricked her eyes. A few minutes ago, she had nearly forgotten about the letters, and RNW. Now she felt cheated.

"You said that was a make-believe persona you described," Nick pointed out. "Why should you care who read it?"

"Because underneath, it was me," Dana said. "Things I couldn't say as myself."

"You were confiding in him," Nick murmured.

"He's not a very nice man, is he?"

The lines of his face grew stern. "He cares very much for you."

"So much that he lets his friends amuse themselves by reading my letters?" She had no desire to eat any more. A squeezing sensation in her chest blocked the hunger pangs.

"Not his friends. Just me." Nick took a sip from his wineglass. "Dana, I'm his emissary to the world. His alter ego. He trusts me to represent him in a wide variety of situations."

"Even with women?" she demanded in disbelief.

"The matter has never come up before," he admitted.

"You're saying he's a hermit?"

"In a manner of speaking," Nick said. "Of course, he didn't know you would turn up tonight, but I expect he would have sent me to meet with you first in any event."

Dana's misery eased, but she still felt unsettled. "He doesn't sound quite normal."

"After tonight, things are going to change," Nick said. "You asked me earlier if you had something to do with his decision to go public. The answer is yes, although he'd have a hard time admitting it. He's tired of skulking around. In a way, this is my last gasp at being RNW's eyes and ears. After tonight, in a sense, I'm out of a job."

"I'm sorry." Dana didn't believe Nick would find himself unemployed for long, but she imagined that any layoff would come as a blow. She hadn't given any thought to Nick's feelings, she realized, only to her own and RNW's. "Do you have other prospects?"

"A few." He leaned back, regarding her over his glass. "I wish we could stop talking about my boss. Frankly, right now, I'm sick of him."

Dana was, too. She wished she had time to sort out her thoughts. They kept circling around and entangling her.

Everything Nick said made RNW more of a puzzle. She felt less and less sympathetic toward the man, particularly after learning that he had shared her letters with his bodyguard. Okay, more than a bodyguard—his go-between.

She smiled.

"What's so funny?" said Nick.

"You're a go-between," she explained. "Like couples used to employ in the old days."

"Have I done a good job of conveying my employer's sentiments?" he asked. "Have I fulfilled my duty?"

"Is that what you've been doing?" said Dana.

"You mean you think I'm acting on my own desires?" he asked teasingly. "Wining and dining you, dancing and putting on costumes?"

"The costumes didn't have anything to do with your desires," she pointed out.

"They do now." His gaze moved tantalizingly down her throat to the formfitting softness of her gown.

A sharp wave of longing rushed through Dana, and she busied herself with her food. Disillusioned as she might be about the self-absorbed RNW, she didn't intend to let herself rebound into Nick's arms.

He was too sophisticated and enigmatic for quiet Dana Grant. She wanted a man for all seasons, not a Romeo for one night.

Nick ate in silence, but she could feel him watching her. Nibbling her asparagus, Dana decided not to let mixed emotions spoil her birthday dinner. It wasn't every day a woman celebrated her landmark thirtieth birthday.

"I wish I could count the expressions that have crossed your face in the last five minutes," Nick said. "What are you thinking?"

Dana took a gulp of wine. White zinfandel, very smooth. "About what the last decade has brought, and what I hope will happen in the next ten years."

"Which is what?" he said.

"The usual," Dana admitted. "A husband and children. I'm not very original."

"That's all?" he quizzed. "No marching across the world stage? Don't tell me you lack ambition."

It seemed a strange comment from a man who hardly knew her, Dana thought, but then she remembered that Nick had read her letters. He must believe a woman who dreamed of being an international detective would want more than domestic bliss.

In a way, he was right. "I suppose I do crave recognition," she confessed. "I like to think I do my work for the love of it, though. I wouldn't want to give it up entirely, although I would like to take time off to be with my kids."

"A commendable attitude," he observed dryly.

"You don't believe me?"

His gaze shifted to a distant point, and she wondered what had drawn him away. "You're a spontaneous woman, Dana. You fling yourself into the moment. Whatever you feel right now I'm sure is genuine. But you might feel differently tomorrow."

Spontaneous? Flinging herself into the moment? Dana found herself reluctant to reveal exactly how mundane a life she led. Nick probably didn't realize that, in addition to having lied about being a detective, she hadn't even visited most of the places she'd written about.

Judging by the ease with which he handled bellhops and the guardian of the costume ball, Nick was a man of the world. She couldn't bring herself to dispel the lingering impression that she, too, was cosmopolitan.

"I'm not so fickle as all that," was her mild response.

"Remains to be seen," he said as he refilled her wineglass.

They finished their meal in companionable silence. Dana kept trying to relax, but couldn't quite achieve it. She was too aware of Nick's nearness, of the way he regarded her from time to time through narrowed eyes, as if trying to take her measure.

Would he be reporting back to his boss? What would he say?

"Well?" she demanded after consuming the last of the ice cream. "What are you going to tell RNW?"

"About what?" he asked.

"You've been studying me as if you were compiling statistics," she said. "How would you describe me?"

A devilish grin flickered across his mouth. "Tempting," he said.

"So you're tempted?" A mischievous streak in Dana made her press on, against her better judgment. "Tempted to do what?"

"Usurp my boss's prerogatives," he said.

Without thinking, Dana reacted as she might have in one of her classes, by defining their terms. "Prerogative, a special right or privilege. Tell me, exactly what special rights or privileges does RNW have where I'm concerned?"

"You sound like you're asking for a demonstration." Nick moved his plate aside.

"Absolutely not. Let's keep this conversation theoretical." Even in the semidarkness, Dana couldn't miss the subtle shifting of his body toward her on the couch.

She wondered how far a sharp tongue could go in holding a man's urges at bay. Although at times Nick came close to intimidating her, she always seemed to emerge at or near the top.

Verbal pyrotechnics were her specialty, although, judging by the intensity with which he regarded her, they were venturing close to the physical realm. Still, she didn't believe a sheltered young woman like herself could tempt an experienced man like Nick beyond endurance.

It was not a contest she would have considered under normal circumstances. At the moment, however, two glasses of wine were percolating through her bloodstream. That, in addition to the late hour and the excitement of their adventures in the blackout, gave her a sense of exhilaration bordering on invincibility.

"All right," Nick said, accepting the challenge. "Let's discuss temptation, theoretically."

"In what way would I tempt your boss?" Dana began.

He regarded her skeptically. "You should be able to answer that question yourself."

"It must be this dress," she said.

"Why would you think that?"

"I'm not usually the seductive type."

He chuckled. "Really? I find that an amazing statement, coming from you."

Okay, so Dana Grant, female detective, occasionally landed in a millionaire's lair or, on one occasion, a potentate's harem. Dana was grateful that the darkness hid her blush as she recalled that particular epistolary episode. "I have an active imagination."

"Let's get back to the part about your dress." Teasingly Nick let his gaze trail down to the exposed tops of her breasts. "Why do you consider it more seductive than ordinary clothes?"

Dana had the feeling that control of the conversation was slipping away. Until she figured out how to regain it, she needed to keep talking. "The material is thin as a handkerchief. And it's cut to display everything in a very suggestive way."

"I can confirm that," said Nick.

A laugh startled from Dana's throat. "Well, it's nothing compared to what *you're* wearing."

"You consider this seductive?" He leaned back, giving her a full view of his broad chest and slim hips. "I didn't think women reacted to men on a purely visual level."

"Of course they do!" Dana gesticulated. "Look at yourself! You have great shoulders, by the way. You must work out at a gym. I can see practically every muscle, including some that ought to be covered by fig leaves."

He chuckled. "You sound as if you've been making detailed observations."

"How could I help it?" Dana responded. "We've been dancing so close we're generating our own electricity."

"I did notice that." Nick leaned forward and traced her jawline with his thumb, raising a series of tiny thrills that shot down her spine.

"Men shouldn't be allowed to dress that way," she murmured.

"I agree," he said, and before she realized it, he had unbuttoned his jacket and tossed it over a chair. Candlelight gleamed off his bronze chest, highlighting its sheen.

Dana knew she should retreat, but she had to touch that firm expanse of skin, just once. Her fingers feathered across his stomach and upper body, feeling a responsive ripple. "I didn't know you weren't wearing anything underneath," she murmured.

"How about you?" he said.

Dana caught her breath at the implication. She'd had to leave off her bra, since it would have shown beneath the neckline.

The first thing that sprang from her lips was a childish remark, such as one of her students might have made, and one she would never, never, have uttered had she given it a moment's consideration. "That's for me to know and you..."

"To find out?" There was more than a glimmer of triumph in Nick's face as he reached out and lowered the dress from her shoulders with one smooth motion, baring her breasts to the cool air. "What a lovely idea."

As his hand cupped one breast and his mouth closed over her nipple, it occurred to Dana that she had just lost their unofficial battle of wits.

Chapter Eight

Dear DG,

What kind of man would it take to awaken you sexually? I've been thinking about that ever since you first mentioned the subject.

My guess is that he would have to be experienced but not calculating. He would need to operate on instinct, tuning in to both your needs and his own.

Whoever that man turns out to be, I suspect he has a revelation in store for himself, as well as you....

Nick's mouth explored Dana at leisure, tasting both nipples before claiming the pulse of her throat, then her mouth. His bare chest covered hers, rubbing softly until she moaned with arousal.

He lowered her onto the couch, their bodies fitting into its curves as if it had been designed for this express purpose. His hands freed her hair from the small chapeau, tossing it and the fluttering veil to the floor.

Dana had never before made love to a man as deft and sensitive as Nick. Her experiences had been confined to one boyfriend in college, whose fumbling could hardly be classified as lovemaking, and a fellow teacher who proved as pedantic in bed as he was in the classroom.

Nick seemed to savor each touch. As he slid the dress from Dana, he knew instinctively how to stroke her so that she never recovered from the initial overwhelming rush of desire.

Her perceptions of him came in disconnected fragments—the tautness of his thighs as he arched over her, the hardness of his back muscles beneath her hands, and the renewed assault of his kisses.

She didn't know this man, and she didn't know herself. Dana had become a wanton creature, eager to blend with him, uncaring of consequences. She wanted to possess Nick, and yet she knew that possession would lead far too swiftly to completion and separation.

Deep inside, she discovered, as he paused to brush a strand of hair from her forehead, she had expected him to hurry past the tender overtures and couple with her impatiently. What could she mean to him, after all, beyond an evening's pleasure?

But Nick was in no hurry. From the way he nuzzled her and responded gently each time she hesitated, he, too, seemed reluctant to pass this first, sweet time of mutual investigation.

Slowly Dana felt something yield within her. The longing for Nick ceased to emanate solely from her body and encompassed her deepest feelings, as well. She wanted to know him as a man, in every sense. She wanted to join him in their own private odyssey to an unknown destination.

If she weren't careful, Dana thought hazily, she might fall in love with him.

In turn, he seemed to care about her response, not just his own. Twice he brought her to the brink of ecstasy and then let her slide back, prolonging her excitement.

But there was only so much a man could take, or a woman, for that matter. When Nick drew away, Dana felt a rush of cold air and a chill of a far sharper nature, followed by a spurt of joy when he returned. He had, she discovered, taken the time to put on a thin masculine shield to protect her. It was apparently one of the extra amenities that came with the hotel suite.

This time, when he came to her, there was no reluctance. Dana had no intention of letting Nick get away again, not even for a moment.

NICK HADN'T PLANNED a seduction. He wasn't even sure it was a good idea. Women could be unpredictable, and in many ways he scarcely knew Dana.

He didn't know the Dominique side of her at all.

She had looked so sweet and mischievous in the candlelight that he hadn't been able to resist touching her. Something about a dare put the devil into Nick, and Dana had definitely offered a challenge.

He had to possess this woman. Nick didn't care whether a man was supposed to think in terms of possession these days. He wanted Dana, and not in any halfhearted way. Whatever her motive might be in continuing to hide her identity, it was most likely similar to his own—a wish to make sure she was appreciated for herself.

How could a man help but cherish her, when she made such delightful noises and responded to him with such passion? Surely she must be aware of her effect on men, and on Nick in particular. But he didn't care how many lovers she had known in the past, as long as he was the one she never forgot.

This moment belonged to him, and Nick intended to make the most of it. He brought out each note of sensuality in his repertoire, and she matched him at every turn, phrase for phrase and crescendo for crescendo.

At some unmarked point, he ceased being the conductor and became a player caught up in the rapture of the music. He had intended to prolong their anticipation even further, but, drawn into Dana by their instinctive harmony, Nick found himself entering her before he quite realized it.

Pleasure shuddered through him. He couldn't believe he was inside this beautiful woman, sharing a duet that united them at every level.

A voice in the back of Nick's mind warned him to hold back, not physically but emotionally. Of all the women he had known, only this one could really hurt him. He throbbed with such need for her that it almost qualified as pain.

Then nature swept away his reservations. Nick grasped Dana and lifted her against his chest, pulling them both into a sitting position. The stimulation was so intense, he almost lost control, but that was one thing Nick had no intention of doing, not yet.

"Hold me," he said breathlessly. "Tight."

As she wrapped her arms and legs around him, Nick stood up and carried Dana into the bedroom. He was still inside her, feeling every twinge of her muscles. She huddled against his chest, so much a part of him that he couldn't imagine letting go.

A single candle gave definition to the bedroom, a vast chamber with a king-size canopied bed and, beyond it, a large whirlpool bath. It was everything a couple could want. He only wished they had days and weeks to explore it.

In the depths of the bed, he rolled her atop him. Dana sat up, hair curling wildly around her delicate face.

A golden sheen bathed her skin. She had a lovely body, slender and firm, with taut, pronounced breasts and straight shoulders. Her eyes contained a hunger that Nick shared ounce for ounce.

In the soft light, a mirror above showed him a golden impression of their bodies locked together, without intrusive details. He watched in fascination as a double image of Dana stirred above him, tantalizing him with the touch of her breasts against his chest and angling her hips to bring him unexpected bursts of elation.

Nick had been careful over the years not to become involved with women who expected more than a brief interlude. He couldn't have done so without revealing his identity, for one thing. For another, he hadn't been ready to yield any part of his independence.

Mastering the business world had been its own aphrodisiac, in a way. Physical exertion in the gym had also provided release.

But what Nick felt now bore no relationship to casual release, or to working off excess energy. He delighted as much in Dana's enjoyment as in his own. He treasured the way her eyes drifted shut, as if the pleasure were almost too much to bear. He found himself watching her in the mirror, not from prurience but from simple appreciation.

The intensity was too much. As desperate as he was to postpone the climax, Nick could no longer subdue the bursts of desire seizing his body. Grasping Dana's hips, he thrust into her harder and harder. She responded with a moan and with swift, rhythmic movements.

Ecstasy burst through Nick. He plunged faster and faster, and a cry of disbelieving pleasure burst from Dana as she arched against him. The moment held, and then the flames gave one last roar and began to subside.

As he drew Dana down beside him, Nick remembered what she'd written in her letter. Was it really possible that she had never experienced this kind of satisfaction before?

He certainly hadn't. Even now, Nick didn't know how to get a grip on his feelings. He wanted more. He wanted to merge with Dana again. He wanted to whisk her away to a private place where nothing could intrude.

It was time, he thought, to end the subterfuge between them. Time to talk seriously about what tonight meant, and where it might lead.

As his breathing quieted, he searched for the words to ease Dana into the truth. It seemed a simple thing, to admit he was RNW, but he suspected she would be angry on learning he'd been deceiving her all evening. Perhaps he could avert her wrath by first pointing out that he knew about *her* deception.

"I've never made love to an actress before," Nick said.

He knew immediately that it had been a tactless way to introduce the subject, judging by the way Dana momentarily stopped breathing.

Her entire body had gone stiff. "What?" she said at last.

"I suppose I should find a more diplomatic way to admit this, but I've known from the beginning that you're Dominique Grant," Nick said.

"What gave you that idea?" She wasn't yielding an inch.

"First of all, my mailbox owner told me," he said. "Then, I had your publicist fax me a photo. Leaving aside the touch-ups and the effect of makeup, it's unquestionably you. That cameo was the clincher."

Dana's hand flew to the ivory pendant still in place at her throat. "Is that why—?" Her voice stopped in midsentence.

Nick cursed his awkwardness. A master of finesse in the boardroom, he possessed precious little of it in the bedroom, he reflected irritably. Dana obviously needed to be reassured that she was attractive for herself, not because of a manufactured image.

"You have a natural glamour. I'm amazed that you seem so unaware of it," he said. "It's part of you—don't fight it. It's what makes you such a success on camera. Other people admire it, and so do I."

She lay staring up at her reflection in the mirror, not seeming to focus on it. Nick wished he could read her mind. From her rigidity, it was obvious he hadn't allayed her anxiety, but he didn't know what else to say.

The words *I love you* came to mind, but he rejected them. He couldn't be sure that he loved Dana, or Dominique, until he knew how much of tonight had been a fluke. It seemed far too unromantic to speak the truth, which was that he felt closer to being in love than he ever had in his life.

When she finally spoke, Dana's voice came out brittle and ironic. "I'm so glad I've brought a little glamour into your life." She rolled away, facing the darkness. "You won't speak of our little rendezvous to RNW, will you? Naturally, you can understand that when it comes to serious relationships, as an actress I need someone who can help my career. Someone with wealth and influence, like your boss."

Her harsh words took Nick aback. Unhappily, he saw that Dana had been feeling not vulnerability but annoyance at having her disguise penetrated.

She had been indulging herself with RNW's bodyguard—the modern equivalent of the lady of the manor bedding the chauffeur. What had she planned to do, keep him on a leash like a pet poodle while she pursued an alliance with his boss? Or simply drop him when it became convenient?

None of this fit with the image he'd formed of Dana tonight. It was hard to believe that even an actress could pull off that much of a character switch. There was something going on that Nick didn't understand.

She was mad at him. He'd grasped that part, all right. But whether she was angry because he'd torn away her mask or for some other reason, he hadn't a clue.

Nick had never paid much attention to writers who claimed a man might outthink his opponents and outmaneuver his enemies, only to be defeated by a woman's heart. After tonight, he would regard philosophers with a bit more respect.

DANA COULDN'T STOP the waves of disappointment from rolling over her. All along, Nick had been attracted to her because he thought she was Dominique. It hurt more than anything she had ever experienced.

Her rational mind insisted there had been real chemistry between them. Maybe so, but she doubted this man of the world would have hired a hotel suite and arranged a birthday dinner for an English teacher.

Still, she wished she hadn't made that spiteful comment afterward. It had been childish to imply that she was killing time with him while waiting to meet RNW. Dana's hurt pride had overcome her better judgment, demanding revenge, but it hadn't made her feel any better.

A lot of things had overcome her better judgment tonight, she admitted silently. She wasn't sure when it had started, or where she could have drawn the line.

At each step, from breaking into Morey's house to jumping into Nick's car, she hadn't been able to picture any alternative. By the time they finished dining and teasing each other in luxurious seclusion, their lovemaking had seemed inevitable, like a force of nature.

Well, Nick couldn't complain. He'd had his fun. He didn't have to know that it had come at Dana's expense.

Unable to lie still, she freed herself from a tangle of covers and went to the whirlpool bath. The water, still quite warm despite the lack of electricity, soothed her as she sank down, and Dana splashed some across her face to still the tears that insisted on clouding her eyes.

Tonight, she had discovered that she could be sexually awakened by the right lover. She only wished that he hadn't turned out to be the wrong lover, as well.

"Dana?" Nick crossed the tile and sat on the edge of the bath. "Sometimes I'm clumsy with words. I apologize if I've said the wrong thing."

"You said what you meant." She fought to keep her voice steady.

"I thought I was complimenting you." Nick sounded so puzzled, she almost wanted to reassure him.

"Then thank you," was all that came out.

"You don't sound very grateful." He lowered himself into the water. "You really are beautiful."

"Everyone tells me that," she managed to mutter between clenched teeth.

"If you want to tell me what made you mad, I'm willing to listen," he said. "I'll even apologize, if I can see what I've done wrong."

Inwardly Dana cringed. After everything that had happened, she couldn't admit that she was just an ordinary woman, someone Nick Lyon wouldn't give a second glance. The impression of beauty, she felt sure, resulted from his having studied the photo of her sister. People had an amazing ability to deceive themselves.

"There's no point," she said with a sigh. "Really."

He brushed some water through his hair, rinsing away the residue of white powder from earlier, then settled back to enjoy a warm soak. "I suppose we ought to get moving, but I don't much feel like it. With any luck, Morey and his goon have given up by now."

"It's a lost cause, anyway." Dana felt her shakiness dissipate as the conversation shifted to neutral ground. "*Heat!* probably has the letters set in type, ready to print as soon as the electricity comes on."

Nick reached over and flipped on the pool's jets. Nothing happened. "Still dead."

"I can catch a cab to my car," Dana said. "You stay here and enjoy the suite."

"I have no intention of giving up that easily." At first she thought Nick was referring to her, but then he climbed out of the pool and began toweling his hair. "I just hope that editor's back in the newsroom by now. It's time for a few threats."

"What could you possibly threaten him with?" Dana asked, refusing to indulge in another round of hurt feelings. Besides, she still wanted to stop the publication, if it was even remotely possible. "I'm sure he's already considered the likelihood of a lawsuit."

"I doubt if he's weighed the likelihood of RNW buying his parent corporation and firing him." Wrapping himself in one of the towels stacked on the tile, Nick moved away.

Dana wasn't sure where he found the slip of paper with the editor's number, but a minute later Nick was sitting on the edge of the bed, tapping it into the phone.

"Bob Worley, please. Tell him Nick Lyon asked for..." Apparently in response to a question, he said, "No, I said 'asked for,' not 'Jasper'... Never mind. Just tell him it's urgent."

As he waited, it dawned on Dana where he'd found the phone number. Their personal possessions must be in the bathroom, which she assumed lay in the sprawling expanse of shadows leading away from the pool.

Grabbing a couple of towels, she went in search of her clothes.

AS HE WAITED for the copy assistant to locate the editor, Nick planned his strategy. He didn't want to bring out the heavy guns right off the bat. Maybe he would offer the exclusive rights to Renfro's identity first, then follow with a threat if that didn't work.

Or maybe he would drive to the newspaper and strangle Bob Worley, just for good measure. At the moment, Nick felt frustrated and angry, as much with himself as with anyone.

He needed a physical outlet. Punching an arrogant editor might just fill the bill.

He should never have been so blunt with Dominique, or Dana, as he couldn't help thinking of her. Obviously, he'd offended her.

The more he mulled it over, the less he believed her remark about reserving serious entanglements for wealthy men. She'd been lashing out at him for some reason of her own.

Nick sensed that Dana felt betrayed, but he couldn't imagine why. She was, after all, the one who had kept a secret from *him*. Since she didn't yet know about his own duplicity, that didn't seem to count—at least in his own mind.

Maybe it would help if he leveled with Dana about being RNW, as he'd intended. But first he had to deal with Bob Worley, who had just picked up the phone.

"Yes?" the editor barked.

"About the letters . . ." Nick began.

"Has that son-of-a-gun millionaire hermit showed up yet?"

"What?" The editor's question, and his irritated tone, didn't make sense.

Not, that is, until Worley snapped, "Damn it, Jasper, I'm tired of you running around like a loose cannon. Who the hell do you think you are?"

Apparently the copy person had mistaken his name, and the editor believed he was Jim Jasper, the reporter at the Top Hat. Nick doubted he would learn anything of value, but he decided to play dumb for a bit.

"Is that a serious question?" he grumbled.

He would use any stratagem he could to bamboozle or intimidate Worley. At the very least, preventing publication of the letters might put Nick back in Dana's good graces. He wanted very much to be on good terms with her, although at the moment he couldn't have said why.

"I don't care how much we're paying you, or whether you *did* get an even better offer from the *National Intruder,*" Worley went on, obviously on a rampage. "Reporters like you are a royal pain in the buttocks. You were due back here an hour ago!"

"Renfro isn't here yet," Nick said.

"Well, where the hell is he? Is that weasely yes-man of his hanging around? Nick What's-His-Name? Get the scoop from him, and bring your incompetent self back here before I come after you in person!"

"Now why would you want to do that?" Nick kept his voice growly. "The power's still off. You're not printing anything yet."

"Because, you idiot, you bozo-brain, you . . ." Worley segued into a series of ear-scorching adjectives before concluding, "You took off with the only copies of the letters!"

Nick couldn't believe it. "What? That's impossible!"

"No, you numbskull, you fleabrain, you..." Worley's vocabulary expanded into X-rated metaphors before he concluded, "You got the originals!"

Nick's mind sifted quickly through the possible scenarios. The editor couldn't be that careless. He must have made duplicates. "What about your copies?"

"They never arrived at the backshop." A note of distress undermined the editor's bluster. "You know me. I'm always scribbling notes on the backs of things. They probably got routed to somebody as a memo, or maybe they're in the shredder. But you were supposed to make your own photocopies!"

Hope leaped into Nick's brain, but he wasn't willing to accept redemption so easily. "I didn't have time. Anyway, what about that shop owner, the one we got them from? He must have copies."

"Maybe, but who can find him?" snarled Worley. "He's not answering his phone."

Now that he had gleaned the prize information that *Heat!* was temporarily letterless, Nick was tempted to hang up on the editor or, better yet, give him what-for. "Weasely yes-man" wasn't the worst name Nick had ever been called, but it rankled.

His good sense, however, warned that he didn't want Bob Worley to know he'd reached the wrong man. Jim Jasper was obviously ignoring his pager or had forgotten it. Otherwise, the editor would have reached him earlier. If Worley realized he was talking to Nick, he would redouble his efforts to contact the reporter, possibly even drive to the Top Hat himself.

"Yeah, well, that jerk Lyon's not here, either. I'll stick around a few more minutes," Nick said. "Then I'll head back."

"Make it snappy." Despite his bluffness, relief colored the editor's voice. "We'll pay for any speeding tickets."

"Okay, boss," Nick said, and hung up.

That was when he saw Dana standing near the bathroom door, wearing slacks and a sweater. From hands planted on hips to legs braced apart, she was the picture of skepticism.

"Why did you refer to yourself in the third person?" she demanded. "And why did you call yourself a jerk?"

Nick filled her in on the conversation. As he spoke, he strolled into the bathroom and dressed in the dark, gritting his teeth as his fingers reminded him of the sorry state of his clothes.

Dana's voice drifted in. "Jasper really has the only copies of the letters?"

"The only copies unless they catch up with Morey Bain," Nick said.

"Nope," Dana answered. "I've got his extra set in my car. His estranged wife gave them to me."

"Perfect." Nick chuckled. "That means, even if the lights go on, we've gained some breathing room."

"Well, not yet," Dana pointed out. "We still have to catch Jim Jasper, don't we?"

From where he stood, she formed a fuzzy silhouette against the light of a single candle. A very shapely silhouette that Nick wanted to take in his arms. He wanted to feel her relax against him, and to see her face tilt upward, and to guide her back to the bed...

He marveled at his own weakness. He had never before let physical attraction get in the way of accomplishing his goals, and his goal tonight was to stop publication of those letters. Especially now that he knew there was still a chance of success.

But he couldn't help being glad that the renewal of hope also gave Dana a reason to stay with him a while longer. And if he could save her from embarrassment, maybe it would atone for whatever he'd said to offend her.

"We'd better get moving, hadn't we?" he said. "There's no telling how long Jasper will stick around."

Chapter Nine

Dear DG,

We've been talking about lovers and sensuality, but I think you'll agree that people have to be friends first. That's what I feel we've become through these letters.

I've never taken the time to talk with a friend this way before. Maybe I've been too focused on business, but personal conversations never much interested me before.

My best buddy is a guy I've known since we were teenagers. We used to get into scrapes in high school. Nothing serious, although I'm sure we gave the principal a few gray hairs.

Mostly we went surfing. The bigger the waves, the better. If the surf was up on a school day, well, school lost every time.

I was the better surfer, but my pal was more colorful. He had this fascination with Alfred Hitchcock, and was developing a paunch even then. He would stand on his surfboard, arms folded, silhouetted against the sunlight, wearing that dour expression, and I could swear it *was* Alfred Hitchcock, making a cameo appearance in his first surfing film.

What about your friends? Is there someone you're especially close to...?

Hitch Rickert grumbled in annoyance as his motorcycle shot between the cars stuck on the freeway. He had to navigate carefully on account of his wide saddlebags, which held a choice of a tuxedo, a dark suit and casual slacks and shirt for Nick.

He could have taken surface streets to the restaurant, but had deliberately chosen the long way around, expecting the freeway to be faster. Usually, at such a late hour, one could anticipate an open road and a surging sense of freedom, and Hitch had been in the mood for a wild ride.

Unfortunately, the blackout had resulted in a bad case of bumper cars. Even so, with careful maneuvering between the lanes of stopped cars, the bike could maintain a steady thirty miles per hour.

Hitch loved the feel of the wind surging through his hair. In this blackout, he doubted any patrolman would bother him for not wearing a helmet. The highway patrol already had its hands full with the fender benders jamming traffic.

Power outages seemed to Hitch to be a judgment on modern civilization, a kind of celestial reminder that man was far from omnipotent. Where would humankind be without all its gadgets and electronic crutches?

Hitch had no doubt where he would be—lounging on a desert island somewhere, with a bottomless keg of beer, a handheld video game and a lifetime supply of batteries.

He liked comfort, which was why he chose to work for his old buddy Nick in a fabulous mansion in Pacific Palisades. He also liked Nick. Hitch refused to work for anyone who didn't meet his high standards of integrity.

Actually, he'd never worked for anyone but Nick, except for a brief stint at a supermarket. That had ended when the manager caught Hitch giving bruised vegetables and dented cans to a bag lady instead of destroying them.

He wasn't looking forward to tonight's announcement. The press and public had pretty much accepted the idea that Renfro Williams was a recluse, and Hitch would have preferred to leave well enough alone.

Once in a while he'd nabbed nosy reporters trying to sneak into the house, but he didn't really have to worry, because the worst that could happen was that they might confront Nick. They would never find Renfro, because he didn't exist.

Renfro was just one of those idiotic names that parents bestow on their kids, for reasons unimaginable to Hitch. And probably to Nick, who had insisted on using his middle name since childhood.

After tonight, that would change. Hitch shuddered, trying not to think about the disruption to his future peace of mind.

A station wagon with Arizona plates, blocked by the motionless welter of cars, had gotten stuck while changing lanes and now blocked Hitch's path. Chaos was setting in, he decided. Mankind's future hung in the balance when an honest man on a motorcycle couldn't cut between the lanes without the risk of smashing into a load of tourists.

With a world-weary sigh, he zipped to the right shoulder and traveled along it. That was illegal, but what cop could blame him?

They ought to be grateful to get one more vehicle off the freeway. He was almost to his exit, anyway.

A few minutes later, Hitch began snarling silently. Dead ahead, the shoulder was blocked by a delivery truck, its emergency lights blinking.

Probably out of gas, he mused dourly. Hitch didn't care much about the plight of one vehicle in this mass of seething motorists, but it had become his problem by dint of the fact that it would be difficult to get around the thing without missing his exit.

He slowed to a halt. A dark-haired young man was leaning against the truck, mopping his forehead. The air had cooled at least twenty degrees from the day's heat, but was still mild.

"Got a problem?" Hitch called.

The driver stared at him with something like terror. In the moonlight, Hitch could see that the fellow was about eighteen and had the wide-eyed look of a visitor who believes muggers lurk behind every billboard in Los Angeles.

"Uh . . . yeah . . ." the driver stammered at last. "I used the call box but nobody's responding. I guess they can't get through this jam."

"Maybe we could push you to the on-ramp." Hitch was reluctant to volunteer for labor, but the panel truck was in his way. Besides, he was beginning to feel sorry for this waif. "Where are you from?"

"Ventura," said the boy. "Oh, gosh, I'm really late. I was due downtown hours ago. I got lost."

"How could you get lost on the way from Ventura?" It was about an hour's drive, but a straight shot on the freeway.

"I got lost trying to get on the freeway in the first place," the driver admitted. "I'm new in the area. Then I had a flat tire, and I had to wait for the auto club, and that was when the blackout hit. I made it this far and then the engine died. I'm going to get fired."

"Your first job?" Hitch asked.

He received a glum nod. "My uncle's got this costume business. The other trucks left earlier. I got loaded last."

"Costumes?" This was getting interesting, even if it didn't have anything to do with Hitch. He was always on the lookout for something that might benefit Nick, and it paid to hear people out.

"Masks. That's what I'm carrying." The driver wiped away more sweat. It couldn't be the heat, because the air felt cool, so it must be nerves. "I'm supposed to deliver them to a party at a hotel, and they've probably given up on me by now. Then I've got a bunch more to drop at some stores early in the morning."

"Got a name?"

"Manuel," said the young man.

"People call me Hitch. Now let's see what your problem is, Manuel."

Leaving his bike, Hitch swung into the truck and flipped on the ignition. It fired up, chugged heavily and began to make banging noises.

"Can you tell what it is?" the boy asked from outside.

Hitch switched it off. "Got a toolbox?" Seeing the driver's blank expression, he did a little exploring and found one beneath the seat. "Let's take a look."

With the help of a flashlight and a set of coveralls that had also been stashed inside the truck, Hitch located the problem as a loose spark plug. Lost in concentration, he didn't keep track of the time until he emerged and realized that he, too, was now late.

Nick probably hadn't arrived yet, either, but the guests would be fuming and fidgety. What they needed was a distraction, Hitch decided.

"I've got an idea," he told the gushingly grateful young driver. "You've missed your party by now, right?"

Elation fading, the boy nodded.

"And judging by your past performance, you've got about as much chance of locating those stores as I do of finding the lost continent of Atlantis in a fish pond," added Hitch.

The driver appeared on the verge of tears.

"My boss will make up whatever money you've lost, if you'll deliver your masks to the Top Hat restaurant," Hitch said. "It's only a few miles away, and you can follow me."

Confusion spread across the young man's face as he struggled to make a decision. The scales seemed to tip back and forth, judging by the way his mouth worked and his ears wiggled.

It was several minutes before he said, "You're sure this guy will pay me?"

Hitch dug into his pocket and produced a business card, slightly smudged. "I work for Renfro Williams," he said, handing it over. "He's rich."

"Good enough for me," said the boy, and hopped back in the truck.

DANA WAS IMPRESSED by Nick's presence of mind. When they were both dressed, he got on the phone and summoned the bell captain. As soon as the man arrived, Nick arranged to have the car brought to the front of the hotel, offering a large enough tip to ensure prompt compliance.

"Let's just hope it hasn't been towed," she said after the man left.

"You think they could get a tow truck out here in the middle of a blackout?" he asked, glaring at his disheveled reflection in the mirror—or what could be seen of his reflection in the gloom. "Trust me. The car will be there."

His take-charge attitude was reassuring. Despite her misgivings, Dana felt safe with Nick.

She knew he was attracted to her for the wrong reasons—or maybe that he was attracted to the wrong woman entirely. Yet she couldn't help trusting him, at least when it came to recovering the letters.

With the costumes tossed over his arm, Nick escorted her out of the suite. Dana was surprised by her reluctance to leave. This place had been a haven, not only from their pursuers, but from the life she had led before.

Here she had discovered a side of herself she'd never known. Something had awakened in her, and as long as she remained in this sanctuary, she didn't have to worry about what to do with her feelings once Nick was gone.

She had always been the sort of person to analyze her actions. When considering colleges and career possibilities, Dana had made lists of pros and cons. Tonight, however, she didn't want to think too much. She wanted to rely on her instincts, and her instincts told her to stay with Nick as long as possible.

In the hallway, the darkness struck Dana afresh with its oddity. Under normal circumstances, modern structures like this were never dark, day or night.

Trekking downstairs, they found the atrium even more crowded with partygoers. Dancers spilled into the corridors, the formal patterns of the waltzes degenerating as each couple worked their own variations.

"Authenticity becomes a victim of enthusiasm," Dana murmured. "It's the costumes, I suppose. They make you feel like a different person, as if you really lived in those times and shouldn't feel constrained to follow a script."

"Ever play a historical role?" Nick asked. "You don't have to tell me, if it's a sore subject. I'm not sure what you mind discussing and what you don't."

Dana answered the question as honestly as she dared. "The only historical part I ever played was the nurse in a high-school production of *Romeo and Juliet,* and that was because the girl who was supposed to play it came down with laryngitis."

"You're very modest." Without hesitation, Nick found his way back to the cloakroom and returned the costumes.

"Not all that modest," said Dana as they reached the hallway again. She'd been directing the school play, as well, but she didn't need to tell him that.

As they headed for the front door, Dana glimpsed Lady Alicia, this time accompanied by a tiny man in a monstrously tall wig. "Without masks we are naked!" she was crying to the man in the red coat. "It is a travesty! I am overset!"

The little man piped up in an indignant tenor, "They have been hijacked! The Hawaiian Gardens Historicals are behind this, mark my words!"

The red-coated host, Sir Allenby, shook his head. "I scarcely think we are the victims of highway banditry. More likely the poor driver is stuck somewhere."

"Fool!" Lady Alicia snapped the man's arm with her fan. "They have taken our masks! What next, I ask you? Our fans? Our chapeaux? Our muslin shifts?"

"I take it conspiracy theories are abounding," Nick murmured as they skirted the confrontation. "I wonder what they make of the blackout."

"They were planning on candlelight," Dana informed him. "I'm not sure most of them know there *is* a blackout."

Before they could make good their escape, the tall woman spotted them. "Not leaving, are you?" she cried. "It's because of the masks, isn't it? You must be so disappointed!"

"No, not really." Dana didn't have the heart to admit that she hadn't planned on attending the ball in the first place.

"We have a prior engagement at the Top Hat." Nick gave a bow. "Thank you and your fellow club members for your hospitality."

"Such poor hospitality it is!" Lady Alicia resumed browbeating the red-coated man. "A pitiful excuse for a ball!"

As Sir Allenby tried to untangle himself, Dana and Nick fled out the door. The street was, they discovered, still cluttered with vehicles, but a valet managed to bring their car around a few minutes later.

She slid into the passenger seat, wishing she had the same uncomplicated mind-set that she'd possessed when they arrived. But her lovemaking with Nick had introduced a whole web of complications that Dana didn't know how to handle.

Part of her wanted to say goodbye and retreat to her condominium to nurse her wounds. A voice inside warned that neither the wealthy RNW nor his worldly right-hand man was likely to become the loving husband that Dana dreamed about, a man who shared her imaginative flights and held her hand as they walked through life together.

Nick wanted a glamorous actress. For his part, RNW would probably prove to be weird beyond belief.

But she couldn't let herself retreat into a cocoon. Dana still wanted to start that new life, the one in which she seized the initiative and went looking for what she wanted. She had to see this evening through to the end.

Feeling off center but determined, she settled back as they shot through the dark streets. On the radio, a commercial segued into the latest update on the blackout, which could best be summarized as no news not being good news.

"And now for our continuing series of vignettes," said the announcer. "An amateur astronomer in Palos Verdes claims to have discovered a comet previously hidden by the glare of city lights and has dubbed it the Constitution Comet, in honor of our founding fathers.

"However, we seem to have a constitutional amendment from two callers in Anaheim Hills, who claim the celestial body is actually a UFO. Mr. and Mrs. Lewis Wilcox allege that the UFO landed in their backyard at three minutes before nine o'clock, hit a power line and caused the massive power outage now affecting the West Coast.

"Keep those stories coming. And now, do you suffer from hemorrhoids? Have you tried..."

Dana turned off the radio. "How far is it to the Top Hat?"

"Just a few miles." Nick continued along surface streets. Apparently he'd decided the freeways could too easily turn into a trap. Judging by their experience driving from South Pasadena, Dana had to agree.

The roads lay eerily quiet, stilled by the late hour and the absence of electricity. Dead traffic lights hung above them like relics of a lost world, requiring caution at every intersection.

They drove in silence, leaving the skyscrapers of downtown and passing through a neighborhood of three- and four-story brick and stucco buildings. At least the darkness blotted out most of the graffiti.

Nick glanced at Dana from time to time, then finally spoke. "You're still not going to level with me, are you? I'd like to know what I said that made you angry."

"*I'd* like to know more about your boss," Dana countered.

"I'd rather—" Nick stopped. "All right, if you insist."

Dana knew she'd taken the cowardly way out, but she wasn't ready to face Nick's reaction when he learned he hadn't made love to Dominique. The hurt was still too raw. "Do you like him?" she asked.

"Well . . ." His mouth twisted in an ironic smile. "We have a great deal in common. He and I get along very well, as a matter of fact. We're practically inseparable."

"You're teasing me, aren't you?" Dana couldn't imagine that Nick was really that chummy with his eccentric employer. "I'm sorry about that remark I made earlier. I'm not holding out for a rich man."

"You mean I might be good enough for you?" The lightness of his tone didn't entirely disguise Nick's seriousness.

Dana turned toward him in surprise. "That wasn't the issue."

"Then what is the issue?"

Did she dare tell him? "There's been some confusion," she said.

"About what?"

"My identity." Dana took a deep breath, intending to blurt out the bad news, but the words got stuck in her throat. If she didn't find something else to talk about, she would sit here harrumphing like an idiot. "I'm, uh, thinking of making a change in my life," she said.

"What kind of change?"

"I'm going to be more aggressive," she said. "I'm going to go after what I want, instead of waiting for it to come to me."

They slowed to allow a station wagon to cross the intersection ahead of them. Dana couldn't read the street signs, but they seemed to be traveling west.

"And what is it you want?" Nick said. "Another Emmy? A film career?"

Dana bit her lip. She wanted to keep as close to the truth as possible, but Nick wasn't going to believe an up-and-coming actress was primarily interested in marriage and children.

"Well?" he prodded. "Are you going to tell me what you want?"

"I want to have it all," Dana said.

He laughed. "Who doesn't?"

Into Dana's mind flashed an image of one of her students, a boy whose goal was to drop out of school and land a job at a garage so that he could get his own apartment. "A lot of people," she said. "They aren't willing to work hard and wait it out, so it doesn't occur to them to dream big. They just go for the cheap thrills."

"I don't mind a few cheap thrills," Nick observed dryly. "Along the way."

"Along the way to what?"

He paused at a crossroads and turned north toward the hills. "That's a good question."

"You mean you don't have goals?" Nick seemed so focused and driven, she had assumed he knew exactly where he was aiming in life.

"I used to," he admitted. "I wanted to be successful in my work. Well, I've achieved that."

"Except that you're getting laid off."

"I am?" He glanced at Dana, then nodded quickly. "Oh, you mean because this is my last night on the job, so to speak."

"Isn't that what you said?"

"I won't have to front for RNW anymore," Nick conceded. "That doesn't mean he won't need my services in other areas."

"Oh." Dana couldn't picture having one's entire career depend on another person's goodwill. Or whims. The notion didn't fit Nick's character. He was too self-confident, too authoritative. She wondered what his real relationship was with RNW.

Then they turned a corner onto Sunset Boulevard. The broad avenue, made famous in films and TV shows, hulked around them, its billboards darkened and its sidewalks empty.

The exception lay directly ahead of them, where a clutch of vehicles jockeyed for position around a double-parked truck. On the sidewalk milled a crowd, the blaze of flashbulbs illuminating elegantly clad men and women.

"Is that the Top Hat?" she asked. "Are all those people waiting for RNW?"

"Presumably so." Nick glanced at the clock on the dashboard, which she could see indicated it was getting close to 2:00 a.m. "Hard to believe they're still here."

"What time were they supposed to be here?" Dana asked.

"Ten p.m."

She hoped the blackout would provide an excuse for Nick's lateness. Was RNW already here?

Then, as a couple of bulbs flashed, she noticed something else. "How come they're wearing masks?"

"What?" Nick peered through the windshield. "Good Lord." He swung onto a side street and found a parking space. "I hope things haven't gotten out of hand."

Dana wondered what that meant, and decided she didn't care. "The important thing is finding that guy from the paper."

"Oh, yes," said Nick, as if he'd forgotten.

BY THE TIME Hitch and Manuel arrived at the restaurant, the natives were getting restless. Food and drink could keep celebrities entertained only so long, even though many of the guests had undoubtedly arrived late themselves.

Following instructions, the panel truck wedged itself between an assemblage of news vans double-parked in front of the restaurant. Ditching his motorcycle on a side street, with the spare clothes locked in the saddlebags, Hitch hurried to the restaurant.

A quick check of the premises and a few discreet inquiries turned up the fact that Nick had not arrived. It also revealed that, if Hitch didn't take action quickly, the guests would be either too drunk or too cranky to care when their host showed up.

He went back outside to join Manuel. "Let's put on masks," he said.

The youth stared at him in dismay. "We're not robbing the place, are we?"

Hitch began to laugh. "Do I look that rough?" Realizing what the answer must be, he said, "No, we're not. Now pick something that speaks to your heart."

Manuel chose a Batman mask. After prowling through the boxes, Hitch chose a kitsch affair, curling with pink ostrich feathers.

"Let's go make an entrance," he said.

As they hopped down to the sidewalk, photographers and onlookers turned toward them. Hitch could hear the buzz of conversation die, then rise again.

"Ladies and gents!" he called as he strode into the restaurant with Manuel tagging behind. "Help yourselves to the masks in the truck. We will all be going incognito tonight!"

Glasses clinked as they were set on tables, and bodies began to shift toward the doorway. Then a man said, "I thought Renfro Williams would be taking the mask off tonight, not requiring us to put them on."

"All in good time." Hitch recognized the man as Harmon Mason, an award-winning director with a reputation for being his own biggest fan.

"We've been waiting long enough already." The man wore the impatient scowl of someone accustomed to being fawned over. He had a thick head of black hair and the kind of chiseled good looks that appealed to women, but not to Hitch.

Then he noticed a familiar-looking woman lingering behind Mason, her hands fluttering as if she wanted to smooth the situation over but didn't dare interfere. She was a knockout, in a sheath dress that sparkled in the candlelight.

The problem was, Hitch had assumed Dominique Grant was the person accompanying Nick in his car. If so, how had she gotten here? And if not, who was with him?

"Bear with me," he said. "Please put on the masks and enjoy yourselves a little longer. There is much ado afoot tonight." The lamps and the mask made Hitch feel distinctly Shakespearean. "In the truck you will find disguises beyond your wildest dreams. Go and transform yourselves, and then the night will reveal its surprises."

As the exodus began, he hoped one of those surprises would be the appearance of his boss. He'd tried to call Nick a short time ago on his cellular phone, but the lines were overloaded and he couldn't get through.

Harmon Mason was among the last to go. "At least that lackey Lyon could have favored us with his presence. This is no way to treat important people."

"Nick?" Hitch bristled at hearing his boss referred to in such an unflattering manner, but decided he had more serious issues to deal with. "You haven't seen him recently?"

He watched the woman for any sign that she had seen Nick, but she showed not a flicker of response. Unless she was a better actress than Hitch expected, she hadn't been near his boss this evening.

"You can see he's not here, damn it," grumbled Mason as he shoved past Hitch.

"I'm sorry. He's kind of distracted tonight." Dominique gave Hitch a half smile and hurried after the director.

Where the hell *was* Nick? What could be so important about recovering letters, anyway? Nick hadn't confided much, just that some letters had been stolen and that they concerned him and a lady. The fax lying on his desk had made it clear who that lady was.

But if Nick was somehow mixed up with this actress, he'd been pretty darn discreet about it. So discreet that neither she nor her boyfriend appeared to be aware of it.

"He's full of himself, isn't he?" murmured Manuel from behind the Batman mask. Hitch had almost forgotten about the young truck driver until now. "But that girl's real pretty."

"That girl is a famous actress," Hitch told him. "Say, why don't you go help people find masks? I'm going to try to call my boss again."

As Manuel departed as instructed, a waiter steered Hitch to a pay phone. He dialed Nick's car, and a recorded voice informed Hitch that the cellular phone customer could not be reached.

He plunked down the receiver in disgust. His instincts urged him to go search for Nick, in case he was in trouble. But Hitch wouldn't even know where to start looking.

Feeling out of sorts, Hitch wandered outside. Fueled by several hours' worth of cocktails, the guests were laughing and shouting as they rummaged through the boxes that Manuel was opening for them. He spotted a network executive donning a fox mask, and a prominent woman banker chortling as she seized a domino supported by a stick.

Hitch hoped his boss would forget about inviting this jam of people back to the estate. It was getting too late for that.

It would be a shame to waste the decorations, the fireworks and the food, which the caterer had left in a makeshift arrangement of coolers and ice-filled plastic bags. But surely a lot of things were going to seed in this blackout. Besides, how would they ever sort out the invited guests from the interlopers in these masks?

A chunky man wearing an ill-fitting suit approached Hitch, holding a pad and pen at the ready. "I need to get your name."

"Why?" asked the butler.

"I'm a reporter for *Heat!*" The man spoke as if the name were certain to impress anyone within earshot. "I might want to quote you, so I need to know who you are."

"People call me Hitch," he said.

"Why?" asked Manuel, who had wandered over to them.

"Because I hitch up my pants a lot," joked Hitch, demonstrating.

"And your name?" the reporter asked Manuel.

"I just drive a truck," said the young man. "You don't need to know who I am."

"Does everyone have to be so mysterious tonight?" demanded the reporter. "I'm way past my deadline. This whole thing is becoming a circus."

"I couldn't agree more," grumbled Hitch. He felt perfectly capable of improvising with this crowd, but he wasn't sure Nick would approve of some of the ideas he might come up with. Anyway, he doubted these stuffed shirts would go for a conga line snaking down the sidewalk, or for dropping beer-filled balloons on passersby—the kinds of activities his biker buddies would appreciate.

"Wait a minute." The reporter tapped his pen against the pad and took a good look at Hitch. The butler could feel those beady eyes ticking off his ponytail, the tuxedo jacket over torn jeans and the huarache sandals. The signs of a true eccentric. "You're him, aren't you?"

"Well . . ." Hitch tried to weigh the pros and cons in a hurry. He didn't want to say outright that he was Renfro Williams, when Nick's stated goal for the evening was to come clean.

On the other hand, letting people get the wrong idea might make short work of this madhouse. Satisfied that they'd met the millionaire, surely they would soon go home.

It was a tempting notion. A little too tempting.

Nearby, a photographer demanded, "You're Renfro Williams?" His flash went off before Hitch had time to reply.

"Really?" Manuel asked. "You're that rich guy?"

"I thought you were with him," said the reporter. "Don't you know who he is?"

"Yeah, well, he said he works for Renfro Williams, not that he *is* him," protested the young man.

"Nick Lyon works for Renfro Williams," said the reporter. "And this isn't Nick."

"Couldn't a rich guy have two employees?" Manuel asked dubiously.

"It's a bit too much of a coincidence for me." The reporter was grinning at his own cleverness. "This guy I've never seen before suddenly shows up and takes over Williams's party. And he's wearing a mask. Thought you had us fooled, didn't you?"

Hitch could hear the buzz rising as word spread through the crowd. Another flashbulb erupted, and then the Minicams swung around. "That's him," someone said. "That's Renfro Williams."

Babble filled the air. He could pick out a few snippets. "You mean that guy?" "He nearly put one over on us, didn't he?" "He's just like I pictured—long hair and all."

As reporters and masked guests clustered around, Hitch decided the mistake was pretty darn funny. He hoped Nick would find it funny, too, because he had no intention of correcting it.

Chapter Ten

Dear RNW,

Until I sat down to think about it, I would have said that I have lots of friends. There are probably half a dozen co-workers and neighbors with whom I chat, go shopping and take in movies.

But truly close? There is one person, actually. However, she guards her privacy with a vengeance and I think she would resent my discussing her in much detail, even without my revealing her name.

Let's just say that this friend is someone I've known all my life. We're so close that at times we have to get away from each other, for breathing room.

She's almost like a mirror of myself, only braver and more confident. She inspires me, but at other times I envy her.

There's no one I can have more fun with, and no one who can irritate me more. Isn't that odd? Now that I'm approaching thirty, I hope I can put such childish feelings aside....

For one of only few times in his life, Nick was having trouble maintaining his concentration.

As they walked toward the restaurant, he couldn't figure out why everyone was wearing a mask. There was an astonishing array of them, some artistic and others comic. In one direction, he saw Mickey Mouse locked in discussion with a witch. The other way, a lady in a checkerboard domino was granting an interview to a TV anchorman.

Maybe it was the darkness, pierced by snatches of light and strained by a cacophony of voices, that made it so hard for Nick to keep his priorities straight. Or it might be the late hour.

More likely, though, it was the distraction of having Dana by his side and wishing they had time to talk about what had happened between them at the hotel. Nick knew there were more important matters at hand. It was just difficult to recall what they were.

He forced himself to think hard. He needed to find Hitch and change out of these torn clothes. That was the first thing. He also had to locate Jim Jasper and take possession of the letters.

None of those challenges was beyond Nick's ability, but the partygoers wouldn't leave him alone. They kept slapping him on the back, demanding to know why he wasn't wearing a mask and congratulating him on the sly way he and his boss had pulled things off tonight.

Nick wished he didn't keep getting the sense that everybody here knew something he didn't. Like maybe the true identity of Renfro Williams.

He was beginning to wonder, in the confusion and disorientation, whether there didn't actually exist another person known as Renfro Williams. Perhaps all these years Nick had only imagined he was fronting for himself. Maybe somehow an alter ego had split off, or had existed the whole time.

It didn't make sense. But not much did tonight.

It was Dana who brought him back down to earth, but not in the manner he would have preferred. She had been listening to the banter of passersby and, particularly, to a TV personality pontificating for a Minicam.

"Renfro Williams?" she asked, stopping short. "RNW is Renfro Williams?"

Nick wanted to say something brilliant and self-assured. What came out was, "Uh, yeah."

Shocked eyes confronted him. "You should have told me."

"Why?" He hadn't given much thought to the fact that she didn't know what the initials RNW stood for. The actual identity of his wealthy boss hadn't seemed important. To Nick's mind, the key issue was whether he or someone else was her secret correspondent. "What's the difference?"

"I knew he was well-to-do," she said. "But not world-class rich. Not famous. Not . . ." She made a futile gesture. "Someone that excites this kind of frenzy."

Frenzy was the right word. Nick felt himself grow cold at the realization that soon he would have to make good on his promise to present the real Renfro to this mob. Then all eyes would turn toward him, along with the cameras. "He hates this kind of thing," he said.

Dana hugged herself, although the air was only mildly cool. "I hate it even worse."

"Do you?" He couldn't believe her. An actress had to deal with cameras and attention wherever she went, at least if she became successful, which Dominique Grant was.

The lady in the faxed publicity photo had posed with confidence shining from every pore. Maybe, he thought, she meant that she hated it when someone *else* was the center of attention.

"I guess I should meet him and get it over with," she said. "Besides, he'll want an update on the letters, won't he? And he might know which reporter is Jasper."

Nick ached to tell her the truth and be done with it. She would probably be even angrier than she'd been in the hotel room, but he could deal with that.

What he couldn't deal with was the pushing and shoving that was thrusting them toward the entrance to the restaurant. This was no time to have a heart-to-heart discussion with Dana.

"Maybe we should find out what the commotion is about." Nick had an uneasy feeling about the noise and excitement. It didn't jibe with his mental image of a group of VIPs awaiting enlightenment.

"Obviously, it's about your boss," Dana retorted. "Isn't that the whole idea of the party?"

"Yes, but he wouldn't make an announcement without me." Only after the words came out did Nick realize how lame the statement sounded.

"You mean your feelings would be hurt?" Dana asked teasingly. "Come on, Nick, you're three hours late."

"It isn't that simple." He stared toward the center of the seething crowd. The glare of the Minicams prevented him from seeing anything but a tallish, stout figure who seemed to be fielding questions. The man appeared familiar, but in the tumult, Nick couldn't place him.

"Well?" Dana said. "Let's go find Jasper."

"Better let me blaze the trail," Nick said. Taking her hand, he began shouldering a path.

The closer they came to the eye of the hurricane, the tighter the bodies were packed. Nick couldn't hear much over the general hum, just some shouted questions.

It occurred to him that an impostor might be claiming to be Renfro, but that was ridiculous. Nobody could hope to carry off such a scam.

"Ow!" Dana gave a painful hop and clutched her foot. "Somebody stepped on me!"

Nick glared at their nearest neighbors, but nobody paid attention. Besides, it was hard to avoid bumping and crunching people and getting bumped and crunched in return.

He was gauging the best way to break through when a newly arrived camera crew plowed by. A piece of equipment barely missed Dana's head. Nick caught her by the waist and hoisted her against him, out of harm's way.

He could feel her quickened breath against his neck, and he relished the soft urgency of her body, reminding him of the moment when he had carried her into the bedroom.

Instantly his masculine senses sprang to alert. The blood began to pound, his muscles tightened, and he could feel an unmistakably masculine response.

Only the knowledge that this was the worst possible place for a display of affection kept him from kissing her. Besides, Dana might not want to be kissed. Most likely she was clinging to him so tightly out of fear.

Nick was about to set her down when, in the wake of the camera crew, people began surging around them, pressing tighter and tighter. Nick could barely keep his balance. A smaller person like Dana could easily be injured.

It wasn't worth the risk. He could find out what was happening in some other way than by getting them both trampled.

Besides, Nick knew that Renfro Williams couldn't have made his announcement, so the tall man must be some kind of entertainer. Or perhaps he was a politician seizing the chance to do a little campaigning.

Retreating from the crowd, Nick lowered Dana to her feet on a quiet stretch of sidewalk. "We'll have to wait until things calm down," he said. "I wonder where the hell Hitch is."

"Who's Hitch?" she asked.

"My..." He stopped on the verge of saying *butler.* "A friend who has my clothes."

Then Nick remembered something he hadn't remarked upon when he parked, but would have noticed under less stressful circumstances. "His bike! It's parked near the car. It registered in the back of my brain, but I wasn't operating on full power."

Dana wore a dubious expression as he pulled her forward. "So what? He wasn't sitting on it, was he?"

"He might have left the clothes in his saddlebags," Nick said.

"Then they'd be locked," she pointed out, limping slightly as she trailed along the sidewalk. "Wouldn't they?"

"He uses a combination," Nick said. "I happen to know the code."

He occasionally borrowed Hitch's bike for a run through the hills and canyons. It gave him a sense of freedom, of escaping his responsibilities. But the exhilaration never lasted long enough.

What he'd felt tonight with Dana was different, Nick reflected as they walked. In her arms, he had experienced a kind of liberty that came from within. He had felt as if the two of them together could stand against anything and find refuge in each other.

Nick wondered how long this natural high would last. The few relationships he'd come close to developing in the past had faded quickly into mutual boredom or annoyance.

But the woman he knew from her letters and from to-night's adventures matched him in so many respects that he didn't think he would ever grow tired of her. Maybe, when he knew more about the actress side of her and why she'd written to him, he would understand whether there was any possibility that these feelings were mutual.

Hitch's motorcycle stood, nose to the curb, half a block from where Nick had parked. With grim satisfaction, he unlocked the saddlebags and, retrieving his flashlight, flipped through the contents.

"What do you think?" Nick was reluctant to pull out all three costumes, knowing he would never be able to fold them properly again. "He's brought a penguin suit, business duds and sports clothes."

"What a dedicated friend. But why ask me?" Dana eyed the folded garments with amusement. "I've never been asked to dress a man before."

Nick swung one leg over the bike, enjoying the virile feel of it. "Too bad he didn't bring black leather."

She laughed. "What would your boss think?"

"At this point, he's probably given up on me," Nick said. "In any event, I'm in no mood for a tux, and business suits make me feel like a kid at Sunday school. I'll take the slacks."

"I'm so glad you asked me to choose," Dana said sarcastically.

"Don't you approve?"

She shot him a mischievous glance, which swept from his face down his chest to his hips. "I think I liked you better without clothes."

At that moment, Nick nearly said to hell with Renfro Williams and his party. To hell with *Heat!* and the letters, too. He wanted to find a private place to show Dana that he preferred her without clothes, too.

A police car turned down the street, cruising slowly as the officer checked them out. Nick had to admit they might appear suspicious, so he made a show of lifting out the slacks and polo shirt and then relocking the saddlebags.

"Let's go," he said. "I can change in the men's room."

They strolled toward the party. The patrol car crept onward, prowling the night for wrongdoers.

Back on Sunset Boulevard, Nick found that a group of street musicians had joined the din. Sitting on the sidewalk with a hat primed for donations, they were torturing a semblance of reggae music from flutes, guitars and drums.

"Are they on or off the beat?" Dana asked. "There's a strange echo around here."

"That's no echo," Nick said. "They're both on *and* off the beat."

He tossed them a ten-dollar bill, anyway. Judging by their leanness, the quartet could use a bite to eat. If they waited for talent to win out, they might starve to death.

The clot of people around the Minicams had thinned. Reporters were drifting off, trying to make connections through their cellular phones. He heard one man cursing and realized the system must be overtaxed tonight.

Nick was contemplating cornering the man and demanding to know if he was Jim Jasper when Dana grabbed his elbow and pulled him forward. "If Renfro Williams is here, I want to meet him and get this over with."

"You make it sound like going to the dentist."

"At least the dentist gives you painkillers."

Nick squinted at the pear-shaped figure at the center of the turmoil. The first thing he noticed was an outrageous mask of curly pink feathers that made the fellow resemble a panda trying to pass as a flamingo.

The panda image came from the tuxedo jacket. How well Nick knew that jacket, and that ponytail, and that tattoo, with its perpetual ode to Phyllis. There was no longer any question as to who was being peppered with questions and showered with attention.

Things began to make sense. Nick still didn't know where the masks had come from, but he could imagine what might have happened on the Renfro Williams front.

When Hitch showed up looking for Nick, people must have gotten the idea he was the eccentric millionaire. The guy fulfilled the image, and Nick supposed his butler was having a good laugh.

He hoped people wouldn't be too annoyed when they learned the truth. As a matter of fact, Nick wasn't sure they would believe the truth. They almost certainly wouldn't bother to come back to his estate for the announcement, now that they believed they had met Renfro himself.

Mask or no mask, Hitch cut an unmistakable figure. Nick was tempted to let his butler pose as him for the rest of their lives.

The only problem was that Hitch couldn't sign Nick's contracts. Too bad.

Then he felt Dana tugging him into the thick of the guests. "What's your hurry?" he asked. "The guy isn't going to vanish into thin air."

"He has to help us find the letters," she said. "He, of all people, will understand."

Except that he doesn't have a clue who you are, Nick thought, or what was in those letters, either.

But it was too late to make explanations now.

"MR. WILLIAMS! I need to ask you about the letters!" The voice came from behind Hitch and belonged to one of the peskier reporters. The fellow had had the audacity earlier to ask why Hitch sported a tattoo with the name Phyllis on it.

Hitch hated questions about Phyllis. Everyone assumed she must be a former girlfriend, but Phyllis had been his golden retriever. He had consented to being tattoed one night after drinking too much, and had impulsively chosen her name.

Possessing an abnormal fear of lasers, Hitch had refused to remove it and instead spent the next dozen years searching for a suitable woman named Phyllis. He had yet to find her.

Besides, Hitch had just noticed Nick wending his way through the throng, accompanied by that actress. For unknown reasons, she had changed into casual clothes. In the darkness, she appeared to have removed some of her makeup, too.

She and her surly boyfriend had disappeared into the restaurant earlier, or maybe they'd left and this was someone else who resembled her. Hitch didn't care what had happened to Dominique Grant, but he would have liked to know what she was doing with his boss now. Or why Nick was squiring a look-alike.

So he turned his back on the reporter and signaled to Nick. In return, he received only a short nod, which might have meant that Nick was annoyed about Hitch's passing for Renfro. Hitch decided to hang loose until his boss made his wishes clear... or fired him.

He didn't regret his moment of glory, though. Those TV hotshots were going to look like monkeys after they went on the air with their phony scoop. It would be a moment worth savoring.

Nick and the woman finally reached Hitch, but he couldn't hear what they were saying, because the reporters were flinging questions at the newcomers. "Hey, Nick, what are you going to do now that you can't front for Mr. Williams anymore?" "Want to make this official, Nick? You know we're not supposed to print anything about Renfro Williams unless we get it straight from the Lyon's mouth!" And "Where'd you get those cute shorts? At least you don't have to worry about ventilation!"

Nick gave the crowd a weak grin and a wave. "I'll talk to you later," he said. "Why don't you guys go embarrass a politician or something?"

"Come on, make a statement!" a man called. "We've got a live feed."

"No, you don't," said another fellow with a smirk. "Your station is off the air. *My* station has emergency status." The two squared off, and a fistfight was prevented only by the intervention of their camera operators.

"I see you got your clothes," Hitch muttered into Nick's ear, indicating the garments looped over his arm. "What're you doing with the, uh, young lady?"

"Long story," Nick hissed back. "If Miss Grant asks you about some letters, say you're concerned."

"I'm concerned?"

"As concerned as she is."

"Sure." Hitch always followed instructions, even if he didn't understand them. That was one thing about working for Nick—he could trust his boss not to do anything stupid. Although, after this fiasco tonight, he might have to reconsider. "How do you want to handle this?" Hitch indicated the ladies and gentlemen of the press. "Want to give them the facts?"

"I'm not sure." Nick wore a bemused expression that Hitch had never seen before. It intensified whenever his gaze fell on the woman who accompanied him.

If Hitch didn't know better, he'd have sworn his boss was in love, or close to it. That was strange, since Dominique had spent most of the evening trailing another man around the restaurant.

But now that he saw her close up, he felt certain this was someone else. A stunt double, perhaps? Her eyes weren't set quite so far apart, for one thing, and she had taken off the rhinestone-rimmed mask he'd seen her wearing earlier. Or hadn't seen her wearing earlier.

Manuel came by with an armload of disguises, and thrust one at the woman. She took it, but didn't put it on.

"What's this?" Nick gestured toward Manuel. His hand came back with a Nixon mask in it.

"I rescued a truck driver," Hitch said. "The kid got lost in the big city. I figured we might as well put these things to good use. The price was very reasonable."

From inside the restaurant, Hitch could hear voices raised in song. It sounded as if they were singing "The Night the Lights Went Out in Georgia" in at least three keys.

"Haven't you figured out who I am?" asked the woman. She appeared to be addressing Hitch.

This must be a trick question. "Dominique Grant?" he said.

She gave a disgusted sigh. "I'm DG," she said.

"Right." Hitch didn't dare exchange glances with his boss to try to find out what was going on. Obviously, this woman expected him to know something, and Nick wanted him to play along.

"Why haven't you been helping us?" she demanded. "We've been chasing all over town trying to get those letters."

"I'm as concerned as you are," said Hitch.

"Have you seen Jim Jasper?" Nick asked. "You know, the reporter from *Heat!*?"

Hitch remembered a reporter asking about some letters. It didn't take a genius to see that there must be a connection.

"He was right behind me." He swung around, but two tourists in varying degrees of plaid stood there snapping photos of the guests. "He's not here now."

"The cellular lines may be jammed, so he might have gone inside to find a pay phone," Nick said. "Dana?"

"I'm coming." She gave Hitch a look of pure irritation, as if he'd done something to anger her, then turned away.

Reading between the lines, he concluded that Nick must have written to her in Hitch's name. Why would Nick send letters and attribute them to his butler?

Then he realized that Renfro Williams must have signed the letters, and now this woman believed Hitch was Renfro.

She obviously wasn't Dominique. Her name was Dana, and Nick had referred to her as Miss Grant, so she must be a sister or something. That didn't, however, explain why a fax of Dominique Grant had been lying on Nick's desk.

Nick and Dana vanished into the building, leaving Hitch to puzzle over this confusing information. He was still sorting out his impressions when a cab pulled up and three people piled out.

They must be pretty damn important, he thought, to snare a taxi during a blackout. Or maybe their appearance had stunned the cabbie into stopping.

One tall, imposing fellow wore a red coat, like a British soldier during the American Revolution. There was another, shrimpy guy in a gigantic wig. But what riveted

Hitch was the woman who hauled herself out of the front seat.

He had never seen anyone like her. Almost as tall as the red-coated man, she wore tier after tier of petticoats beneath her flowing skirt. Her large bust nearly spilled from her low-cut bodice, above which loomed a large, expressive face covered with powder, rouge and fake black beauty marks. It was topped with a white wig that put spun sugar to shame.

This was a woman worth noticing, a creature from another era—or another planet entirely. She was so far removed from the everyday grind that the world around her took on an air of unreality.

"We've come to warn our friends!" she announced in stentorian tones. "Someone followed them from the hotel! Thank goodness I stepped outside to get a breath of air and saw it! Now where might they be—a man in torn shorts and a pretty young woman? They said they had an engagement at the Top Hat. This is the Top Hat, is it not?"

People stared at her with mouths agape. Hitch guessed she must be referring to Nick and Dana, but couldn't bring himself to send this vision sailing away so soon. "Who are you?" he asked, awestruck.

The woman's mouth formed an original shape as she frowned at him. "Where did you get that mask?"

"This?" Hitch's hand flew to the feathered concoction. "From that truck."

The red-coated man produced a larger-than-life-size grimace. "Why, that's the company! Some of those must be our masks!"

"Pilfered!" cried the bewigged woman. "Highway banditry! I knew it!" She advanced toward Hitch, laying about her with a Japanese fan.

He stood his ground, frozen in a kind of ecstasy. This woman seemed to have emerged from one of his fantasies, except that she went beyond anything Hitch could have conjured up by himself. He tried to picture her on the back of a motorcycle, and knew the sight would lay waste to the city.

She reached him and whacked him lightly across the knuckles. "You, sir!" the woman demanded. "Return our property to us!"

It took a moment before Hitch could find his voice. Then he managed to say, "May I ask your name?"

"Lady Alicia!" she snapped. "As if it were any concern of yours!"

Hitch gave a deep sigh, one that rose from the depths of his soul. "Would you consider changing it to Phyllis?" he asked.

DANA COULDN'T BELIEVE how unappealing she found RNW. She had tried to prepare herself for almost anything—arrogance, indifference, stoniness. But this fellow bore no conceivable relationship to the man with whom she'd corresponded for so many months.

I've come to depend on our "conversations" to free me from the narrow realm in which I both rule and am imprisoned. Could that rotund blusterer with the scraggly ponytail and shabby tuxedo jacket have written such poetic words?

We would meet as equals, the force of both our personalities bringing us together with an explosion more brilliant than fireworks.

Far from an explosion, there hadn't been so much as a flicker of interest on either side. Renfro Williams hadn't examined Dana as if she were his heart's true companion.

He'd glanced at her with a touch of apprehension, like a man facing a landlord to whom he owed rent.

Disappointment sat heavily on her spirit, mingled with disbelief. This *couldn't* be RNW.

But, of course, he was. Camera crews and famous guests—even in their disguises, Dana had recognized several television personalities and two business titans—couldn't be mistaken.

By comparison to Renfro, Nick struck her as romantic and tender. He cleared her path into the restaurant, his strength protecting her from the crowd, his hands gently steering her around loose chairs that loomed in the uncertain light.

She wished he were the one who'd written the letters. But in the end it didn't matter, because she was the wrong woman for him.

As they wedged their way through the packed bodies, Dana was grateful for the mask. She'd put it on after two people called her Dominique.

The mistake galled more bitterly than ever, because it reminded her that Nick wanted someone Dana could never be. The real Dana Grant wasn't glamorous, or daring, or brave. She wasn't Dominique, no matter how many people got them confused.

In her reverie, Dana nearly ran into Nick. He had come to a dead stop, partially blocking her way.

They stood near the middle of the large dining room. Candles flickered on the tables, making everything shadowy and vague.

Another room opened to their right, separated from the one they were in by a waist-high partition. It was impossible to see into its depths, but Dana could hear the clinking of glasses and the chatter of many voices.

By now, the mood had become boisterous as guests acted out the characters of their masks. Winston Churchill pontificated in one corner, although she thought she heard him saying a most inappropriate "One if by land, two if by sea!"

An Indian princess was singing one of the songs from *Pocahontas* to a circle of admirers, who mostly seemed fascinated by her designer gown, with its peekaboo cutouts. Two men in Humpty Dumpty masks had linked arms and were dancing a cancan to music that only they could hear.

Dana could already picture the T-shirts that would be hawked on street corners: I Survived the Great Blackout. But would she survive, and if so, in what condition?

"Listen." Nick spoke close to her ear. "I'm going to find the men's room and change clothes. The telephones should be adjacent, so I'll check for our friend Jasper. You ask around. Maybe somebody knows who he is."

"Sure." Dana refused to show how intimidated she felt by the raucous behavior of the guests. Tonight, she told herself, she wasn't Dana Grant, she was DG, international detective.

As Nick moved away, she felt momentarily adrift in space. Resolutely Dana turned and began making contact with the masked figures around her.

To her polite "Excuse me," the first man she encountered grunted, dropped his head on his table and began snoring. A second man shrugged and said, "Gotta get another drink."

Dana gritted her teeth and went on. Nobody knew who Jim Jasper was, but most people tried to be helpful. Several drew her into their conversations as if she were an old friend.

"What do you think of Renfro Williams?" asked a tall woman in a stunning caftan and a sequined mask.

"He reminds me of an old hippie," Dana said honestly.

"Hippie?" burst out a blond woman wearing the rubberized face of a cat. "Who cares? The man is rich beyond belief! I'll take that kind of hippie any day!"

"You'd have to wait in line, honey," said a third woman.

"You guys don't mean it," Dana said. "You wouldn't marry a man just because he's rich."

"Rich?" said the third woman. "That's only part of it. Influence, power... and did you notice the muscles under that jacket?"

"I wonder who Phyllis is," said the lady in the caftan.

Dana couldn't imagine why Renfro Williams had ever felt lonely. He certainly wouldn't be, after tonight.

And she didn't care. That was the amazing part. The man she had met outside the restaurant seemed so divorced from the letter writer she'd been worrying over that she didn't even want to get to know him better.

What's wrong with me? Dana wondered as she continued searching for the reporter. Am I really that fickle?

She passed a group of men discussing the power outage. One speaker in a Frankenstein mask felt sure it was sabotage and thought he could get a script out of it.

A short, intense man insisted he was already writing a script about a blackout and that the second fellow was trying to steal his idea.

"You can't steal a generic idea," retorted Frankenstein. "Everybody in Hollywood's going to be writing blackout scripts after tonight. The question will be who gets into production first."

Their voices rose in argument. Dana moved on.

It was no use searching any further for Jim Jasper in here, she decided. Since the throng was thinning slightly, it might be worth taking another swing outside.

Dana was heading for the exit when a woman in a shimmering sheath dress and a rhinestone-trimmed half mask came around the partition from the second room. Dana sidestepped quickly to avoid a collision and said, "Excuse me!" even though she didn't believe the near mishap had been her fault.

"Excuse me!" said a voice with the exact same inflection, at the exact same time.

They were the same height and the same build, Dana saw. For one bedazzled moment she had the illusion that she had come face-to-face with herself.

Chapter Eleven

Dear DG,

You appear to have a far more complicated relationship with your friend than I have with mine. From your tone, perhaps you feel estranged from her just now? But we never know the strength of our feelings until they're tested, do we?

I didn't realize how deeply my loyalty ran until one day when I was seventeen. My friend and I had been surfing on a beach that a local gang had staked out as their turf.

My buddy came out of the water first, and was confronted by two tough-looking fellows armed with knives. They weren't paying attention to me, and I suppose I could have fled, but it never occurred to me.

Without a moment's thought, I ran at them, yelling and wielding my surfboard as a shield. They hesitated. Through lucky timing, a police siren sounded a few blocks away, and the thugs ran off.

I hope I never find myself in such a situation again. As we grow older, we become more aware of our own mortality. Would I hesitate? Would my own mind betray me with doubts?

But I don't suppose you have to worry about courage. Not when you confront murderers and jump out
of airplanes as part of a day's work....

Dana realized she should have expected to see her sister
here. The party was apparently a major event, and it had
begun late enough that Dominique might have been planning to attend after their birthday dinner.

Still, she heard herself asking, "What are you doing
here?" just as her sister posed the same question. With almost identical gestures of impatience, they both pushed
their masks up.

Darn it, were they that much alike? Focusing on her
sister's glamour and confidence, Dana had never been
aware how much they sounded and thought the same. And
looked similar, since she assumed her thunderstruck expression matched Dominique's.

Well, not that similar. Dominique wore a glittery, close-
fitting gown with a rhinestone-studded mask. Dana knew
she must resemble the country cousin in her plain black
mask, cotton sweater and slacks.

Her sister was obviously waiting for a reply. "I'm trying to get those letters," Dana explained. "Do you know
a reporter named Jim Jasper?"

"I saw him outside earlier...." Dominique broke off, her
mouth dropping in horror. "You mean *Heat!* has the letters? No wonder he kept trying to corner me. I figured he
wanted to ask about Harmon, so I begged off."

"He's got the letters with him," Dana volunteered. "If
I can get them, we're home free."

"I don't know where he is now. Oh—" Dominique's
expression altered from anxiety to appeasement as a man
approached.

Beneath his Zorro mask, he had the sleek good looks of an actor. Or, in this case, a former actor; Dana had seen Harmon Mason's photograph enough times to recognize the noted director and erstwhile box-office star.

"What's this?" His gaze traveled from one to the other of them. "Some kind of joke, Dominique?"

"Harmon, I'd like you to meet my sister, Dana."

The man gave a brusque nod, his attention already shifting to other figures in the room. "I need to talk to Myford Raines about a new production company he's forming. Excuse me."

Dana grimaced at the departing figure. "Is he always so rude?"

"He's conducting business," Dominique said. "You have to remember, these parties aren't just social occasions in Hollywood. They're a chance to make contacts and do deals."

That was no excuse for bad manners, Dana reflected, but refrained from criticizing the man further. "Since you know what Jim Jasper looks like, would you mind coming outside with me?"

"Not at all," Dominique said.

As they headed for the exit, Dana hoped her sister would identify the reporter quickly and then go in search of her inattentive boyfriend. She didn't want Nick to see them together, not yet.

Tonight was magical, a special time when the rules had been put on hold. She didn't want the magic to end any sooner than it had to. Maybe, just once more, he would pick her up and save her from the crowd. Or dance with her, or hold her close.

On the sidewalk, the dwindling group of guests had been joined by passersby and tourists. As the two of them emerged into the flash of camera bulbs, Dana heard someone call, "There's Dominique Grant!"

Dominique maintained a dignified silence. Subtly, however, she stood a little straighter, and after a moment she tossed back her hair. As always, she seemed more alive before an audience.

Dana didn't see how anyone could spot the reporter in this crowd. With no streetlights to help, and the glare of flashbulbs adding confusion, it was almost impossible to sort one figure from another.

Except for Renfro, of course. He maintained an imposing presence at the storm's center, shaking hands and giving high fives. The man wasn't shy in the least. He appeared to be enjoying himself immensely.

The woman beside him caught Dana's eye. She blinked, but the image remained. There couldn't be two Lady Alicias in one universe, let alone one city.

"I can't believe it," Dana said. "What's she doing here?" And why did Renfro Williams have his arm around the woman's waist?

She recalled Nick telling Alicia that they were headed for the Top Hat, but that didn't explain why the woman would abandon her costume ball and follow them. Then Dana noticed Sir Allenby, frowning at the truck double-parked in front.

"The masks!" she cried.

"What?" said Dominique.

"These masks! I'll bet some of them were supposed to be part of the Colonial Ball!" Dana shook her head. "I can't imagine how they ended up here."

"Renfro brought them," said Dominique, busy signing autographs for a couple of delighted fans.

RNW had hijacked a truck full of masks? Events had definitely taken a left turn from reality this evening.

"Over there!" As her fans departed, Dominique raised herself on tiptoe and pointed to the far side of the gathering. "That's Jasper! He just hung up his flip phone. It looks like he's heading for Renfro."

Dana glimpsed a heavyset man with a khaki shoulder bag dangling at his side. "The letters!" she said. "They must be in there. And if he just talked to his editor, he might know they're the only copies."

"Then let's go get him," said Dominique.

Dana caught her sister's arm. "Dom, you don't have to do this. You've been a big enough help already."

Her sister shrugged. "You can see what Harmon's like. He can't bear to let anything get in the way of his making movies. If there's a scandal and he finds the press underfoot, he'll never forgive me."

"It isn't your fault."

"It won't matter."

Then he doesn't deserve you. Dana bit her lip. She knew how headstrong her sister could be—and how useless it was to argue with her. "Then let's go talk to Jasper. Maybe when he sees us together, he'll accept the fact that someone mistook me for you."

"I've got a better idea." Dominique raised one hand slightly, a gesture that said, *Big sister is taking charge.* "You keep close to the building and I'll circle around the outside. Just in case he doesn't persuade easily, one of us can grab the bag while the other one tackles him."

"What will we do with it?" Dana asked.

"Rip those letters into eensy-weensy shreds," snapped Dominique.

Dana had to smile. "You look like you could eat him alive."

"It's crossed my mind."

In a way, this was even better than a birthday dinner. Dana felt as if they were kids again, marshaling their pals in a series of *Star Wars* skirmishes across the neighborhood. "Go get 'em, Princess Leia."

"Give 'em heck, Luke Skywalker."

Dana had always wished *she* could play Princess Leia, but now, as then, there was no question who would prevail. "May the Force be with you."

"Likewise," said Dominique, and skirted toward the curb.

Dana turned to take an inside route, and that was when she saw Nick. He was staring straight toward her, wearing a glazed expression.

He couldn't have missed seeing her and Dominique together. With a sinking sensation, Dana realized the magic had just come crashing to a halt.

THINGS WERE BEGINNING to make sense.

The one possibility that had never occurred to Nick was that Dana had been telling the truth about being Dominique Grant's sister. The resemblance between them was remarkable, but after seeing them side by side, he knew he could have told them apart anywhere.

Dana had a more natural stance, a less self-conscious tilt to her head and a more open way of gesturing. Then there was that modest habit of ducking her head and smiling upward at an angle.

No wonder she'd been upset at learning that he'd made love to her while under the mistaken belief that she was Dominique. No wonder she'd been offended by his admiring references to glamour.

The little knucklehead thought he wanted that kind of nonsense. She didn't realize he was attracted to her in spite of it.

Nick would have been willing to march up to Dana and tell her, but he doubted she would believe him. He could see from the way she and Dominique were talking that Dana was deferring to her sister.

She must have grown up in Dominique's shadow. He supposed Dana would have a hard time accepting that he preferred her as she was. And he certainly couldn't explain himself in front of Dominique without revealing a lot of embarrassing personal details.

He wanted to talk to Dana quietly, in a private place where he could soothe away her doubts with caresses. This was not the sort of explanation a man wanted to make on a sidewalk with half the world looking on.

From the corner of his eye, he spotted Hitch getting chummy with Lady Alicia. Hitch was kissing her hand and making a courtly bow; it was a most uncharacteristic show of deference, but then, Hitch had never been concerned about how onlookers reacted to his behavior. For her part, Lady Alicia was too busy snatching masks off people to notice him.

The masks. Somehow the history buffs must have tracked them. At least now Nick knew where the darn things had come from, if not how Hitch had managed the mask-napping.

Beyond them, Nick could see a man who appeared to be a reporter zeroing in on Hitch. From the sidewalk, Dana was heading for the man, who Nick guessed must be Jim Jasper.

Here was their golden opportunity to retrieve the letters. Once that was done, there would be plenty of time for recriminations, clarifications and reconciliations.

Nick hurried to catch up.

LADY ALICIA'S FAN cracked over Hitch's head. "You may stop kissing my hand!"

He straightened. "Yes, my lady."

"Now where are they?" the woman demanded.

"The other masks?" He had gathered by now that the lady of his dreams was connected with the costume devices, although in what manner Hitch couldn't determine.

"No, fool, the man in the torn shorts and that lovely young thing with him!" cried Alicia. "There was a man following them. Two men, to be precise." She squinted into the darkness. "They must be lurking about. Come, come, fellow! Speak!"

"They'll turn up," said Hitch. He felt certain by now that Nick wasn't going to fire him for posing as Renfro. From the way things were going, Nick didn't seem that eager to seize the spotlight, anyway. Maybe he'd changed his mind about going public.

Hitch couldn't imagine himself continuing to play the role of Renfro Williams, but for tonight it was a gas. Lady Alicia, however, didn't seem to care about millionaires any more than she did about conventional manners.

"Turn up?" she demanded. "Turn up where? In a pudding? In my soup? I need to find them now!"

Nick must have gone inside to change his clothes. "Let's check in the restaurant," said Hitch.

Before he could lead his lady indoors, however, a hand clamped over his arm. "Mr. Williams!"

It was that pest of a reporter who'd been asking about the letters earlier. "Can't you see I'm busy?" said Hitch.

"I don't think you're too busy to talk to me." The man puffed up his chest. "I'm Jim Jasper from *Heat!* I want to discuss the letters you wrote to Dominique Grant."

Hitch's brain executed some fevered clicking and whirring, like a Las Vegas slot machine coming up cherries. Letters, avidly pursued by Nick. Dominique Grant, who managed to be in two places at once but was actually her own sister.

He came up with two cherries and a lemon. Hitch could see that Nick must have written some letters to Miss Grant. Love letters, apparently. But why would Dominique Grant be escorting that idiot director if she had the hots for Nick, and how had her sister gotten mixed up in this?

"I never wrote any letters," said Hitch, sticking to the truth.

"Oh, really?" The man pulled a sheaf of papers from his knapsack. "What do you call these?"

Hitch plucked one and held it up, but couldn't read it in the dark. He could, however, make out the initials RNW.

A bit obvious, he thought. It wasn't like Nick to make the bonehead mistake of using his own monogram. Still, there must be a lot of RNWs in the world.

With the help of copious squinting, Hitch deciphered the initials of the addressee, DG. Ah, yes, that was why Dana had announced that she was DG and expected Hitch, or rather Renfro, to react.

So the letters had been written to Dana, not to Dominique. But why hadn't Nick told her the truth about being Renfro? It was too confusing for Hitch.

"My brain feels hot," he said.

"I'll bet it does," sniped the reporter.

"Stand back, man!" Lady Alicia whopped the fellow with her fan. "Can't you see he's ill?"

"He's been a naughty boy," said Jasper, unabashed. "Writing mash notes to an actress. He never imagined we'd catch on, but you can't fool *Heat!*"

"Utter bosh," said Hitch. "I'm in love with Lady Alicia."

"Me?" The woman paused from fanning him back to health. "We've only just met, sir."

"I love you!" Hitch clutched his hands over his heart. "And nobody else."

The reporter was scribbling rapidly. "You're turning out to be quite a Romeo, Mr. Williams. May I ask this lady's name?"

"Alice Frammell," barked Lady Alicia. "I'm a clerk-typist for Wrigley Personal Hygiene Products, if you must know."

"I never use anything else," said Hitch.

"They make *women's* personal hygiene products!" boomed the love of his life.

"I'll have a sex change," said Hitch.

Then he noticed two women approaching the reporter from opposite sides. Or rather, the same woman was approaching twice. No, they were dressed differently— Dominique and Dana, together at last . . . sort of.

"You have something of mine," said the one in the striped sweater.

"Excuse me?" Jasper's head swiveled from one to the other, stopping as he faced the woman in the glittery gown. "Ah, Miss Grant! I've been looking for you!"

"We've been looking for *you*." Grabbing the letters from his hand, she began tearing them into strips.

"Hey!" Jasper shouted. "What are you—"

The woman in the sweater ripped the bag off his shoulder and pulled out several more sheets of paper, shredding them as well. "I think this is all of them."

"We've got other copies of—" The reporter's voice broke off. "Oh, my God. That's why Worley insisted I bring them straight back. Give those to me!'' These last words emerged in a roar.

''Not on your life,'' said the Miss Grant in the glittery dress, stepping off the curb to get away.

That was when Hitch spotted a van rocketing toward her, a van painted with the name of a mailbox store.

ELATION SOARED through Dana. She and Dominique had destroyed the letters. The scandal was averted, and they were both safe.

Then she saw the van bearing down on her sister. Even as she cried a warning, she could picture Dominique's body crushed beneath the wheels, her life snuffed out by a tragic accident.

Only this was no accident. That van belonged to Morey Bain. Dana flung herself forward, but her muscles seemed to respond in slow motion.

The van swerved from its collision course and braked sharply. Leaning out, Morey grabbed Dominique and hauled her through the side door, sending bits of paper fluttering into the street.

''Gotcha!'' To the driver, he yelled, ''Move it!''

It took a moment for the van to gain speed again. In that instant, a slim figure in a Batman mask jumped from the double-parked panel truck onto the rear bumper of the van. It was the man who'd been distributing masks earlier—Manuel, someone had called him.

Braced against the bumper, Batman clung to the back door handles as the vehicle accelerated down the street. In one gut-wrenching moment, they were gone.

''Dominique!'' Dana ran into the boulevard, as if she could stop the vehicle by sheer force of will. How could this have happened? Hadn't the idiots noticed they'd seized the wrong woman?

But then, Morey had believed Dana was Dominique all along. As far as he was concerned, he'd captured the *right* woman.

What could he possibly hope to gain? He'd just kidnapped a woman in front of dozens of witnesses, Dana told herself as cars swerved around her. The man was risking a long prison sentence.

She remembered the deposit slip in her pocket. Did it mean more than she'd assumed?

Nick caught her arm, hauling her onto the sidewalk. "You crazy woman, it won't help if you get yourself killed."

"We've got to catch them!" she said.

"Damn right." He turned to Renfro Williams. "Hitch! The keys to the bike!"

The billionaire reached into his pocket and, meek as a lamb, tossed the keys to his right-hand man. "We'll follow in the truck."

"Do that. And call the police!"

Nick raced down the sidewalk, not waiting for Dana. But she had already grasped his purpose, and begun her own race to the motorcycle. They wouldn't be able to stop the van, but at least they could keep it in sight. On the bike, even a traffic jam wouldn't hinder them.

In the silence that had fallen over the crowd behind them, she could hear a man impatiently calling Dominique and then snapping, "What do you mean, kidnapped? Well, if it's mistaken identity, they'll let her go, won't they?"

Obviously, Harmon Mason was not going to ride to the rescue.

Nick leaped onto the bike, revving it to life. Dana flung herself on the back, wrapping her arms around him as if her life depended on it.

As they shot down the street and careened onto Sunset Boulevard, she realized that it did.

Chapter Twelve

Dear RNW,

This may sound odd, after the adventures I've described, but I don't picture myself as brave.

I honestly don't know what I'd do if the life of someone I loved were in danger. If it were a child, I think I would instinctively do anything to save him or her.

In any other situation, though, I might be too aware of my own limitations. I hope not. Like you, I want to do what's right. I suppose I'm less afraid of dying than of failing to uphold my principles.

But that's easy to say. We can't always control our reactions on the spur of the moment.

As you said earlier, we don't know the depth of our own feelings until they're tested....

The roar of the motorcycle and the pounding rush of pavement beneath them marked the boundaries of Dana's world. She could feel nothing but Nick's hard body entwined with her arms. The wind shut out everything else.

Nick had changed into slacks and a shirt made of some soft fabric. She could feel his muscles tensing as he steered the bike, and smell the earthy masculinity of his perspiration. It had a clean tang that reminded her of the moment after they'd made love.

The memory sent tingles along Dana's nerve endings as she recalled his slow kisses and the way he'd stroked her into a smoldering fire. Now they were united again, as close as if they were in bed, but with an entirely different purpose.

She wished she could read his thoughts. He'd seen her with Dominique. Had he been disappointed? Was he eager now to meet the genuine article?

She tried to tell herself that it didn't matter. The important fact was that Dana had put her sister in danger. Saving Dominique was more important than her own personal feelings.

It was hard to imagine, even now, that Morey Bain could truly harm anyone, but she knew it was possible. He'd fired at them in the hotel garage, and pursued them to outrageous lengths. The man was a maniac.

Even so, he must have some plan. Where was he taking her sister?

Through eyes half-shut against the onrushing night, Dana determined that they were heading west along Sunset Boulevard. Not far past the restaurant, the road changed from a leisurely wide avenue to a series of sharp curves where traffic picked up speed.

From the jarring drag of the pavement, she felt as if they must be traveling ninety miles per hour, but that might be an illusion. She had no standard for judging. It wasn't as if she spent every day clinging to the back of a motorcycle, chasing bad guys through the streets of Hollywood.

The notion made Dana smile. This was definitely something her alter ego might have done. How thrilling it sounded, to tackle danger and laugh in its teeth.

The smile faded. Speaking of teeth, hers felt as if the fillings might rattle loose at any moment, and the wind chilled her fingers until she could barely maintain her grasp on Nick.

This was a good way to get herself killed. That was one thing characters in Dominique's soap opera didn't have to worry about. Even when the writers did let them die, a rush of viewer mail could bring them back from the dead by some miraculous twist of fate.

Dana hoped Nick could see better than she could. One thing she knew for sure—no scriptwriter was going to put the pieces back together if they crashed.

They careened through an intersection to the accompaniment of honking horns. They must have run a light, she mused, and wondered whether it had been yellow or red.

Dana could feel their pace quickening, and realized they must not have been traveling as fast as she'd thought. Or else they were passing the hundred-mile-an-hour mark, a speed at which the tiniest bump could send them airborne.

She prayed that they were closing in on Dominique. Not that two people on a motorcycle could accomplish much, other than keeping tabs on the van. But maybe they would spot a police cruiser, or the van would run out of gas before they did.

Something had to give. Dominique couldn't die because of a bunch of letters and a silly scandal that might have embarrassed that self-absorbed director Harmon Mason.

Dana no longer cared what ridicule her students and fellow faculty members might heap on her. She doubted Dominique cared about anything except getting out of this mess alive, either. There was nothing like a life-or-death situation to put matters into perspective.

As her body began to adapt to the unfamiliar forces of acceleration and wind, Dana peered over Nick's shoulder. They were passing multimillion-dollar homes that had become blacked-out castles in the moonlight. She could see only a blur ahead, but then the traffic thickened and everything slowed and came into focus.

The van was only a few vehicle-lengths beyond them, prowling behind a Porsche and a Lexus that did not seem inclined either to yield or to speed up. A rear door in the van flapped open, and Dana wondered whether the daring young Manuel had managed to get inside. She hadn't seen him lying on the road, thank goodness, so perhaps he was safe.

A pothole sent the van lurching, and the other rear panel flew open. As the motorcycle swerved around the hole, its headlight raked something moving inside. Dana could just make out two figures flailing at each other.

They kept losing their balance, however, as the vehicles shot around the steep curves near UCLA. From the way the fighters wavered and stumbled, she doubted anyone was landing much of a blow.

Dana's stomach clenched as she reflected on how fragile her sister was, and how easily a thug like Morey could hurt her. But the two figures looked blocky, not feminine. Apparently, the man in the mask was defending the damsel in distress. Silently she cheered the young man on.

The motorcycle pushed closer. In the glare of its headlight, Dana spotted a shape huddled on the floor of the van, wriggling to avoid being stepped on. It had to be Dominique. She must be terrified, and perhaps bruised from all the jostling.

How dare Morey treat her sister that way! Dana felt as if she could fly over the handlebars and punch the jerk's lights out. Common sense and gravity kept her rooted in place, but her thoughts flew ahead, seeking a solution.

The guard must be driving. She wondered why he was going along with this insanity. Morey had a way of being persuasive, she recalled, and she supposed he must have made up a plausible story.

He'd certainly fooled Dana. She had never suspected him of anything but kindness in all those months when he volunteered to take her mail to the main post office as a special favor. She had never imagined his motive was to gain access to her outgoing letters, as well as the incoming ones from RNW.

Or perhaps Morey had simply bribed the guard. A lot might depend on whether the fellow was a ruthless mercenary or a nice guy who'd been duped.

Dana snapped out of her reverie as, ahead of them, one of the combatants fell to his knees after receiving a blow. After a heart-stopping pause while he struggled to rise, the other man smacked him on the head, and he collapsed.

Dana recognized the victor from his thick trunk and short legs as Morey Bain. He had, apparently, knocked out Manuel.

How had a seemingly innocent quest managed to endanger so many people? If Dana had foreseen what might happen, she would never have entered that house in the first place.

Please let the poor guy be all right, she prayed silently. And Dominique. Dana would have done anything in her power to save them.

But the person who could help them wasn't her, it was Nick. And apparently he had a plan.

He gave the bike more gas as they shot alongside the van, trying to maneuver abreast of the driver. She guessed that he was hoping the guard would be ripe for quitting this deadly game, if they could get close enough to shout an explanation.

But the car ahead of them refused to budge. Nick tried to angle between the two vehicles, but there wasn't room, not on this twisting route. They were forced to fall back, half a length behind the van.

A stocky figure appeared in the open back of the vehicle. Dana thought Morey was going to reach out and close the rear panels.

Then she saw something in his hand. Something that glinted in their headlight as he took aim.

NICK HOPED Hitch hadn't gotten stuck in traffic somewhere behind them. He needed reinforcements, and he needed them soon.

He dropped back and changed lanes to make it harder for that creep Morey to get a fix on them. The guy lowered his weapon, and Nick wondered whether the man had really meant to use it.

Nick didn't intend to find out. Not with Dana clinging behind him, about to turn into a human projectile if they crashed.

Oddly, he wasn't worried about his own safety. The adrenaline pumping through his arteries had erased any sense of vulnerability. He simply couldn't imagine a trajectory that would carry that bullet into his body.

Macho arrogance, no doubt. Sometimes it served a useful purpose, Nick mused. And sometimes it made fools of otherwise sensible men.

They were coming to the freeway, and he braced himself for an abrupt turn, not knowing which on-ramp the driver would choose. To Nick's surprise, the van swept along, making no attempt to change course.

They weren't taking the freeway. Why not? The only explanation that occurred to him was that Morey Bain had a specific destination in mind and it lay due west.

Nick had been trying to second-guess his quarry since they left the restaurant. Unfortunately, he knew nothing about the shop owner and, therefore, no likely scenarios offered themselves.

Morey had left the torn letters scattered along Sunset Boulevard, which meant he either didn't see them or didn't care about them. He might have been after Dominique— or, more likely, Dana—all along.

Was there something she hadn't told Nick? In view of the various versions of reality they had created for each other, that seemed possible. But she would have told him when they got on the bike, he felt sure, if she knew anything that could help her sister.

It struck him that he didn't really know much about Dana. He'd been so convinced she was Dominique that he'd tried to fit everything she said into the wrong mold.

He had no idea what her dreams or goals were. In fact, he didn't even know her occupation. They had been as intimate as two people could be, and yet they remained strangers.

The enigma was mutual, of course. She believed Hitch had written those letters, and Nick couldn't tell her otherwise over the roar of the motorcycle. This was hardly the moment for true confessions, anyway.

He wished they could go back to that hotel suite and start over. For one thing, the pressure of her body against his was stirring up instinctive longings that had no respect for adverse circumstances.

Mostly, though, he wished they could talk. He wanted to come clean with her. He should have done that in the first place, instead of trying to stay in control.

But then, hadn't he spent the past thirty-five years gaining and keeping control over every aspect of his existence?

Even assuming a second identity had been a form of control. Renfro Williams had remained untouchable, almost superhuman. Meanwhile, Nick had been free to hear and observe things that people would otherwise have hidden from him—and to use that knowledge to fortify his power.

It was an insight that Nick found startling. In the middle of chasing his quarry down Sunset Boulevard, he found himself yanked into a reassessment of his life.

For more than a decade, Nick had pushed aside every contrary impulse in an effort to dominate his industry and everyone around him. He had abandoned relationships with women and with friends—other than Hitch. His singular focus had been to acquire and to rule.

He had succeeded beyond his wildest dreams. The problem was, his success might cost him everything that mattered.

Trying to find a mate through correspondence had been one more way to stay in the driver's seat. Although he had told himself he was seeking a potential wife, the fact was that by keeping his identity a secret, he'd retained the ability to cut off contact at any time.

What Nick hadn't counted on was becoming so fascinated with his correspondent that he yearned to meet her. In recent months, he had begun imagining what DG might look like and how she would fit into his world. He had pictured a perfect union of minds and bodies—but always on his terms.

Everything had fallen apart the moment they collided at Morey Bain's house. Dana had a way of doing and saying the unexpected, and turning Nick's world upside down. He couldn't control her, no matter how hard he tried.

And he *had* tried, Nick admitted ruefully. He'd withheld information, taken charge of their quest and maneuvered Dana into a hotel room. He had convinced himself he only wanted to get to know her better, but what idiot would believe that? In retrospect, he didn't even believe it himself.

Tonight he had learned that there were some things that couldn't be handled with a show of importance and a large check. Maybe a lot of things.

Nick blamed himself for dragging Dana and her sister into this mess. Dana would never have gone to such lengths on her own. She might have ventured as far as the newspaper, but she certainly wouldn't be speeding on a motorcycle behind a van carrying her imprisoned sister into the Palisades.

The Palisades. It was a hilly, canyon-ridden region between Beverly Hills and Malibu. Rough terrain lay ahead.

The road had narrowed and was curving even more tightly than before. Since the other cars had vanished onto the freeway, the route belonged only to the van and the motorcycle.

Morey Bain was bracing himself in the open doorway again. Those stubby legs must give the guy a better-than-average sense of balance, because Nick didn't see how he could help being thrown to one side.

At least the creep seemed to have set aside his gun. It must have been an idle threat, although Nick couldn't be sure.

Staying this close to the van was risky. But once Dominique left their sight, there was no telling what might happen to her.

Nick would rather see his intimate letters spread over every tabloid in the nation than let Dana's sister come to harm. He knew the woman clinging to him must be full of regret. Well, so was he.

Damn his ego. Damn his determination to find a lover by mail to protect himself from fortune hunters. The only good thing was that, by some undeserved stroke of fate, his machinations had led him to Dana.

He had to prove himself worthy of her respect, and the way to do that was to save her sister. With an irrational fury, Nick determined to take charge of this mess again—at any cost.

He knew he would triumph. The adrenaline rioting through his bloodstream told him so.

"Dana!" he called over his shoulder.

He felt rather than heard her answering "Yes?" close to his ear.

"Do you know how to drive a motorcycle?"

"I . . . guess so." At least he thought that was what she said.

For all he knew, Dana might work as a stuntwoman. She certainly would make a perfect double for her sister. In any case, lots of people knew how to ride a motorcycle.

Nick shouted against the wind, hoping she could make out his words. "I'm going to try to jump inside. You'll have to scoot forward and grab control."

It was a crazy idea. If every instinct in Nick's body hadn't been shouting for him to prove himself to Dana, he would never have tried it.

It might be a modern-day version of the caveman clubbing the saber-toothed tiger to impress his wild-haired mate. Well, one caveman, coming up.

Nick felt Dana's hands tighten around his rib cage as he shot the bike forward, darting along the right side of the van. It was a deception intended to make Morey clear out of the doorway and hurry toward the front.

With any luck, the scoundrel would be staggering toward the passenger window, intending to stop an imminent boarding attempt, Nick thought as they zipped around another series of curves. As soon as they came to a straightaway, he dropped back abruptly and tensed for a leap into the rear of the van.

Behind him, he could feel Dana's muscles tighten, as well. She seemed to be preparing herself to move, so apparently she had understood his instructions. She would need to boost herself onto his seat and seize the handlebars instantly to keep the bike stabilized.

It couldn't possibly work. But with his masculine imperative drumming out his fears, Nick saw no alternative.

This would take split-second timing, and the split second was now! Nick's brain issued the call, but something held his muscles in check. Before his conscious mind even registered what was happening, his body knew that things had gone horribly wrong.

Morey Bain hadn't gone to the front of the van. He'd maintained his post between the open rear doors. And he was holding the gun.

Light and sound blasted toward them. From some distant planet, Nick became aware of the bike plunging aside, smashing through a hedge and leaping into a field.

Had he been shot? Nick couldn't tell if he was in pain or simply had become one huge blob of suspended sensation. Hell, he wouldn't even have taken odds on whether he was still alive.

The bike roared across the pasture, cutting an ugly swath through the soft grass. A series of horse jumps stood affixed to the ground, as if deliberately placed there to foil trespassers who careened through hedges on motorcycles.

Nick wrenched the handlebars, cutting around a white fence. The cycle skidded in a hail of dust and grass clumps, like a power mower gone mad, and spun at a ninety-degree angle. Dana uttered a cry and flew through the night like a wild bird.

Nick fought to stop the bike so that he could help her. But the damn thing had a mind of its own, tearing off as he struggled to regain his grasp on the controls. He knew he could do it with a few seconds of unhindered concentration.

If only there weren't a tree dead ahead, zooming toward him much too fast.

DANA HAD BELIEVED, perversely, that the power of her will was stronger than centrifugal force and would keep her attached to Nick. Then the cycle skidded and her grasp tore loose.

A sense of unreality cushioned her soaring arc across the meadow. Landing knocked the wind out of her, and she lay motionless.

She became aware of the pain in her shoulder a fraction of a second before she heard the cycle crash. Her pain disappeared instantly.

Scrambling to her feet, Dana loped across the field. Moon and stars turned the landscape into a surreal setting, pierced by the unnatural gleam of a single headlamp.

It wasn't moving. It emerged from a point very close to the earth, where the cycle must be lying on its side.

"Nick?" He had to be here somewhere. It didn't occur to Dana at first that he might be seriously injured. She still hadn't absorbed the reality of the wreck. "Where are you?"

Then she saw the crumpled shape lying a few feet from the bike.

The cycle itself lay twisted around a tree. Nick apparently had bailed out just before impact, but he lay terrifyingly still.

Dana repeated his name several times as she knelt beside him. She touched his shoulder, and felt a faint shudder. Then the movement stopped.

"No!" She wanted to flip him onto his back and listen for breathing, but she remembered reading that trauma patients shouldn't be moved. In the case of spinal injury, jarring the nerves could cause paralysis.

Dana gazed frantically around. A screen of trees probably hid a house, and common sense urged her to call the paramedics. But she couldn't move. The shock of the accident and her own tumble, combined with an overwhelming sense of dread, locked her muscles in place.

In the moonlight, she could see sweat-dampened hair clinging to Nick's temple. Instinctively she reached out to touch him, but then she drew back. Even the slightest disturbance might worsen his injuries.

He had to be alive. Dana could feel the warmth of his body in the cool air, and she thought she detected a faint movement that might have been breathing. Or it might have been her own vision wavering as her heart hammered.

This was where her bravado had led them both, to this field and this tragedy. Why had she ever believed it was all right to pretend to be something she wasn't?

Dana had thought she was being straight with herself earlier, recognizing the fact that she was no intrepid detective. But when honesty counted and the chips were down, she'd tried to fool Nick again, and this was the result.

In that crucial juncture, when he had told her to take over the bike, she should have refused. She had known deep inside that she couldn't do it. Maybe nobody could. But at least an experienced stunt rider would have acknowledged the limits of her own ability.

Feeling the damp coldness of the ground seep through her slacks, Dana tried to reconstruct that point in time. She had felt, in defiance of all logic, that she *could* take over the cycle and hold it on its course. Images from movies had flashed through her brain. Too bad they hadn't reached as far as her body.

She wasn't sure what had gone wrong. In the rush of wind and the concentration on her task, she hadn't paid much attention to what Nick was doing, except that he was preparing to launch himself into space.

Dana had started to leap forward, only to find herself colliding with Nick's back. She must have misgauged the timing.

Vaguely she recalled hearing a loud noise that might have been the sound of them crashing through the hedge. The events had happened so quickly, they'd become jumbled in her mind.

She took a shuddering breath and gazed at the man lying inert on the grass. Tonight she had come to know every inch of him, from his rugged face and broad shoulders down to his slim hips and straight legs.

Memories played through her mind of the way he'd held her in bed, of his body poised over hers with such confidence and vibrancy. She wanted him back. She wanted to hear his voice, see the sparkle in his eyes and feel him near her, beside her, inside her.

With a jolt, Dana realized that somewhere between burglarizing a house and chasing Morey Bain down Sunset Boulevard, she had fallen in love with Nick Lyon. It was a useless emotion. It couldn't restore him to health. It certainly couldn't save his life or Dominique's.

It was no substitute for actually being the woman he believed she was, the brave and resourceful alter ego she had created. A creature who had just come crashing to earth, bringing Nick with her.

Dana ran her hand lightly over his arm. "I'm sorry," she murmured.

A slight movement sent her heart skittering around her chest. With a moan, Nick opened his eyes and stared at a clod of dirt. Then he muttered several profanities.

"It hurts, huh?" Dana said.

"Like being run over by Attila the Hun and his Mongol hordes," Nick groaned.

"That's Genghis Khan," she corrected. "He was the one with the Mongol hordes."

He lifted his head with visible effort. "What are you, a history teacher?"

"English," she said. "I teach high-school English."

Slowly Nick raised himself to a sitting position. "No wonder you write so well."

Dana's joy at seeing that he'd escaped serious harm yielded to renewed dismay. "You really shouldn't read other people's letters."

"Other—? I've been meaning to talk to you about that." He ran his hands across his chest. "Was I shot?"

"No," she said. "I fouled you up. When you were trying to leap."

He frowned. "That's not the way I remember—"

"We've got to get to a phone." Dana jumped to her feet and brushed off her pants. The motion sent twinges through her shoulder, but she couldn't bother about that now. "We need to let the police know where Dominique is.

Maybe they can catch them." She gestured toward the row of trees. "There's probably a house back there."

"A mansion, you mean." Nick shook his head, then winced. "You think people who live in a place like that are going to let strangers into their house in the middle of the night?"

"It's an emergency!"

He released a painful breath as he stumbled to his feet. "Let's hit the road. There's a better chance of getting somebody to call 9-1-1 on a car phone."

He'd been right about most things so far, hadn't he? Besides, there might *not* be a house behind those trees. "All right."

They stumbled across the field and along the furrow left by the cycle, supporting each other over hillocks. A slight rise leading to the hedge formed a major obstacle, and Dana's shoulder throbbed as she helped hoist Nick upward.

Ironically, the ache reminded her how glad she was to be alive. And especially how glad she was that Nick was alive.

Only when they reached the pavement did it occur to either of them that they should have searched the saddlebags for a flashlight. "I can't believe I didn't think of it," Nick muttered. "My head feels like steel wool."

"I'll go back."

"Just wave your arms," he said. "The point is to get help."

Headlights raked them, and Dana signaled frantically, but the luxury car skimmed past. The motorist didn't even slow down.

Traffic was sparse, and the next two drivers proved equally unwilling to stop. By then, Dana was ready to move into the middle of the road and risk getting hit.

Before she could force her stiff body into motion, she heard the rattle of a truck. If only... It couldn't be...

Then it came around the bend, and Dana recognized it. The mask truck!

Brakes squealed as Renfro Williams leaned out the window. He had removed the feathered mask to reveal a leonine head and overlarge, almost bulging eyes. "Is that you? Nick? Are you all right?"

Nick nodded shakily as Renfro flung open the door. With more than a little help, the two of them were soon tucked inside the vehicle.

"I think we lost them," Dana said, long-suppressed tears threatening her composure. "He's gotten away with my sister."

"We'll find them," the white-wigged woman said grimly from behind the wheel. "If it's the last thing we do."

"Go get 'em, Phyllis," said Renfro.

Chapter Thirteen

Dear DG,

Your letter about risking your life for others brought on a lot of conflicting emotions.

To my surprise, I found myself wanting to shout at you that it's the man's job to put himself in danger. An antiquated idea, isn't it? The strength of my reaction surprised me, because I think of myself as a man of the nineties.

The chivalrous ideal held that it was the woman's place to sit sweetly at home in her tower while the man tilted with dragons. Of course, I'm sure reality was quite different.

Women have always had to protect their families, to cope with hard situations, to struggle for survival. It doesn't surprise me that you, or any other woman, would display courage.

What surprises me is that, even while I understand intellectually that men are no braver, my instincts demand that I protect you.

So if you run across any dragons, please let me know....

Nick didn't see the reporter at first. Jim Jasper was sitting on a box in the back, jotting in a notebook. When he spotted Nick, Jasper gave him a coolly assessing glance and went back to writing.

Nick overcame the urge to boot the man out of the truck. They didn't need some snoop interfering on a touchy mission like this. On the other hand, they could hardly leave the guy in the middle of nowhere.

Lady Alicia, or Phyllis, or whatever her name was, drove with breakneck abandon. At this rate, it was a toss-up whether they would catch Morey Bain or break the sound barrier first.

"Sorry it took us so long," Hitch said apologetically as he helped Dana wedge herself into a corner and find a strap to hang on to.

"It's a good thing, actually." Nick tried not to think about how many parts of his body must be bruised, chipped or scraped. "A few minutes earlier and you wouldn't have seen us."

"Any idea where those brigands might be heading?" asked Lady Alicia.

"I'm afraid not," Dana said. "Morey's house is no-where near here."

"By the way—" Hitch swiveled to face Nick "—what happened to my motorcycle?"

"Wrapped around a tree," said Nick. "Sorry."

The big man's face crumpled. "You wrecked my bike?"

"Don't worry, Hitch," Nick said soothingly. "I'll buy you another one."

"With saddlebags?" asked the butler.

"Lots of them," said Nick.

He caught Dana's befuddled gaze. "*You* have to buy *him* another cycle?" she asked. "And how come you call your boss Hitch?"

"Would you want to be addressed by a silly name like Renfro?" Nick demanded.

Hitch drew himself up. "Excuse me!"

"Renfro, Shmenfro!" said Lady Alicia. "Stop whining and help me find our quarry! I can't see hide nor hair of them."

As Hitch turned his attention to the road, Nick noticed Jasper pulling out his flip phone. The man dialed, then grimaced and snapped the thing shut. "I can't believe the circuits are still busy. I've only gotten through once all evening."

"Imagine," Dana said. "Other people have the nerve to make urgent phone calls when you've got gossip to report."

Jasper fixed her with a disdainful stare. "And who exactly are you?"

"I'm the one who wrote the letters," Dana said.

The man blinked. "Which letters?"

"The ones you dropped all over Sunset Boulevard. Or did you manage to pick them up?"

"He didn't have time," Hitch called from the front. "He couldn't miss the kidnapping of Dominique Grant."

"Goodbye, letters," Nick said with satisfaction. "The only copies, too. You can tell your editor for me that he should make sure who he's talking to on the phone, Jim. I didn't appreciate his referring to me as a weasely yes-man."

"You talked to Worley?" Understanding dawned in the reporter's eyes. "So that's what he was jabbering about. Well, it's only a temporary setback. Our informant should be able to provide duplicates."

"Morey Bain?" Dana shook her head. "He's the guy who kidnapped my sister, you idiot."

The reporter stopped fiddling with his pen. "Excuse me?"

"Not only that," said Dana, "but why would you want letters written by Dominique Grant's sister? Morey Bain got us confused. And, by the way, he doesn't have another set. I took them."

Jasper ground his teeth before responding. "I can recreate the letters. Key phrases, anyway. Don't forget that half of them were written by Renfro Williams. You may not be anybody, lady, but he's big news."

"Hitch didn't write those letters." Nick knew he was skating on thin ice, but he'd been seeking a chance to tell Dana the truth. This was far from the ideal setting, but it was the best he could do. "I did."

"You?" snapped Jasper.

"You wrote them?" Dana demanded.

"He did," Hitch confirmed.

Nick supposed he ought to go one step further and explain that he was really Renfro Williams, but he wasn't ready to do that in front of a reporter for *Heat!* Not without considering all the angles.

There was no time for further conversation, anyway, not with Lady Alicia uttering a whoop of delight in the front seat. "A trail!" she cried. "Milady has left us a trail of crumbs!"

"Crumbs?" Jim Jasper left his box seat and came to peer between the seats. "You can't see crumbs at night."

"Not literally," crowed the driver, wrenching the wheel and sending them all skittering at a ninety-degree angle. "Her mask!"

Leaning forward, Nick glimpsed something sparkling in the road. Apparently Dominique Grant had tossed her rhinestone-bedecked mask into the cross street to show where the van had turned.

He didn't like to think how Morey Bain must have reacted if he had seen that thing go flying out the back. Right now, Nick didn't like to think about anything that might be happening to Dominique Grant.

DANA HUNG ON TIGHT as they veered around the corner. The night's events had pushed her close to the panic point, but at least the sparkling mask gave them a chance of reaching her sister.

And she had a few precious seconds to recover from her shock. Nick had written those letters. Nick, the man she'd believed was nothing like the poetic soul she'd come to feel so close to during the past months.

In a way, it was a relief to realize that the eccentric Renfro was not her correspondent. But that didn't mitigate her confusion.

Why should Nick have written about feeling isolated? The man appeared to know everyone in Hollywood and, obviously, went everywhere.

She no longer had any idea what kind of man he was, except that he couldn't be trusted. It might have helped her state of mind if that realization made him less attractive, but it didn't.

Nick was staring out the windshield, unmindful of Dana's reaction to the bombshell he'd dropped. She wondered whether he would ever have confided in her, had it not been for his need to dissuade the reporter.

"You know," Hitch said from the front, "this road is beginning to look familiar."

"Of course it looks familiar," snapped Nick. "It's the way home."

"Home?" Dana said.

"He's heading for the estate." Nick took a deep breath. "Apparently Morey Bain is planning a little party at Renfro Williams's house."

DOMINIQUE WAS GLAD to see the young man in the Batman mask stirring on the floor of the van. She had crept over and checked his pulse, so she knew he wasn't dead, but she'd feared he might go into a coma.

Now she laid one hand on his temple, hoping he would remain where he lay. If he sat up, that nasty man in the polyester suit might deck him again.

Tending to the fallen warrior had given her an excuse to slide nearer the rear doors. Thank goodness her captor, whom his driver referred to as Mr. Bain, hadn't noticed when she tossed her mask out.

She had considered bailing out the back herself, but on reflection, it had seemed like a poor idea. The van would stop, and the men would give chase. She had zero chance of escaping in her heels and gown. And there wasn't likely to be anyone else coming after her now.

Dominique's heart contracted as she recalled the sight of her sister's motorcycle caroming off the road and through the hedge. She prayed that someone would reach Dana in time to get her to a hospital.

Perhaps Harmon Mason had followed. His Jaguar was perfectly capable of overtaking the van, and if he'd seen the motorcycle, he could summon help on his phone.

But that seemed a faint hope.

Tonight, Dominique had viewed him in a different light. Until now, they'd met in small restaurants and at his home, where there were few interruptions. Harmon's focus had been almost exclusively on Dominique.

Well, that wasn't quite true. He'd spent most of the time talking about his upcoming pictures and long-range plans. She had found the subject so fascinating that she didn't consider how self-absorbed the man's conversation was. Tonight, she had noticed it keenly.

He'd also been rude to Dana. Dominique had defended her boyfriend out of loyalty, but that was more consideration than he'd shown her.

His only concern had been to impress the money men who could help his plans. She'd felt like a tagalong child, a most unfamiliar sensation.

Still, Dominique couldn't help imagining that Harmon might come through for her. Lots of people had difficulty integrating their public and private personas. Maybe, now that the chips were down, Harmon would show that he cared.

Otherwise, she'd gotten herself into this mess for nothing, and Dana, too. Dominique didn't believe her sister would have gone to such lengths to retrieve the letters if not for fear of ruining her romance with Harmon.

She wished she knew exactly what Bain's connection was to the letters. She assumed there must be one, based on the timing of his attack. The possibility that a deranged fan had coincidentally driven up in a van bearing the name of a postal-box company and snatched her just as she got her hands on the letters seemed remote at best.

"I think we lost them," commented the driver, a gangly fellow in his mid-twenties who wore a blue guard's uniform.

"I'm not paying you to think," snapped Bain.

The driver shot him an irritated glance. "Look, I can use the extra money, but I need to be sure you're on the up-and-up. I don't want any trouble with the law."

"For kidnapping me?" Dominique snapped. "You bet you'll have trouble with the law!"

"Shut up!" Bain clenched his fist as if considering a blow. "I told you, she cheated me in a business deal. It's all under the table. Why do you think she hasn't called the police before now?"

"Because I haven't had a chance!" Dominique had no intention of keeping silent, regardless of the implied threat from Bain. Winning over the driver appeared to be her best chance of escape.

"Sure you have," the gangly fellow replied. "I've been chasing you all evening."

"That was my sister!"

"What do you mean, your sister?" snarled Bain. He had a round face with watery eyes, not the kind of angular visage that Hollywood producers would choose for a villain. "How stupid do you think I am?"

"Dana Grant wrote those letters," Dominique said. "Not me. They aren't worth anything."

The man uttered a couple of vulgarities before responding, "Except that she was writing them to Renfro Williams. Did you know that?"

Dominique had to admit she didn't.

But her words must have dismayed her captor. He gritted his teeth and absently fingered the stock of the gun protruding from his shoulder harness. "You aren't the one who broke into my house?" he said at last.

"Dana broke into your house?" Dominique couldn't picture it. Her little sister had always shrunk from taking risks.

In their growing years, it had been Dominique who faced down the school bullies and lied to their parents about attending a pajama party when they had really been going to an Elton John concert. She had been the one willing to break the rules to achieve her goals, with Dana following timidly.

Apparently her kid sister had changed. Then the image of the motorcycle careening through the bushes flashed into Dominique's brain, and she shuddered. Maybe Dana had changed a little too much.

"Did she tell you what she stole?" growled Bain.

Dominique shook her head.

"She didn't give you anything?"

"Certainly not."

The man's mouth twitched. "We have to go back!"

"Why?" asked the driver.

"Because she took something of mine that I need," the man snapped. "I figured she'd hand it over by the time we reached her boyfriend's estate, if only to save him from discovering her dead body on his front lawn."

"Dead body?" the man said. "Hey, wait a minute! I never agreed—"

That was when they heard the jouncing noise behind them, a truck engine splitting the quiet night, along with the grinding of large gears in inexperienced hands.

Dominique didn't know anyone who owned a truck, but there wasn't much traffic on this side road. She had to keep her hopes up.

"I think we've got company." Bain removed the gun from its holster. "Turn into that driveway."

"I don't want anything to do with this," said the guard.

The pistol swung toward his head. "You don't have any choice," said Bain.

DANA FELT a flash of hope as they turned between stone posts onto a broad driveway. Surely Morey Bain wouldn't have brought Dominique to such an obvious place if he planned to kill her. Surely he intended to let her go, once he got whatever it was he wanted.

Dana hoped it was nothing more than the deposit slip, although she couldn't see what value that had. Or maybe he intended to blackmail Renfro Williams. Whatever it was, they could come to terms.

"I want everyone to stay in the truck," Nick announced as they followed a bend in the driveway.

Ahead, Dana could make out the silhouette of the van, parked beneath some trees. Beyond it, a great house sprawled across the landscape, a stone facade giving it the appearance of an old English manor.

"Splendid!" said Lady Alicia. "I thoroughly approve of this house."

"Would you like to live here, Phyllis?" Hitch asked hopefully.

"I won't live anywhere except on my own terms!" she replied.

"I'm not staying in any truck," the reporter told Nick, ignoring the other couple. "I'm coming with you. The letter story's blown, but this one could be even bigger."

"The man has a gun," Nick said. "Is a byline worth dying for?"

On the point of heading for an exit, Jim Jasper hesitated. "You're sure about that? The gun, I mean?"

"Dead sure. Don't worry—I'll give you a detailed account. I'm used to issuing press releases, remember?" Nick thrust past Hitch and opened the passenger door. "I'm going to find out what he wants."

"I'm coming, too." Dana angled behind him.

"No." He jumped down and turned, his chest blocking her exit. "You're not risking your life again."

"It isn't up to you." Dana no longer cared about impressing Nick by pretending to be an adventurer. The only thing that mattered was saving Dominique's life. "She's my sister."

Their eyes locked. "It won't do her any good if you get killed."

"You don't even know for sure that he has a gun," Dana told him challengingly. She didn't see how she could push

Nick aside; he was too strong. But the minute he turned, she would have a clear field.

"Why do you think I crashed the motorcycle?" he asked in amazement.

"Because I messed up." Until this moment, she hadn't doubted it was her fault things had gone wrong.

"Because an English teacher didn't suddenly turn into Evel Knievel?" he asked. "What nonsense. Didn't you hear the shot?"

Now that she considered it, Dana did recall hearing a loud noise. "I thought that was just us crashing through the bush."

"Trust me, it was a gun," Nick said. "Now will you stay here?"

"No," she said.

A half-dozen emotions crowded across his face. In only a few hours, Dana had come to know him so well that she could identify them—frustration, concern, annoyance, tenderness, anger. And respect. "Then stay directly behind me. If somebody has to take a bullet, it's going to be me."

"Okay." Dana knew she would get nowhere if she didn't make this concession. "Let's go!"

He lifted her down, his arms lingering around her longer than was strictly necessary. She came to rest tight against him, and realized she was in no hurry to move, either.

She tried to absorb the fact that they might be facing death. Maybe this was goodbye. It seemed to her they had barely said hello.

Finally Nick stepped back. "We're going to walk straight up the driveway," he said. "Obviously, they know we're here. It might make them jumpy if we try to conceal ourselves."

Dana nodded. Words wouldn't budge through the lump in her throat.

It was one thing to behave with spontaneous bravado. Walking up the asphalt at a deliberate pace, knowing that a kidnapper with a gun waited ahead, was another matter.

As she trudged along, Dana became acutely aware of her physical senses. Through the rubber soles of her shoes, she could feel the hardness of the blacktop. Occasionally a tiny stone skittered away, its noise abnormally loud. From behind the house she thought she heard muted voices, but it might have been the summer breeze, or a dog growling.

Starlight bathed the landscape with eerie clarity, turning shadows into substance. The scent of roses drifted through the air, a cloud of fragrance that spoke of mystical gardens in long-lost kingdoms.

Night birds called from the trees, and Dana remembered Nick's description of walking in the canyons near his home. Her mind, so long attuned to the idea that Nick was merely representing RNW, now tried to integrate the man she knew with the letters she had been reading these past months.

It was Nick who had written of power and solitude, of dreams that came true but lost their magic in the process. Watching his broad back proceeding ahead of her, the shoulders square and the head high, Dana knew that this man was no hired lackey.

He's RNW. Renfro Williams. That other man must work for him. Hitch. He must be the friend who looked like Alfred Hitchcock on a surfboard.

Dana didn't know why Hitch had pretended to be Renfro, or why Nick continued to hide his identity. It hurt that he hadn't told her.

Tonight, she recalled, the reclusive Renfro Williams had planned to unveil himself. No wonder Nick had been so certain the announcement wouldn't be made until he arrived.

He'd been pulling off this deception for years. It was impressive, really. Nick had been pretending to be someone he wasn't for a lot longer than she had, in front of the press and the public and the entire business world.

Maybe, she thought, she had pulled off her fraud, too. She had imagined herself to be brave and, like the Cowardly Lion, she had been.

She'd broken into a house, run from an armed and dangerous man and tried to take control of a motorcycle traveling at high speed. It was Morey Bain's gunshot, not Dana's awkwardness, that had forced them to crash.

She no longer felt afraid, merely a little nervous. She just hoped she was strong enough to save Dominique. And to face whatever the future might bring in a world empty of her make-believe lover.

Ahead of them, the van's rear doors stood open. Dana spotted a movement and halted at the same instant as Nick.

"Stay back," he muttered.

"I can't see," she hissed.

"There's nothing to see."

"There will be." She peered around him in time to observe a shape that glittered in the moonlight. It was Dominique, twisting as she staggered out of the van and half slid, half fell to the ground.

One wrist was clamped in the grip of Morey Bain, who jumped down beside her. In his other hand, he held a gun. To Dana, it looked enormous.

As soon as Morey caught his balance, he pressed the barrel to her sister's temple. Dominique's lips clamped, more from impatience than from fear. Dana realized she had to intervene before her sister took action and got herself killed.

She stepped to one side, away from Nick's protective shelter. "I'm the one you want," she said.

Nick reached for her. "I told you—"

Dana dodged away, her eyes fixed on Morey Bain. What a monstrous toad he was, hulking over Dominique's delicate figure. "I'm right, aren't I? You were looking for me."

"Have you got it?" he demanded.

What if the deposit slip *wasn't* what he sought? Or suppose he intended to keep Dominique as a hostage while he made his getaway?

Dana couldn't afford to take either of those chances by handing over her meager bit of evidence while he still held her sister. "Yes," she said. "I'll make you a deal."

"Dana!" Nick growled.

She darted forward before he could stop her. The gun barrel swung toward her, and she hesitated. "Let my sister go. I've got what you want, so take me."

"Dana!" Dominique gasped.

"This isn't your problem," Dana said.

"It's *our* problem!" said her sister.

"If he needs a hostage, he can have me." The words sounded ferociously brave. For an instant, Dana wondered where they'd come from. Then she remembered that she'd spoken them, and wondered if she had taken leave of her senses.

It was too late to retreat, though. Too late to do anything but walk straight into the lion's den. Or the weasel's lair, in this case.

Nick started after her, but the gun shifted position, aiming at his heart.

"You." Morey reached out and caught Dana's arm. "Get over here."

At the same time, he released Dominique, who stumbled toward Nick. Dana felt the cold muzzle of the gun nudge her temple.

"You'd better have it," Morey said, "or you've written your last love letter, sweetheart."

Dana didn't know which upset her more, the reminder that Morey had read her correspondence, or the fact that she probably didn't have what he wanted and was about to get killed.

She decided that getting killed won, hands down.

Chapter Fourteen

Dear RNW,

I enjoyed the image of you as a knight in shining armor, slaying a dragon and depositing it at my feet. Well, perhaps not actually killing it, but capturing it and turning it over to a wild animal park. A live dragon would be very special indeed!

You were right when you said women have always had to be brave. It's just that it wasn't the kind of bravado that poets write epics about.

Sometimes it's the small steps—defying outdated rules, standing up for what you believe, or risking embarrassment for a good cause—that take the greatest amount of courage, don't you think?

Nick thrust Dominique behind him. "Get into the truck," he growled.

To his relief, she hesitated only briefly before obeying. At least one sister in the Grant family had some sense.

He couldn't believe Dana had deliberately put herself in danger. Nick would gladly have surrendered himself instead. Now he had to endure the almost unbearable sight of Morey Bain poking her with that gun, when every ounce of his character demanded that he attack.

Nick understood just how great a risk she was running. He knew that neither of them possessed whatever it was Morey Bain sought. They hadn't taken anything except a deposit slip, and that was worthless in and of itself.

"How much do you want?" Nick demanded.

"You're offering a ransom?" Morey Bain leered at him. "How quaint. All I want is what's already mine."

"Kidnapping a woman is a bit excessive, don't you think?" Nick knew he was stalling. He kept hoping he would come up with a brilliant plan.

Bain snorted. "You wouldn't dare turn me in, not unless you want to go to jail for burglary."

Nick thought about the reporter sequestered in the truck, living proof that they didn't care about publicity. He hoped Morey wouldn't find out about him anytime soon. "We need an assurance that you'll let her go...."

"You're in no position to make deals!" Bain jammed the gun against Dana's temple so hard she flinched. "Hand it over!"

Dana glanced at Nick uncertainly. He wanted to rush in and grab her, but the gun was too close. Hell, if Bain wasn't careful, the damn thing might go off by accident. "Give it to him."

Dana made a face and fished out the deposit slip. "Here."

Bain glared at it. "What's this?"

"It's the only thing we took from your house."

He thrust the slip into his pocket. "Like hell. You've got my bankbook. It was on the desk, and it's gone."

"Why would I take your bankbook?" Dana demanded. "I couldn't withdraw anything unless I had your signature. Besides, I wouldn't steal your money, even if you did get it by swiping my letters."

The thickset man uttered a coarse laugh. "Your letters? That's peanuts, lady, and you know it. I'm sure you've checked the balance by now. Where is the damn thing?" He clamped harder on her arm.

She looked so slender and fragile next to that thug, Nick felt his fury approach the boiling point. He had to restrain himself, for Dana's sake, but he didn't know how long his willpower would last.

"I don't have—oh!" Her face brightened. "I know where it is! My foot hit something, but I couldn't find it in the dark. I must have kicked the bankbook under your desk, Morey."

"Liar!" He twisted her arm behind her, inducing a tiny yelp.

Despite her pain, Dana kept talking, holding him off. "Where'd you get all that money anyway?"

With any luck, Nick thought, the reporter had reached the police on the flip phone. He braced himself to lunge forward as soon as Bain heard sirens, to forestall him from fleeing with Dana.

"You'd be amazed what people put in letters," sniffed her captor. "You're not the only person with information they want to hide."

"You've been blackmailing your clients!" Dana gasped. "That's awful!"

"The best part is, nobody dares turn me in." Morey Bain gave Nick an evil grin. "And neither will you."

"Then what are you worried about?" Dana asked him. "You can always get your money, even without a bankbook."

Nick already knew the answer. The book was evidence. This was the kind of money that didn't get reported to the Internal Revenue Service, who had an unpleasant habit of putting people in prison for that type of oversight. "He doesn't want to go to jail for tax evasion."

"What about murder?" Dana demanded. "If he shoots me, he'll never get away with it."

"I thought we could hush this whole thing up," Morey snarled. "I never meant to hurt anybody. But I spent some time in prison once, for forgery. No way I'm going back there. You're going to help me, lady, or I don't care if we all get killed."

"You need to think this through, man," Nick said placatingly.

Morey shoved Dana toward the side of the van. "She's coming with me. If that bankbook isn't at my house, you're history, lady."

Nick stepped forward in protest, but the gun was tight against Dana's temple. He couldn't risk provoking a shot at this range.

He had never felt so helpless. Nick wanted to hold Dana safe in his arms more than he wanted all the things he'd worked for in his life. Without her, the house was an empty shell and the business empire a soulless machine, churning out money that could buy nothing he needed.

Then he heard the one thing he had been praying would not intrude. It was the sound of Jim Jasper's voice as he jumped from the truck.

"What's going on? I can't see a damn thing!" Apparently the reporter had poor night vision. He bumbled forward as if unaware of Dana's imminent danger. "Oh, hey, are you Morey Bain? I'm Jim Jasper from *Heat!*"

Bain's small eyes fixed on Nick in disbelief. "You brought the press?"

Now the man understood. They weren't trying to hide their burglary. That meant they wouldn't hesitate to call the police, either.

Morey Bain's time had just run out. And so had Nick's.

A roar ripped from his throat, wild enough to make Morey freeze in momentary confusion. That was all the time Nick needed to throw himself forward to save the woman he loved.

NICK'S SHOUT startled Dana, but she had already seen from the quivering of his muscles that he was going on the offensive. She took the only way out—she sat down hard, slipping out of Morey Bain's grasp.

For an instant, the gun wavered between her and Nick. Suddenly, so fast she almost couldn't register it, Nick executed a kick at Morey's elbow.

Then the world exploded.

Dana had never realized how loud a gunshot could sound when it originated inches from your ear. Her first thought was to wonder where Morey had hidden the cannon.

Then bodies came flying toward them. Dana, trying to shield herself with her arms, caught only fragmentary glimpses of what appeared to be a circus acrobatic act.

From the van, Batman bailed through the rear doors and the blue-uniformed guard leaped out the front. At the truck, Dominique, Lady Alicia and Hitch hurled themselves from the cab, overrunning the befuddled reporter as they stampeded toward Morey Bain.

Where was Nick? For a heart-stopping moment, Dana thought he must have been shot, but then she saw him land a right uppercut to the shop owner's jaw. From this angle, Nick's fist looked huge, and Morey appeared to rise at least four inches off the ground.

Then both of them disappeared beneath the onslaught of bodies. A quick roll along the ground was all that prevented Dana from getting trampled underfoot.

When she recovered her bearings and sat up, she could see Morey pressed against the van, eyes bulging with fear. Nick was lashing his wrists behind him with packing twine, and Dominique was whacking him in the face with her sequined evening bag.

"Oh, don't ruin it!" cried Lady Alicia, clapping her hands in dismay.

"How could you ruin a face like that?" demanded Dominique, landing another blow.

"I meant your reticule!" said the bewigged woman. "It's smashing!"

"What, this?" Dominique stopped pounding Morey and examined her purse. Worked in delicately shaded colors, it had probably cost a bundle. With a shrug, Dana's sister removed a few items and tossed it to Alicia. "It's yours. I appreciate the risk you all took in coming after me."

Finally, from down the road, came the shriek of sirens. "What took them so long?" grumbled Nick, still hanging on to Morey Bain.

"It's only been a minute since I called them." Hitch brandished a flip phone. "I had to pinch it off that reporter. He wouldn't let us use it."

"Don't tell them anything!" begged Jasper, who had been standing on the sidelines making notes. "Once they file a report, everybody will get the story! It's my exclusive. *Heat!* will pay you, I promise."

"We shouldn't talk to the police?" Dominique demanded. "That's why you wouldn't let them call? Are you crazy?"

"Do you think anybody cares about your money?" added Hitch.

Jasper gazed slowly around. "I suppose I could write a first-person account," he said.

"Just don't try to paint yourself as the hero," said Lady Alicia, "or I will personally pound you into tea cakes!"

The man sighed. Dana almost felt sorry for him.

THE GLARE of police headlights and the flash of blue dome lights transformed Nick's front lawn into a scene from a movie. It was, unfortunately, not the kind of movie he wanted to see tonight. He was more in the mood for *An Affair to Remember* than for *Lethal Weapon*.

What Nick wanted was to gather Dana against his chest and soothe her with sweet nothings. Then he would carry her into the house and ply her with the food and drink left behind by the caterer, who, judging by the absence of her distinctive trucks, had given up and gone home.

To Dana, he would admit the stark terror that had shot through him when he thought she was going to die. His fingers would brush the hair from her face, and coax a smile from her lips, and then he would lean toward her and...

Except real life kept getting in the way. There was Morey Bain, wriggling angrily against his ties and yelling that he was the victim of hoodlums. And Lady Alicia, threatening to wreak bodily harm on the creep. And Hitch, who kept trying to talk the costumed lady into moving into the house this very night, lock, stock and sequined purse.

There were so many people to deal with. Since he was lord of the manor, the responsibility fell to Nick, and it was heading for him now, in the person of the police officer in charge.

That gentleman, a thirtyish African-American with military bearing, strode across the lawn. "I'm Sergeant George Burns," he said, with no trace of a smile. "But believe me, I'm no comedian. Now what's going on here?"

Everyone started talking at once. This was a relief to Nick, who appreciated the delay in having to identify himself. He needed to tell Dana his real name first, even if it wouldn't be during a leisurely encounter softened by sweet nothings.

Dana stood near her sister, hugging herself and gazing into space. After handing his captive over to Sergeant Burns, Nick came alongside.

Before he could open his mouth, she said, "I know you must be Renfro Williams."

"He is?" said Dominique.

"It's a game they play," Dana told her.

"Not anymore." Nick wished he could penetrate her stoic gaze to find out what she was thinking. "How did you figure it out?"

"Let's just say it became obvious," Dana said.

Before he could question her further, George Not-the-Comedian Burns began separating everyone so that his officers could interrogate them. That reminded Nick that he also had a motorcycle accident to report before some Palisades homeowner awakened to find a motorcycle wrapped around his tree and traced it to Hitch.

The next hour passed in a blur. There were no lights other than those from the vehicles, and the harsh glare added to the sense of confusion.

Nick yearned for his usual floodlights, but it appeared that the aliens or ferocious power-eating squirrels or whatever it was that had cut the West Coast grid were still holding the authorities at bay.

Manuel the truck driver, sans Batman mask, strode around with a pleased grin. Apparently, the daring of his rescue attempt had redeemed him from the shame of getting lost with a load of masks. It must also have compensated for the large bruise on his chin.

Sam, the guard, was spilling every detail of the night's chase, portraying Morey Bain as barely one step above Vlad the Impaler. He was obviously trying to get himself off the hook, and Nick guessed he would succeed.

Lady Alicia held an officer enthralled as she described the night's events in melodramatic terms. According to what Nick could make out, Morey Bain had stolen the masks, kidnapped half the guests at the Top Hat and single-handedly blacked out the West Coast.

Bain, with handcuffs replacing the twine, yelled repeatedly for his lawyer until an officer stuffed him into the back of a squad car. Noises continued to emanate, muffled into a background hum.

Jim Jasper had reluctantly set aside his notebook and was providing information to an officer, who kept shaking his head, as if amazed that a reporter could have observed so little.

Nick supposed he could still find a way to withhold his identity from the reporter and keep the police report confidential. If you had enough clout, you could do almost anything. But it no longer seemed important to pose as Nick Lyon, right-hand man.

He was tired of maintaining iron control over his domain and everyone around him. There were more important things in life, as he had discovered tonight.

So, after Jasper finished making his statement to the police, Nick gave him another scoop. The man's mouth worked compulsively as he scribbled down the real story of Hitch, the masks and Nick Lyon, who was right-hand man to himself.

In the morning, Nick decided, he would call some of the more respectable representatives of the press. He wanted to make sure they printed an accurate description of how things had gotten confused tonight, so that he wouldn't antagonize the guests who had spent the evening shaking hands with his butler.

Jasper made a few more notes and then dialed his flip phone, dancing on the balls of his feet the whole time he was talking. Nick hoped he gave his editor a headache.

He turned away to see Hitch hovering over Lady Alicia, plying her with soft drinks brought from the house and addressing her as "my little Phyllis." Finally Sergeant Burns demanded, "Why are you calling her Phyllis? I thought her name was Alice."

"It is!" boomed the lady in question.

"But she's going to change it," said Hitch.

"I am not!" stated his ladylove. "I happen to like my name."

Hitch touched his throat. "But, darling, you have to match my tattoo. How would it look if we got married with the wrong name on my neck?"

Lady Alicia smacked him with her fan. "They can remove those things with lasers," she said. "I recommend it!"

In the glare of headlights, Nick saw his butler swallow hard. "I guess it's time I tried it," Hitch said.

At last the car with Morey Bain departed. One of the officers followed with the postal-shop van, which would be impounded as evidence, leaving only Sergeant Burns to finish taking Dominique's statement.

Nick's head was buzzing, and he felt stiff from today's exertions. Now that the adrenaline had ebbed, he was becoming aware of throbbing bruises along one side of his body where he'd landed after being thrown from the motorcycle.

He needed to be alone with Dana. There were so many gaps to fill and explanations to make, and he didn't want to bother with any of that. He just wanted to kiss her.

Sergeant Burns snapped his notebook shut. "I guess we're done for now."

Thank goodness, Nick thought. Peace and quiet, at last.

"I'm glad we could help," said Dominique Grant—right before she fainted onto the grass.

DANA RUSHED to her sister's side, filled with self-recriminations. Why hadn't it occurred to her that Dominique might suffer from delayed shock? The woman had been through a horrible experience tonight.

So had Dana, and she supposed she might collapse at some future time, when events struck home. In a few days or a week, her knees might buckle and she would hit the floor at the supermarket. One thing was for sure, she would never manage to do it as gracefully as her sister.

Nor right in front of Nick, either. He was bending over Dominique, lifting her in his arms, talking softly, as if trying to coax her back to consciousness. He looked incredibly strong and resilient, considering what he'd been through tonight; but then, Dominique tended to bring out that side of men.

Dana was dismayed to recognize her emotion as jealousy. How could she possibly feel that way toward her sister?

True, Dominique was the kind of woman who belonged in this fabulous house, with this powerful and important man. But Dana had never begrudged her sister anything, and she didn't intend to start now.

Still, as she watched Nick murmuring to Dominique, the logic of it cut into Dana's heart. For most of the evening, he had believed Dana *was* her sister, even while they were making love. It seemed only natural that Dominique should be the one to end up in his arms.

A lifetime of self-doubts assailed Dana. Most likely she was suffering an emotional reaction to trauma, she recognized, but the knowledge didn't help much. A horde of adolescent insecurities rushed back, as if they'd been amassing for years at the frontiers of her self-respect.

How could she compete with a glamorous actress? Why did she imagine she could stand as an equal beside Nick, who ruled this estate, and a virtual kingdom besides? Dana might be brave and daring in her fantasy world, among her books and letters, but she had overextended herself tonight.

At last Dominique's eyes fluttered open. "Harmon?" she whispered, in a tone so trusting that it broke Dana's heart.

"I'm sorry," Nick said. "He's not here."

Dominique stared at him for a moment. Then she said, "That self-centered son of a gun. I hope he trips over a camera cord and brains himself."

As Nick lowered her to the ground, George Burns strode to Dominique's aid. "We can take you to the hospital, ma'am," he said.

She waved her hand. "No, thank you, Sergeant. I want to avoid publicity as much as possible."

"Then I'd be happy to drive you home," he said.

She regarded him dubiously. "You don't smoke a cigar, do you?"

"I'm not the comedian, ma'am."

"Then I should be delighted to accept your offer," said Dominique.

She turned to Dana. "Thank you. I know what a risk you took coming after me."

"This whole mess was my fault in the first place!" Dana protested.

Her sister smiled. "If I hadn't insisted on playing Princess Leia, I wouldn't have put myself in danger. You and that good-looking man of yours were doing fine all by yourselves."

"Does that mean I get to play Princess Leia next time?" Dana teased.

"Whenever you want." Dominique gave her a hug before departing with the sergeant.

Manuel volunteered to take the others back to the restaurant in his truck, with Hitch riding along to retrieve Nick's car. They went with some reluctance, as if leaving a party, but Lady Alicia was yawning, and the guard kept shaking his head to keep his eyes open.

Dana knew she ought to go with them. From the restaurant, someone could give her a ride to South Pasadena, or she could call a cab.

The long habit of avoiding difficult situations nearly set Dana's feet moving toward the truck. Besides, her shoulder ached where she'd fallen from the cycle, and she told herself she needed to rest.

Nick was busy directing traffic as the remaining police car departed and the truck stirred to life. She should leave while she had the chance, Dana thought.

Now that the letters had been destroyed and Morey captured, the evening's work was done. Nick's mind must already be turning to other responsibilities and future challenges. Or perhaps, simply, to sleep.

The truck inched forward and, guided by Nick from the center of the driveway, turned around. She needed to hurry, before it straightened and picked up speed.

Dana didn't move.

She wasn't held in place by any conscious decision. It was as if, deep inside, a voice had shouted, *Enough!*

It sounded a bit like the fearless Dominique of their childhood days. But it wasn't her sister, not this time. The voice, finally and forever, belonged to Dana.

She needed to find out what would happen. This was the first day of the rest of her life, as the cliché went. From now on, Dana was going to go after what she wanted, even if she ended up with mud splattered on her face.

And so, at two-thirty in the morning on July 5, her shoulder smarting and her stomach quivering, Dana Grant stood her ground.

Chapter Fifteen

Dear DG,

I understand what you mean about small steps taking courage, but I certainly don't find them more intimidating than the prospect of risking my life.

Whenever I make policy or propose a new venture, I'm almost certain to draw criticism. And when I'm forced to confront someone over a problem, the result can be blown tempers and hurt feelings. The prospect doesn't please me, but it doesn't frighten me, either.

Maybe I'm just insensitive, but I can't imagine being afraid of someone's reaction to me. Not as long as I'm doing what I believe is right . . .

As Nick watched the truck drive away behind the police car, he felt both exhausted and hungry. But what he wanted most was neither rest nor food.

He needed to hear Dana say that she forgave him for his lies, and for assuming she was Dominique.

Without the headlights for illumination, he couldn't read her expression as she stood in the driveway. She wasn't running to throw her arms around him, but neither had she leaped aboard one of the vehicles and made her escape.

Every part of Nick's body smarted, twinged or throbbed. It occurred to him that both he and Dana probably needed a physical therapist and a trauma specialist more than they needed each other.

It took him all of ten seconds to decide otherwise. Even as Nick's thoughts drifted over their evening together, the demands of his body shifted.

He needed Dana in every way a man could need a woman—even ways he shouldn't feel after bashing a motorcycle into a tree. His arms ached to hold her, except that at this point he didn't think he could pick up even the love of his life without dropping her.

The love of his life. That was a scary phrase. It meant that his future happiness rested in someone else's hands.

Nick Lyon never yielded control to anyone. But tonight, Renfro Nicholas Williams had been born again, and he was going to do things differently. Starting now.

"Would you like something to eat?" It might not be the most romantic opening, but to Nick it seemed a reasonable start.

Moonlight caught the startled widening of Dana's eyes. "Eat?" she said.

"It's been a while since we had dinner," he pointed out. "We could celebrate your birthday again."

"It isn't my birthday anymore," she said.

"We could celebrate being alive."

Slowly, Dana nodded, but she didn't speak. Nick tried to think of a way to resume the spontaneous chatter they'd been spouting for hours, but drew a blank.

He was surprised how awkward he felt around this woman he'd been touching and interacting with for nearly six hours. He started to take her elbow, but she flinched, so he settled for leading the way inside.

Maybe she was sore from the accident. Or mad at him. He wouldn't blame her, Nick admitted silently.

What a mess he had made of those precious moments at the hotel after their union. She had deserved more from him, but he hadn't realized it then.

Dana wasn't the kind of woman he usually encountered, Nick reflected as he unlocked a side entrance. All evening she had showed no interest in the company of glitzy people, and she appeared more intimidated than acquisitive toward his enormous house.

The only thing about him that had impressed her were the letters, Nick reflected. Those words had come straight from his soul, bypassing the social facade. She liked the part of him that was most himself, the part that didn't interest other people.

It might ease the tension now if he said something deep and meaningful, the kind of phrases he'd written in their correspondence. But all Nick could manage was, "The caterer probably left enough for an army."

"Caterer?" Dana asked.

"I was planning to invite everyone back from the restaurant to make my announcement here," Nick said. "In restrospect, it seems a bit pompous, doesn't it?"

She didn't answer.

The silence was driving Nick crazy. He tried to tell himself Dana was just worn-out and maybe shell-shocked. He shouldn't take it personally.

But he did.

Nick led the way through the oversize den and down a hallway into the restaurant-style kitchen. A wash of moonlight through the window gleamed off stainless-steel sinks and butcher-block islands.

Every surface was covered with plastic-wrapped trays of hors d'oeuvres and finger foods sitting in beds of partially melted ice. There were mounds of shrimp and crabmeat, arrays of fruit balls and fresh strawberries, tiny sandwiches, stuffed mushrooms, quiche, congealing Swedish meatballs, asparagus spears and caviar, cheeses, chicken wings and squares of cheesecake and carrot cake.

Additional food had been piled into coolers, no doubt also packed with ice. Nick had requested in advance that the food be kept cold, knowing it might have to sit for an hour or so before being consumed.

"This is going to waste?" Dana asked in dismay.

"Not if we eat it," he said.

She leaned against a counter, as if too overwhelmed to make a start. "I can't believe nobody's going to eat most of this food. We should take it to the homeless."

"The homeless already live here," Nick said. "Hitch keeps hiring them."

"Exactly what does Hitch do around here, anyway?" she asked.

"He's my butler."

"Kind of a weird butler. But he's your old surfing buddy, isn't he?"

"I see you're putting the pieces together. You're good at puzzles, aren't you?" It was a relief to shoot the conversational breeze with Dana again, even at this hour and in an unlit kitchen. "Shall we dine?"

"There's nowhere to sit," she said.

"Let's take some of this stuff outside," Nick proposed. In addition to the lack of table space, the air-conditioning had been off for hours and the room felt stuffy. "There are tents in back, along with buckets of champagne. I guess they left them outside, since I don't see them here.''

Dana hefted a tray of hors d'oeuvres. "I'll start with these.''

Nick copped a platter of seafood. "Here's my first course.''

They went out together, taking turns shouldering open the doors, which didn't cause as much pain as Nick would have expected. For some reason, his body didn't hurt so much anymore, or else he was getting used to it.

Behind the house, the lawn had taken on a fairyland charm. Beneath the moon, the red-white-and-blue theme had turned to pearl and silver. Sprays of balloons danced from the backs of chairs, and huge bouquets mingled their scents with those from the rose garden.

Nick thought he heard low voices around the side of the house, but when he listened more closely, they were gone. Probably his live-in staff had left their windows open in a distant wing and were discussing what the police cars might have been investigating and why the party had been canceled.

"This is really your house?" Dana asked as she set her tray on a white wrought-iron table. "What do you need so much space for?''

"Dreams," Nick said as he sat down.

She cocked him an inquisitive look. "You've made them all come true, haven't you?''

"Not yet," he said.

Dana ducked her head, as if refusing to believe what he'd implied. Nick wondered whether she was modest, or didn't want to go further with their relationship. He found that hard to imagine.

Not that he was an egotist. There were plenty of women in the world who would gladly turn their backs on Nick, as himself or as Renfro or both. But Dana had demonstrated in the hotel suite that she wasn't one of them.

She busied herself sampling the food. "This is fabulous. I feel so selfish."

"Why?" The canapes *were* good, but Nick didn't feel guilty, since he'd paid for them.

"Lots of people are hungry tonight."

"Name three."

She chuckled unwillingly. "I guess I am laying it on a bit thick, aren't I?"

"Enjoy yourself," he said. "This is the first peaceful moment we've had in hours."

He should have known he'd spoken too soon, because at that moment, the fireworks went off.

They started with two huge bangs and a couple of whistling rockets that showered the sky with blue and white stars.

"I don't believe it." Now Nick understood what the voices had meant; the pyrotechnics crew were hanging around. They had probably heard the door slam as he and Dana came out and decided to fulfill their contract so that they could go home.

"Where did those come from?" Dana asked, holding a miniature sandwich in midair as if she'd forgotten it.

Red, white and blue fanned across the sky like a peacock's tail. The colors struck Nick as incredibly bright, especially in contrast to a world turned gray.

"I arranged them," he said. "They were supposed to go off hours ago. The neighbors will be furious."

"Don't be silly," said Dana. "Most of them probably missed their fireworks tonight, especially if they planned to watch on TV. This should be a treat."

She didn't know rich people. They wanted the world to operate on their timetables and no other, Nick reflected.

At least he knew what to do with the leftover food, champagne, flowers and balloons. He would have his employees deliver Care packages to the entire neighborhood tomorrow, and have Hitch deliver generous portions to the homeless shelters, as well.

It would make a good peace offering. Besides, rich people loved getting free food.

The sky was blossoming with colors that must have been visible for miles. Nick leaned back, relishing the splendor of the display.

He hadn't expected to enjoy the food or the pyrotechnics. For months, as he planned his unveiling, Nick had anticipated a miserable experience, something to be suffered through and pushed out of memory as quickly as possible.

Instead, he felt the special quality of this moment keenly. There *was* magic here tonight, and not just in the sky.

All his life, Nick had lived for some future point at which the world would rest in his palm. Well, here it was.

He wanted to freeze time. He wanted to watch forever the play of childlike delight across Dana's face as it tilted toward the heavens.

With her, everything Nick owned became shiny and new. He wanted to share everything at once—the Picasso in the living room, the mosaic floor in the entryway, the cloverleaf whirlpool spa hidden in the garden.

Other people had designed them, and until now he had admired them on an esthetic rather than a visceral basis. Now he wanted to wallow in what he'd accomplished, to let the luxury soak into his pores, and to give it all to Dana.

Overhead, white and green and blue and red constellations formed and reshaped themselves amid the boom of explosives. Hadn't the ancient Chinese believed fireworks scared away bad-luck demons? Tonight, he could believe it.

"I've never had my own fireworks display," said Dana, and then shot him an uneasy glance.

Nick touched her hand. "What's wrong?"

"It isn't really for me, of course," she corrected. "I just feel as if it is."

"If you like, I'll have them come back tomorrow night specifically in your honor," Nick offered.

"The neighbors would kill you!"

"I'll buy them earplugs," he said.

Beneath an umbrella of scarlet and azure lights, she gave him a crooked smile, then ducked her head shyly.

Couldn't she see how much he cared about her? But then, Dana was a woman who responded to words rather than visual images. She might possess terrific intuition, but when it came to romance, she would never believe anything that wasn't expressed verbally.

He needed to tell her how he felt. But Nick had no experience in baring his soul.

Acknowledged as an expert in negotiations and public relations, he could summon euphemisms and interpretations at the flick of an eyebrow. But deep-down honesty...now that was harder.

Before he could organize his thoughts, a white circlet of fireworks bloomed behind Dana, turning her into an angel. "You're wearing a halo of stars," he said.

She rested her chin in her palm. "I feel like a kid who just emerged through the looking glass."

Her words made Nick reflect. "Actually, I *don't* feel like a kid, for a change. I feel like a man who's finally come of age."

"You?" Dana asked. "After all you've accomplished?"

"This is my coming-out party tonight," Nick said. "A man isn't truly himself until he gives the most important part of himself away. His heart, Dana."

She gazed at him in rapt silence beneath an exploding mandala of colors. Her eyes were full of questions, but she said nothing.

Nick had to keep going. He couldn't let his habit of playing his cards close to the vest interfere now. This was the time to reveal his aces, hand over his kings and yield to the queen of hearts.

"I've been holding you at bay all night," he admitted. "It was easier to play hide-and-seek than to let you see who I am inside. I come from a middle-class family. I wasn't a very good student, and nobody voted me most likely to succeed. But somewhere along the line, I inherited or developed a ruthless ambition to control everything around me."

"Ruthless?" Dana asked.

Nick nodded. "I don't mean underhanded or unethical. But I've pursued my goals single-mindedly, and avoided getting close to people along the way. The only problem with being king of the world is that, all by yourself, it isn't much fun."

Dana's smile took in a fountain of color erupting above them. "I think it's lots of fun."

"Of course it is," Nick said. "Now that you're here."

As she waited, her face turned red and blue and yellow beneath the flashes. He knew he was expected to say something further, but he couldn't figure out what it was.

"That's all?" she asked, finally.

Brilliant sweeps of poetry danced just beyond his grasp. *Say something, anything.* "Aren't the fireworks terrific?" he asked.

"Oh, Nick." She let out a long sigh. "You're hopeless."

"Give me a sec," he said. "I'm thinking."

The hidden pyrotechnics geniuses chose that moment to unleash their greatest triumph. An American flag burst into the sky, stars and stripes shimmering in place.

At a distance, a trumpet began playing the national anthem. Scattered applause from half a dozen points ricocheted off nearby hills.

Not only his neighbors, but half of West Los Angeles, must be observing this magnificent, enormous, vainglorious demonstration of Renfro Williams's wealth.

Not only watching, but each contributing in his or her own way, strangers brought together for one singular moment. What had been intended as a publicity stunt had turned into the kind of special occasion that broke barriers between people and opened their hearts.

That was when Nick realized what he had left out.

"I love you," he said as the stars and stripes twinkled one last time and fluttered to earth.

"I COULD really use a back rub," said Dana.

It hardly seemed the appropriate response, when Nick had just declared his love. But her throat had a knot in it, her stomach was pummeling the hors d'oeuvres, and her shoulders were so stiff she could barely move.

"Here?" he asked.

Dana gestured toward a lounge chair. "That will do, if you don't mind," she said. "Unless you're too sore, yourself?"

"Never." Nick stood up gamely.

As she walked over and flopped onto the lounger, Dana realized she was buying time. She needed to make sense of what had happened, these past few minutes.

Far from rejecting her, Nick had fallen in love with her. This went contrary to every expectation.

She wasn't supposed to win the first time out. She almost felt disappointed that her new leaf had been turned so quickly.

Relationships were supposed to grow, she mused as Nick's strong hands kneaded the muscles of her back. But hadn't this one been developing for months, in between the tall tales and the deceptions?

The two of them had led each other a merry chase. They had been, she realized, like two grumpy pandas being dragged to mate at a zoo, each refusing to concede its territory, even as it felt the inescapable attraction.

"What does that mean?" she asked at last.

"What does what mean?" He hesitated, then resumed probing the tenderness in her back.

Dana could feel the tension easing out of her. "Being in love. What does it mean to you?"

"Lying to each other, giving each other the runaround and rubbing your back for eternity," Nick responded promptly.

"We've already done that."

"Then I guess we'll have to get married," he said.

She hadn't mistaken his intentions. He'd meant what he said, in the most traditional and wonderful manner. So why was she lying here getting a massage instead of jumping for joy?

Gradually Dana realized what was wrong. Unlike other little girls, she had never planned her own wedding. She had only imagined what she would wear as maid of honor at Dominique's wedding.

There was no law that said the older sister had to go first, she reminded herself, and started to laugh.

"What's so funny?" Nick sounded affronted.

"I was wondering if Dominique would mind her kid sister getting married first," Dana said.

"She can be maid of honor and walk down the aisle with her Emmy," he grumbled. "Then she'll get as much attention as she wants."

Dana's laughter turned to giggles. "Can't you just see it? There'll be Lady Alicia in her wig, and Hitch in his tuxedo jacket, and Manuel in a mask. I absolutely draw the line at that guard, though."

"Does this mean the answer is yes?" Nick asked.

She took a deep breath. "I guess it does."

"You guess?"

Dana rolled over to face him, which was a mistake, because his hands automatically stroked her breasts before he realized what had happened. Then he let his hands drop— a very gentlemanly action under the circumstances.

Dana owed it to Nick to be as frank as he was. "The only problem is, this isn't really me tonight."

"It isn't?" Nick cocked an eyebrow.

"I'm not...I'm not what I seem." Regretfully Dana pulled herself into a sitting position. "I'm just an English teacher who writes fanciful letters."

"You mean you don't always go on wild-goose chases by the light of the moon?" he asked in mock dismay.

Dana refrained from poking him in the ribs, but only because she suspected his torso must have turned into one big bruise by now. "This isn't a joke," she said. "It's true—I'm not adventuresome."

"You prefer to get your excitement from books and ideas," he suggested.

"Well, yes." Now that she'd started talking, the words came more easily. "I'm the last one to volunteer for anything, the least likely to speak up, and I can never figure out what to do until a crisis is past. I think matters over a few times before I act. Sometimes I think them over for so long that I forget what I was thinking about."

"Dana, I don't need a woman who's hooked on risk taking." Nick's eyes burned into her, more in chiding than in anger. "You were brave when you needed to be. We all have to face our share of trouble, whether we seek it or not. It takes as much courage to stare adversity in the face as to hunt down criminals or jump out of airplanes."

"Don't remind me." Dana shuddered. "Those letters were awful. I can't imagine how I had the nerve to make that stuff up."

"They weren't awful." Nick fluffed her hair lightly. "They brought us together."

Then he did what she wanted most. He scooped her against him and began covering her mouth with kisses.

They started soft and slow, and then his tongue parted her lips.

White light blurred her senses. Dana wanted to yield to a flood of delightful instincts, but something tickled at the edges of her hearing. A clicking, then a buzzing.

"What's going on?" she asked, lifting her head.

"The power," Nick muttered in disgust, and Dana realized the whiteness had marked not an emotional response but the end of the blackout.

Amid a low electrical hum, lights flooded the lawn, turning it bright as a summer's day. A few dozen yards away, the house glowed from every window.

"I don't believe it." She'd been hoping to get the power back all evening, and now she didn't want it.

"*Heat!* can finally go to press," Nick grumbled.

"And all those other newspapers, with their photographs of Hitch," Dana reminded him.

Nick groaned. "They'll be furious."

"I think it's funny."

"They won't."

"They made the assumption," Dana pointed out. "Besides, you'll be a hero for rescuing Dominique. Don't worry, Nick."

"I'm too tired to worry." He gave her an incandescent smile that put the electric lights to shame. "And too happy. Now let's go somewhere dark and quiet."

Dana was delighted to cooperate.

Chapter Sixteen

Billionaire Marries His Pen Pal
A *Heat!* Exclusive
By Jim Jasper

Somewhere in the South Pacific—Billionaire Renfro Nicholas Williams and Dana Grant, sister of soap-opera star Dominique Grant, were married this week on a private island.

The couple met by mail when the bride, a high-school English teacher, answered the groom's personal ad.

The wedding was held in this remote location in an attempt to avoid the press. However, your intrepid reporter was able to secure a position on a neighboring island to witness this memorable event.

Dozens of guests were flown in for the occasion. According to information secured from a source among the serving staff, these included high-school faculty, family members and Dominique Grant herself.

As *Heat!* readers know, Miss Grant broke off a romance with Oscar-winning director Harmon Mason after he failed to come to her rescue when she was kidnapped during the Fourth of July blackout.

She arrived with her new boyfriend, stand-up comedian Joe Sasser. The couple were seen holding hands, and Miss Grant was observed to laugh at several of Sasser's jokes, a sure sign of infatuation.

This reporter, who managed to charter a small boat, can also relate that, with his own eyes, he saw guests dressed in colonial costumes, apparently unmindful of the tropical heat.

The best man was the groom's longtime friend and butler, John "Hitch" Rickert. Rickert is best remembered as the man mistaken for Williams by most of the media—but not this reporter—on the Fourth of July.

He escorted his fiancée, popularly known as Lady Alicia. She is known for driving the truck in which they, along with Williams, Dana Grant and this reporter, pursued and rescued Dominique Grant.

Her captor, businessman Morey Bain, last month pleaded guilty to kidnapping in Los Angeles Superior Court. He still faces federal charges of mail theft and tax evasion.

Rickert and Lady Alicia, popular guests on late-night talk shows, are said to be recording a new version of "Eighteen Wheels and a Dozen Roses." Remember, you heard it here first!

The wedding took place at night and was off-limits to the press. However, according to my exclusive source, it was staged in a tropical garden. The groom and best man, the ushers and the bridesmaids, all wore white. The bride wore red, white and blue.

The ceremony took place by torchlight in honor of the blackout during which the couple met.

A definitive cause of the power failure remains to be

determined. Official reports attribute it to a computer malfunction, possibly brought on by a virus.

However, *Heat!* is aggressively pursuing rumors that either sunspots or high-school hackers were to blame. We will continue to investigate the rampaging rodent theory, as well.

Wherever and whenever news happens, or is reputed to have happened, or might be about to happen, you can count on us to be there first!

MILLION DOLLAR SWEEPSTAKES

SWP-M96

HARLEQUIN®
AMERICAN ✦ ROMANCE®
®

Maybe This Time...

Maybe this time...they'll get what they really wanted all those years ago. Whether it's the man who got away, a baby, or a new lease on life, these four women will get a second chance at a once-in-a-lifetime opportunity!

Four top-selling authors have come together to make you believe that in the world of American Romance anything is possible:

#642 ONE HUSBAND TOO MANY
Jacqueline Diamond
August

#646 WHEN A MAN LOVES A WOMAN
Bonnie K. Winn
September

#650 HEAVEN CAN WAIT
Emily Dalton
October

#654 THE COMEBACK MOM
Muriel Jensen
November

Look us up on-line at: http://www.romance.net

MTTG

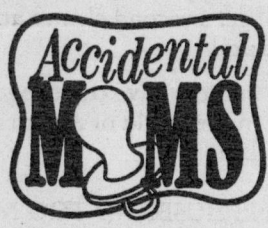

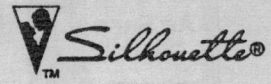

HARLEQUIN® and **Silhouette®**

are proud to present...

HERE COME THE

GROOMS™

Four marriage-minded stories written by top
Harlequin and Silhouette authors!

Next month, you'll find:

Married?!	by Annette Broadrick
Designs on Love	by Gina Wilkins
It Happened One Night	by Marie Ferrarella
Lazarus Rising	by Anne Stuart

ADDED BONUS! In every edition of
Here Come the Grooms you'll find $5.00 worth
of coupons good for Harlequin and Silhouette
products.

On sale at your favorite Harlequin and Silhouette
retail outlet.

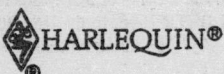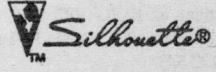

HCTG996

Free Gift Offer

With a Free Gift proof-of-purchase
from any Harlequin® book, you can receive
a beautiful cubic zirconia pendant.

This stunning marquise-shaped stone is a genuine cubic
zirconia—accented by an 18" gold tone necklace.
(Approximate retail value $19.95)

Send for yours today...
compliments of ⬧HARLEQUIN®

To receive your free gift, a cubic zirconia pendant, send us one original proof-of-purchase, photocopies not accepted, from the back of any Harlequin Romance®, Harlequin Presents®, Harlequin Temptation®, Harlequin Superromance®, Harlequin Intrigue®, Harlequin American Romance®, or Harlequin Historicals® title available in August, September or October at your favorite retail outlet, together with the Free Gift Certificate, plus a check or money order for $1.65 U.S./$2.15 CAN. (do not send cash) to cover postage and handling, payable to Harlequin Free Gift Offer. We will send you the specified gift. Allow 6 to 8 weeks for delivery. Offer good until October 31, 1996 or while quantities last. Offer valid in the U.S. and Canada only.

Free Gift Certificate

Name: _____

Address: _____

City: _____ State/Province: _____ Zip/Postal Code: _____

Mail this certificate, one proof-of-purchase and a check or money order for postage and handling to: HARLEQUIN FREE GIFT OFFER 1996. In the U.S.: 3010 Walden Avenue, P.O. Box 9071, Buffalo NY 14269-9057. In Canada: P.O. Box 604, Fort Erie, Ontario L2Z 5X3.

FREE GIFT OFFER   084-KMF

ONE PROOF-OF-PURCHASE
To collect your fabulous FREE GIFT, a cubic zirconia pendant, you must include this
original proof-of-purchase for each gift with the properly completed Free Gift Certificate.

084-KMF

Merry Christmas, Baby!

A romantic collection filled with the magic
of Christmas and the joy of children.

SUSAN WIGGS, Karen Young and
Bobby Hutchinson bring you Christmas wishes,
weddings and romance, in a charming
trio of stories that will warm up your
holiday season.

MERRY CHRISTMAS, BABY! also contains
Harlequin's special gift to you—a set of
FREE GIFT TAGS included in every book.

Brighten up your holiday season with
MERRY CHRISTMAS, BABY!

Available in November at
your favorite retail store.

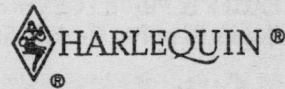

HARLEQUIN ®

®

Look us up on-line at: http://www.romance.net   MCB

You're About to Become a *Privileged Woman*

Reap the rewards of fabulous free gifts and benefits with proofs-of-purchase from Harlequin and Silhouette books

Pages & Privileges™

It's our way of thanking you for buying our books at your favorite retail stores.

PROOF OF PURCHASE
Offer expires October 31, 1996
HAR-PP175

**Harlequin and Silhouette—
the most privileged readers in the world!**

For more information about Harlequin and Silhouette's PAGES & PRIVILEGES program call the Pages & Privileges Benefits Desk: 1-503-794-2499

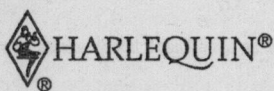

HARLEQUIN®

HAR-PP175